LOVE
NEST

LOVE NEST

Andrew Coburn

MACMILLAN PUBLISHING COMPANY

New York

Macmillan Publishing Company
866 Third Avenue, New York, N.Y. 10022
Collier Macmillan Canada, Inc.

Library of Congress Cataloging-in-Publication Data

Coburn, Andrew.
Love nest.

I. Title.
PS3553.023L6   1987   813'.54   87-1519
ISBN 0-02-526560-1

This novel is a work of fiction. Names, characters, places and incidents,
are either the product of the author's imagination
or are used fictitiously.
Any resemblance to actual persons, living or dead,
events or locales, is entirely coincidental.

10 9 8 7 6 5 4 3 2 1

Printed in the United States of America

For my wife, Casey Coburn,
and our kids, Cathleen, Krista, Lisa, and Heather.

ACKNOWLEDGMENTS

Phyllis McGovern, the late Stanley Greenhalgh, and
Trentwell Mason White, Ruth Hitchings, Julia Danley,
Bella Copolla, Peter Skolnik, Ned Chase, Dominick
Anfuso, and everybody at Bishop's, for help past
and present.

LOVE
NEST

One

William Rollins had a solitary drink at the bar in Rembrandt's Restaurant in Elm Square. The square was in the prosperous and prideful town of Andover, twenty miles north of Boston. The restaurant was in a former funeral home, Lundgren's, where twenty years ago Rollins had wept over the twin caskets of his parents. He might have stayed for another drink had the young bartender not placed the telephone in front of him and quietly informed him that he had a call. The peremptory voice on the line said, "Get over here."

He did not hurry. He handed over a small plastic disk to the girl in the cloakroom, deposited a modest gratuity in the dish, and waited with catlike calm for his coat. He was neat and trim in a vested suit, wore amber-tinted eyeglasses, and had the bloodless look of a corporation lawyer. When his coat came, he checked the pockets to make sure his scarf and gloves were there. He trusted no one. From the corner of his eye he noticed a familiar face or two in the queue waiting for tables, but he strode away without speaking. His temperament did not favor his being the first to offer a greeting. Aloofness was a virtue.

His car, babied from the day he bought it, was an eight-year-old Mercedes in near-perfect condition. He drove it slowly through a set of lights into downtown Andover, which was mostly closed up for the night. Male manne-

1

quins in worsteds and tweeds, smiling placidly through the glow of Macartney's display windows, suggested solid citizens of the town. Lem's Coffee Shop, which closed at six, was a mere slat of light. Citizens Bank, where he had several accounts, stood shrouded in darkness except for the glimmer of the electronic teller. The clock outside the bank told him the time, eight-twenty, and the temperature, twenty-seven degrees Fahrenheit.

The night held all the chill of November, a month he loathed. His parents had perished in November. The only poet he read with feeling called it "the month of the drowned dog." He saw it as a ghastly time, each day sinking inward, nothing growing, nothing alive, the year diminished to a stub. A couple of Novembers ago he had contemplated ending it all and would have done so had his mother not murmured from the grave, *Don't be a fool.*

He cruised through a second set of lights at the Gulf station. The red brick of the post office loomed on one side, the glass front of Barcelos Supermarket on the other. He accelerated when Main Street began its rise toward Phillips Academy, of which he was an alumnus, friendless during his four years there, his status awkward as a day student. Had it not been for his mother, he never would have stuck it out.

Beyond the academy grounds he turned right onto Hidden Road, soon fastened onto Porter Road, and a few minutes later veered down a choice cul-de-sac. He coasted into a circular drive lined with the woolly nighttime shapes of shrubs and left his car near a three-stall garage. Grass deadened his steps in his shortcut to the front door. The house was a brick colonial, formidable in its dimensions and pretentious in its colonnaded front. The voice that had summoned him was Alfred Bauer's. Bauer's wife opened the door.

"Hello, William."

2

He stepped in and stood under a chandelier. "I'm expected."

Harriet Bauer smiled with lips pushed out by large, handsome teeth that were always visible. She was fair-haired, big-boned, somewhere in her late thirties, with a broad Germanic face and wide-apart eyes. She was wearing a sweat suit, which did not surprise him. The Bauer family was into body-building—Nautilus, aerobics, yoga, calisthenics. Beneath her baggy suit was a belly like an iron plate and a sturdy pair of endless legs that would have suited a dancer. Her husband, who had turned fifty, could execute push-ups on one arm, and their strapping sixteen-year-old son looked murderous when bare-chested. She said, "Alfred will be with you in a minute."

"He made it sound urgent."

"Yes," she said, her smile curiously bright, as if nothing in the world could discompose her. He knew she could achieve a high through her own physical activity. "Come," she said.

The house was skillfully laid out, one room developing grandly into another, with furniture of eye-catching lines and cheerful colors. A mirror wedged into white oak recorded his passage into the study, where fiery logs gave a blush to the walls. As she helped him off with his coat he smelled the liniment she had rubbed on herself and found the odor disconcertingly pleasant.

"Can I get you something?" she asked, and he shook his head, his ear keyed to an insistent pounding high in the house, a kind of thump and clatter muffled by distance, which took him a second or two to fathom: her son's stereo. He raised his eyes.

"It all sounds so angry, so . . . desperate. Not music at all, is it?"

"Kids love it."

"Yes, it sells," he concurred, aware of nuances in her

3

manner, none he could quite figure out, though he had known her and her husband for ten years, had been in business with them for three, and was privy to secrets; some they had divulged, others he had divined. Unused to being kept waiting, except by them, he said dryly, "I'm never really positive who's in charge—you or Alfred."

"That's something you shouldn't worry about."

He agreed with a curt nod and sat down. She remained on her feet, her legs smartly spaced, the drawstring on her sweat pants pulled tight.

"The young woman who did typing for you last summer, you remember her, don't you?"

"Yes," he said, guardedly.

"She was special to us, William, but what was she to you? Anything?"

"A name in my Rolodex. She wasn't much of a typist, and I quit calling her. Why do you ask?"

Abruptly Harriet Bauer moved closer to the fire, which infused her with its glow and sparked a dry glitter in her hair. She regarded him at length. "She seemed the sort you'd have taken an interest in."

"No," he lied.

"I'll accept that with a reservation."

"Do as you please."

"And assume you won't be too upset to learn she's dead. Apparently she was murdered."

He felt his lips go dry. At the same time he was aware of the sudden and silent presence of Alfred Bauer in the doorway, but instead of looking in that direction he leaned his face toward the fire, as if the pattern of flames held meaning. He said something to Harriet Bauer but in a deformed voice that curled in on itself and limited its clarity.

She said, "My son knows. We told him straight off. That's why he's playing his music. His shrink says it shields him."

4

Rollins peered up at her through his tinted spectacles as his right shoulder sank to one side, as if the future held only absurdities. "How," he asked in a short whisper, "how did it happen?"

"We don't know all the facts yet."

"Where?"

"The Silver Bell. That makes it awkward, of course. For all of us."

He shuddered outwardly. Inside he wept. He watched the long curve of Harriet Bauer's hand sweep hair from her forehead. He said, "It has nothing to do with me."

"Do you really believe that?"

At the moment he believed in nothing. Nothing was real except the vibrations emanating from the faraway stereo. That and a blend of fragrances. Firewood erupted on the grate and effused its essence, the minty breath of liniment hung cool. Alfred Bauer had not budged from the doorway, but the bay rum on his shaved jaws wafted its bouquet well into the room.

"You're not simply our lawyer, William. You're our associate."

Something seemed to touch him, to gather him in the chair, as if the young woman for whom he had denied feelings were giving him a posthumous embrace. "Yes, I will have something. Bourbon, please."

"Alfred anticipated that." Her tone altered slightly. "By the way, don't ever underestimate us."

Alfred Bauer, soft on his feet like a heavyweight in fighting form, stepped into the room with a glass of Old Grand-Dad in his hand. Chest pelt shone like armor from his half-open shirt. His head was bald and domelike, his eyes an improbable baby blue, his voice a muscular baritone. He said, "William would never make that mistake."

* * *

5

With an expression of strain and a restless stance, Detective-Sergeant Sonny Dawson said, "Jesus, I don't have the stomach for this."

"You think I do?" the medical examiner said, bending over the bed on which the abused body of a young woman lay flat and narrow, her dark auburn hair spread wide over a pillow. "I mean, do you think I like it? This kid couldn't have been more than eighteen."

"Nineteen," Dawson whispered to himself.

"What?"

"I'm agreeing with you."

The bed was queen-size, and the room was in a rear of the Silver Bell Motor Lodge, which was girded by spruce and pine in the Ballardvale section of Andover, near Interstate 93. The young woman's leather shoulder bag was on a night table but held no identification. Suede boots stood beside the chair where her clothes had been tossed. Her underpants were nothing more than a cobweb. Her jeans were designer, her charcoal sweater monogrammed with an M. Her coat was in the open closet, nothing in the pockets except a pouch of keys.

"She must've been sweet," the medical examiner said and traced a gentle finger over her bruised face. The eyes were open. "She died hard."

"I can see that."

"Not an ounce of fat on her, nothing to cushion the blows. Look, you can tell ribs are broken."

Dawson went into the bathroom, where an aging uniformed officer named Billy Lord was dusting for prints. "Can I use the sink?" Dawson asked and without waiting for an answer ran water and doused his face. Then he flashed a crooked smile. "What's the matter with me, Billy? Am I getting old?"

"I don't know, Sonny. You forty yet?"

"I'm getting there."

"You got no belly. That says something."

"I don't eat a lot."

"Seems to me you're in pretty good shape."

"Not at the moment." He ripped off some toilet paper and patted his face dry in front of the mirror. His eyes, unmistakably green, gave him a zealous look. As a student at Boston University, a neat beard exalting his features, he had resembled a youthful Christ. Now, nearly twenty years older, the face clean-shaven, lean, and economical, honed sharp at the edges, he looked every inch a cop—with the possible exception of his hands. They were long and expressive, tooled, it would seem, for gentle business. He ran one through his dark hair. "Town like this shouldn't have homicides, d'you know that, Billy?"

"Town's growing, has been for years. Can't stop it, Sonny. You could stand in the middle of Main Street and blow your whistle, developers would run you over. Who'd pick you up? Me and the chief maybe, no one else."

"But I can bitch. I'm allowed to do that." He tossed the sodden tissue into the wastebasket. "How are you doing there?"

Officer Lord looked up with large, flat eyes. Hunkered down, he had the body of a bullfrog. "Not terrific. I think everything's been wiped."

"Keep at it," Dawson said and rubbed a crick in his neck while continuing to stare at himself in the glass. Again he pushed back his hair, but it quickly reverted to its natural fall, damp and limp over his forehead. Then he opened his check sports jacket and hiked up his trousers, which were burdened by the weight of his holstered revolver. He seemed to be delaying his return to the victim.

"Sonny!"

His name rang in his ears. It came from the medical examiner who was preparing to leave. Dawson stepped swiftly out of the bathroom and gazed at the bed. "That was fast."

The medical examiner closed his black bag and reached

for his overcoat. "All I have to tell you at this point is she's dead." He struggled with his coat. "Help me, huh?" Dawson helped him. "You probably want to know how long she's been dead. I don't know. Maybe three hours. You want to know the cause? Probably internal hemorrhaging. Whoever beat her didn't hold back. The weapon? I'd say bare fists."

"Can't you close the eyes?"

"Why? I'll only have to open them again." The medical examiner shifted his bag to his other hand. "What's the matter? You've seen bodies before?"

"Not many." Dawson stared at the stillness of the distorted face, at the austere lay of the limbs, at the rigidity of the toes. His voice went strange. "What d'you think, Doc, is that a person anymore?"

"Don't ask me silly stuff."

Dawson's crooked smile returned. "You know what my last case was? Obscene calls. Teacher from the high school was getting one a night, same muffled voice. Turned out to be a kid in her class."

"That's not surprising."

"But it's ironic."

"Why's it ironic?"

"Just is, Doc."

They tramped to the door together. The medical examiner raised his coat collar. He did not have much hair on the top of his head, just wisps, and he had a staved-in appearance, which made him look older than he was. "It's been a lousy month, Sonny. My wife missed Megabucks by a single digit, and our dog died, a blessing really. The poor thing was crippled up and half blind. And, of course, Reagan was reelected. That says a lot about the country's mentality. Oops, I should be careful. You probably voted for him."

"In a moment of madness."

"Maybe you'll luck out and live to regret it." The medical examiner smiled and threw open the door. Three cruisers were parked in a straight line, their dome lights bubbling blue in the chill air, and farther away officers in fur-collared jackets were questioning guests. An ambulance waited nearby. "You know, Sonny, I think she was a hooker."

"I know she was."

The medical examiner, who had stepped out into the cold, glanced back in surprise. "How do you know?"

"I did her a favor once."

"Then you know her name."

"Melody," he said.

After placing another log on the fire, Harriet Bauer left her husband and William Rollins to themselves, mounted wide stairs, and followed a long, airy passageway to her son's room, where stereo speakers hung from the walls. Hard rock pounded at her from every side. "Turn it down!" she shouted. He did, but not enough. "Turn it off!"

"You said *down*," he protested in a voice that caught.

"Now I mean *off*," she said, semaphoring the words. He obeyed, and the sudden silence was as much a shock to her ears as the music had been. "How are you doing?"

"Fine," he said, standing flat-footed in a yellow T-shirt and tight corduroys that pulled at his crotch. He was a farfetched copy of his father, with a shock of white-blond hair and a child's face levitating over an explosive chest, with muscles shifting in his long arms. He had strength but no grace, no agility, no swift step, only a clumsy one.

Regarding him doubtfully, she said, "I can tell you're not."

His ears, like his father's, had large lobes that colored

9

first when he flushed. Baby whiskers pricked his chin, which was prominent, like her. She knew he was fighting tears, a battle he had always been urged to win.

"I know what you're feeling," she said and saw his lower lip tremble.

"I'm not feeling anything."

"We'll all miss her."

He shied away from her, stumbling. His room was a mess. Books and magazines on the floor. An accumulation of clothes. Nike sneakers with long, trailing laces. She caught up to him.

"We all loved her, baby."

"Don't talk about her."

"We don't have to." She flurried fingers through his soft-spun hair, easily picturing him bald like his father and knowing too soon he probably would be. "But I think we should."

"*You* didn't love her."

There were fleeting instances when she regretted having a son, though a son had been her burning wish. She remembered the delivery, forceps required, his cry an eerie one, his breath not yet smelling of the world when he first came into her arms. She remembered his greedy mouth, her finger trying to satisfy it, and the nurse, impatient but not unkind, telling her it was not her finger he wanted. The irony of her reply passed well over the nurse: *You'd think I'd know.*

She said gently, "You're wrong, Wally."

If there was a response she did not hear it. His head was turned, his eyes on a wall, as if he needed noise from the stereo.

She said, "When you're grown up and ready for marriage, it'll be a princess."

"When's the funeral, Mom? When are they gonna fling her into the grave?"

10

He was a hair's breadth from hysteria, and she said no more.

When she returned to the study William Rollins had his coat on. Some bourbon remained in his glass, and he downed it. Her husband came away from the fire with a smile, scratched his chest, and said in his rich voice, "William and I have reassured each other. Nobody has anything to worry about. Unfortunate what happened, but it happened."

Rollins glanced behind him.

"I'll take it," she said and relieved him of the empty glass before he could place it on the imposing book cabinet of carved cherry, somebody's heirloom she had paid top dollar for at a Beacon Street auction in Boston. "Every business has its problems."

"That's what I told him. Right, William?"

"Words to that effect," Rollins murmured.

She peered at him and said, "Do you want another drink, one for the road?"

"I've had enough."

"Wise of you to know that," Alfred Bauer said. "Harriet will see you to the door."

They did not speak until they reached the foyer, where Rollins placed himself impassively under the chandelier, adjusted his spectacles, and fixed his scarf. Harriet Bauer freed the bolt in the lock and gripped the doorknob without turning it. Her smile, planted inches from his face, revealed her gums.

He said, "You smell like a gymnasium."

"Does that offend you?"

"You know it doesn't."

"Are we sparring?"

"Don't we always?"

"Are you making a pass?"

"Hardly," he said.

"Why not?"

"It would amuse you."

"No," she said, "it would amuse Alfred. You're such a neat package of a man, William. Quite unreadable when you want to be. Are you an alcoholic?"

He shook his head.

"Good. That would have worried us. Are you queer?"

He gathered himself to reply but then did not bother.

"I didn't think so, but Alfred wondered."

"Then why didn't *he* ask me?"

"Some things I do better." She opened the door and cold air barged in. A wind had kicked up and sounded like church voices swelling into a hymn. She said, "You're taking this very well. I know in my bones Melody meant something to you. I'm bothered I don't know how much."

"Who killed her?" he asked quietly.

"That's the big question." They each listened to a stampede of leaves. "Let's hope it wasn't one of us."

He stepped past her, braced his shoulders, and glanced back. Her smile was faint.

"Someone must tell Rita," she said.

The name chilled him.

"You do it," she said.

He started to speak, but the door closed on him.

The ambulance attendants shuffled in, bundled the body in a red rubber bag, and carted it away on a litter. With his back to the empty bed, Sergeant Dawson telephoned Chief Chute at his home and apprised him of events. The chief, who had dozed off while watching television, said, "Take it slow, Sonny. I'm not all that alert yet. Tell me again about the tip."

"Dispatcher said it was a muffled voice, could've been male or female or even a kid's. All it said was somebody

12

was dead at the Silver Bell, room forty-six. A cruiser in the vicinity got there in minutes."

"We got the voice on tape?"

"Yes," Dawson said. "Billy has taken pictures and is still dusting, and later he's going to vacuum. I've got guys checking the other units, but it seems nobody saw or heard anything. Most of the units on this side are unoccupied."

"Tell me about the victim."

"The body was lying unclothed on the bed. Somebody with strength had worked her over. Her face was messed up, but I recognized it. She wasn't local."

"Thank God for that. So who was she?"

Dawson had wrapped the telephone cord around his wrist. Meticulously he freed it. "Melody," he said, and there was a sizable pause from Chief Chute.

"Sonny, I'm sorry."

"Everybody used her, absolutely everybody." Rapidly he regretted his words. Stretching the cord to the fullest, he carried the phone to the window and separated the drapes. The moon, at its influential fullest, beamed in like a voodoo eye.

"Sonny, I hate to ask you this, but it's important. You can lie a little if you want, but I've got to have an answer. Did you ever . . . I mean—"

"I know what you mean." He was quiet for a moment. "No, Chief, not really."

Chief Chute's sigh filled the phone. "I remember when life was simple, the town little. 'Course I wasn't chief then, just a plain old patrolman having a coffee at Lem's and talking to the girls from town hall. Did I ever tell you that's how I met my wife?"

Dawson closed the drapes.

The chief said, "I don't suppose you've notified the district attorney. Do it, Sonny, do it now."

"I was hoping you would. I was hoping you'd convince him to let me take charge of the case."

"Sounds like you already have."

"Tell him we'll sew it up for him. Tell him I've already got leads."

"Would I be telling the truth?"

"More or less. I'm ninety percent certain it was the Bauer boy who made the call."

The chief's intake of breath was sharp, and Dawson could picture him digging his toes into his slippers and smoothing his fuzzy hair. His voice was low. "The Bauers scare me."

"I can handle them."

"And the Italian woman, Rita whatever her name is. Can you handle her?"

"I'll use kid gloves."

"No pun intended, but she's a heavyweight in every sense of the word."

"I realize that."

"You're not planning on hiding anything, are you, Sonny? I mean anything major."

"You trained me too well for that."

"No, Sonny, neither of us are what you could call trained. We play it by ear. That's what scares me the most."

"I want only what's best for the town," Dawson said in a colorless tone. "Trust me."

"I've always trusted you, Sonny. Why should I stop now?"

Dawson put the phone away and then looked into the bathroom, where Officer Lord was still in a crouch, a smudge of gray powder on his nose. "Did you hear all that, Billy?"

"No, Sonny. I never listen in on other people's conversations. But I'd like to give you some advice. If you don't mind. If you won't get mad."

"I'm listening."

"You've got to learn to cover your ass."

* * *

14

Leather-and-chrome furniture and potted plants of a lush variety marked the lobby of the Silver Bell. The night clerk, a retired fire fighter named Chick, lifted his rumpled face when he heard the doors open and fidgeted when he saw who it was. "I don't know anything, Sonny. I swear to God." In the crosshatch of a weathered cheek was a black mole that jiggled like a spider in its web when he spoke. "You want, I'll sign a paper."

Sergeant Dawson splayed his fingers against the edge of the reception desk. "Take it easy. As far as I know, we've always been friends."

"Always!" the clerk affirmed. He had chalk white hair and the blazing eyes of an insomniac. His employment was an act of charity by the manager, Mrs. Gately.

"You know who it was, don't you, Chick?"

"I knew her only a little, that's the truth. She signed in late last night, no luggage, alone, like always. I said two words to her, that's all."

"What were the words?"

"Hello."

"That's only one. What's the other?"

"I forget." His mole twitched. "Sonny, why are you doing this to me?"

"What name did she use?"

"Barbra Streisand. She liked to make jokes. Time before it was Tina Turner. I didn't know who Tina Turner was till somebody told me. Sonny . . . I can guess how you feel."

"What are you talking about?"

"I know you went out of your way for her."

"No, it's like you said, Chick. You don't know anything. Where's your boss?"

"Waiting for you. I called her, she came right over."

Dawson turned on his heel and walked beyond the reception counter, past a potted plant and a charcoal sketch of a raptorial bird. The clerk called after him.

"Sonny!"

15

"What?"

"Hang loose."

Dawson did not knock on the office door, simply opened it, strode in, and smelled coffee, freshly made. The delicate pot was on a tray, part of a service set, cups and saucers included. "I suspect a long night," Mrs. Gately said from the shadows of her desk. A gooseneck lamp with a slender fluorescent tube cast the only light, mostly on her well-structured face. "Help yourself."

He lifted the pot and, not bothering with a saucer, poured coffee into a cup. The cup was china, the silver sterling. "I rate."

"No," she said. "I do."

He dribbled cream, stirred, and took a cautious swallow, eyebrows bent in. Mrs. Gately rose soundlessly and stood, with polished fingernails grazing the desk, a trim and shapely figure in a navy blue blazer and a straight gray skirt, the skirt tight across her hips. Her hair, stylish in its curl and cut, possessed striking tones of silver. Her nose was aquiline. She had a kind of grave beauty that needed no smile and prospered with age. She was nearly fifty.

"There's not much I can tell you."

"You surprise me," he said, his mouth down at the corners.

"What do you expect, Sergeant? Tears? I don't cry for anybody."

He remembered her husband's funeral, the wake at Lundgren's, and the quick service at Christ Episcopal Church, no tears then either. He said, "I thought she'd stopped coming here."

"That's what you wanted to think."

Her voice had become cold and measured. His seemed twangy. "Who was her client?"

"Assuming she had one, how would I know? Her arrangements were discreet."

"Where's her car?"

16

"Look in the lot. Gold Mazda. She was doing well."

"Did you talk with her?"

"Briefly. Late this morning. I told her to behave herself."

He dropped his cup. He did not think that he meant to, but there, suddenly, probably on purpose, were the broken bits, with some of the spill on his shoes. "I'm sorry," he said and started to stoop.

"Leave it," she said rigidly, and he straightened and sidestepped the damage. She slipped away from the desk, diminishing her face to shadow. "We don't like each other, do we, Sergeant?"

"Not at the moment."

"Perhaps we blame each other."

"I was doing my job."

"You were suspect."

He kneaded his brow, as if his mind were sore. In the secrecy of his mind, Melody shimmered. Whole and healthy, her wealth of auburn hair swirling past her shoulders, she smiled at him. "Do you know what I wish, Mrs. Gately? I wish we could be open with each other."

"I told you months ago I don't trust policemen. I don't trust their motives or their mentality, but for some reason you think you're different."

"I am."

"Why? Because they call you *Sonny*? Because they love you at Lem's? Because you seem to care for people? Sorry, Sergeant, it doesn't wash."

"I thought we were on the same side."

"The same side of what? The tracks? Hardly."

"Don't be a bitch, Paige."

She bristled, not at the epithet, but at the use of her given name, which was her mother's maiden name, the family one of Andover's oldest. Taking slow steps, she carried herself closer to him. "Do you remember a long time ago I told you Melody was messed up, really messed

17

up? You asked what it was—drugs?—and I told you straight. Men, your age."

"And Bauer's."

"That's right, Sergeant. Your rival."

"Don't make it sound dirty."

"What was it?" She took another step forward, her mouth severely set, as if her words had a bad aftertaste. The toe of her pump crunched china. He could smell her scent, faintly cinnamon. "You have interesting eyes, Sergeant. Green. Real green. That's what attracted her."

"So much you don't understand."

"You'd be surprised."

"I wanted what was best for her."

"Be careful of what you say, Sergeant. You have the right to remain silent."

He tightened as her ironic face half smiled, the movement of her bright lips scarcely perceptible. He looked for sympathy of a sort in her eyes. It was there all right, but it was not real. It was parody. Without warning she grasped the lapels of his check jacket.

"I could kill you."

Here and there threads gave.

"Let go."

Then a noise wrenched them both around, she swiveling hard on her heels. The door had opened, and the knit face of the night clerk peered in at them, eyes flaring. "What do you want?" she snapped.

"Something I forgot to tell Sonny." The voice was sheepish, apologetic. "About the Bauer boy."

"I would guess he already knows."

"Tell me later, Chick," Dawson said.

The face withdrew, some disappointment in it, and the door closed with a gentle click hardly heard. Mrs. Gately moved back a pace, cords shifting in her throat, as if a grim part of her were taking control of the whole of her. She

18

said, "The boy is in his teens. The idiot years. It would be best to leave him alone."

"I don't think that will be possible."

"Then you'd better know what you're doing."

"I've dealt with the kid before."

"This is different."

"Yes, much," he said grimly and gave her a look conveying the sympathy she had denied him. "You should have stayed in real estate, Paige."

"Do you know who his godmother is?" she shot back, and he nodded with the irony of a cardplayer who had saved an ace.

"That could be more your problem than mine."

Her face darkened, seemed to seal up. She spoke in a voice that was rock hard. "You owe me for a cup."

He said, "You've cost me a jacket."

William Rollins left his Mercedes on the street and trudged reluctantly up the moonlit walk, which took a jagged route around shrubs planted on graded levels, a tough shovel in the winter. The house was a custom-designed contemporary built twenty years ago on ledge, the windows of varying sizes and shapes, a fancy of the original owner. Nearly every window was ablaze. The current owner, Rita Gardella O'Dea, who lived alone, stinted on nothing.

At the door he pressed the button and, with a shiver of anxiety, the cold driving at him, listened to chimes. He knew there would be a wait. Rita O'Dea never hurried, except perhaps to church to light candles for the souls of her parents and her brother. When the door finally swung open, he greeted her from bent shoulders, as if the passing minutes had pressed upon him.

"Don't just stand there," she said.

He hustled in, worked his way by her as she closed the door with a firm thrust. She was sheathed in a turquoise

19

robe and was robustly overweight, with great charcoal eyes
that had a way of smashing into him and knocking him
either into place or out of it. Her heap of black hair was
jolted up by a ribbon. "I'm sorry to disturb you," he said.

"I was watching TV. That's *not* disturbing me. You
watch TV?"

"Sometimes."

"I watch it a lot." Her shadow hovered. "Well, Willy,
what's up?"

It was a name he detested and felt he did not deserve,
but he dared not correct her. She was the sister of a slain
Mafia leader and an exile from Boston, her behavior eccentric, her moods unpredictable, her whims many. In her
large, full face, sweet in repose, was the sulk of a child and
in her voice the wail of a baby.

He said, "A matter to discuss."

"Something serious?"

"Yes."

"Then let's not stand here."

She took him through a room that had been redecorated. It was light and airy, Scandanavian, the furniture a
glossy teak, the white pelts of animals tossed on the floor.
He felt her smile.

"You like it?" she asked, looking back. "I got rid of all
the wop stuff. The shades with fringes, all that shit. Somebody should've told me."

Nervously he adjusted his glasses. "What you've done
is marvelous."

"Should be. I paid enough."

She directed him into the spacious kitchen, where pun-
cheons of gleaming oak formed counters and the copper
of hanging pots and pans resembled weaponry. Every cu-
linary convenience, from a double microwave oven to a
Cuisinart food processor, seemed within the sweep of her
large arm.

"Sit down," she said, and he sat at a trestle table, his

20

coat still buttoned but the collar lowered. She laid out a dish, cut generously into a chocolate walnut cake, and said, "Have a slice." It was a slab. Which he did not want. He had no sweet tooth and never had, not even as a child. "Try it." He picked it up in his hand, for there was no fork, and ate from the side of it. No napkin. He licked his fingers. "Well?" she asked, and he brought his head up.

"Delicious."

"Better be. I put everything in it." She loomed over him with her hands buried to the elbows in the capacious pockets of her robe. "You said it was serious, so is it bad? I hate bad news."

What bothered him the most at the moment, absurdly, were moist crumbs that had fallen on the lap of his coat. When he tried to brush them away, he made a smear. His anxiety mounted.

She said, "If it's a problem you can handle, I don't want to hear about it."

"Some trouble at the Silver Bell."

"Tell Alfred."

"He sent me." He wanted to get out of the chair, but she was in the way. "Melody is dead."

The blood left Rita O'Dea's face. Watching her hands rise slowly out of her pockets, he expected the worst, but her voice was soft. "Hold me."

He struggled up and, as much as he could, embraced her.

Two

Twenty years ago, when Paige Gately's husband took sick and she got into the real estate business, Andover was in the midst of a housing boom. The Lawrence *Eagle-Tribune*, which displayed its Andover news prominently, proclaimed that builders were changing the face of the town. "Developers," the reporter wrote, "are gobbling up the green, subdividing it, and erecting houses in areas that were once poultry farms, fruit orchards, meadowlands, pine groves, lovers' lanes, swamps, and gravel pits."

"It's only the beginning," warned the planning board chairman, whose sentiments were echoed by the building inspector, who feared Andover would become a bedroom town of Boston. In reality, it already was.

The houses in varying stages of construction were garrisons, Georgian colonials, redwood contemporaries, flung-out ranches and splits, handsome Capes, outsize gambrels and saltboxes, and what the reporter called "California wingdingers with glass fronts, cedar ceilings, and ominous overhangs." There seemed nowhere in the town's sprawling thirty-two square miles that something wasn't going up.

Acreage off River Road, which included the old Henderson farm, was being parceled into thirty-eight lots. The site contained peach trees, Scotch pines, fields of loosestrife, and patches of sugar-fine sand and overlooked Wood

Hill, which itself was under development, several of the houses already erected and landscaped. Atop the hill, Paige Gately pointed out to a prospective buyer that on a clear day one could see the Prudential Tower in Boston, some twenty miles away. The customer, put off by her aloof good looks and icy smile, eventually went to another broker and bought a place on Reservation Road, where the houses were being built in a strikingly modern manner under the confines of cluster zoning.

The planning board chairman was an avid proponent of such zoning, which arranged house lots like pieces of pie around a delicacy of groomed grass, flowering shrubs, and ornamental trees. "A tiny park, so to speak," the chairman said at a public hearing. "All you have to do is travel to a few sites to see that it works."

The building inspector was less enthusiastic about such zoning but praised the cul-de-sacs that went along with it—"nonthroughways traveled only by the mailman and the residents themselves." One such cul-de-sac, in a choice part of town near the academy, was Southwick Lane, where a ranking Raytheon executive hired an architect to design a brick-front colonial along manorial lines. Four years later, when he went to work for the Nixon administration in Washington, the executive sold the property to Alfred Bauer, who, among other ventures, had a hidden interest in a string of health clubs under investigation by Boston vice squad detectives.

Another area of construction, dramatic in its variety of houses, was the land around Wild Rose Drive, which included Strawberry Hill Drive, once the site of the biggest berry farm in the county. It was here, competing hotly with other brokers, that Paige Gately sold her first house, to an engineer for a Texas-based corporation that had transferred him into the area.

Many in town damned the developers, but some expressed admiration for their ingenuity. On what became

Oriole Drive, a contractor drove his equipment over pure ledge and, to the building inspector's amazement, succeeded in digging and dividing the rock and grading it into lots, on which he interspersed colonials with ranches—the East with the West.

Over on North Street, in order to use a scrap of back land, another contractor built a house that squatted in Andover but faced the tiny and deprived city of Lawrence, which for some complicated reason, provided the utilities. Andover, however, collected the taxes.

Regulars in Lem's Coffee Shop noted, without surprise, that no development, not yet at least, was taking place in the vast tract that meandered off Woburn Street and spread beyond Ballardvale Road. This was the so-called Tea Coupon land, which had hundreds of owners of lots within lots—dating back some seventy-five years when the Grand Union Tea Company promoted itself with coupons redeemable in parcels of plots the size of postage stamps.

Nearby, however, houses were going up on the hundred-acre triangle that once had been the Anderson poultry farm; and in the town's south section, underground utilities and storm sewers were installed in a lush development off Wildwood Road, where Paige Gately brokered a number of houses, some a few times over, angering other agents because she worked on a commission two or three points below the prevailing rate and would shave another point to save a sale.

Farther south, a contractor was developing prime land off Gould Road bordering Harold Parker State Forest and Field's Pond, where the high honk of Canadian geese was a haunting sound. A banker friend of hers steered a well-heeled client her way for one of the grander properties and later, out of earshot of the client, placed a soft white thumb against her cheek and whispered, "I still think about you."

This was also the neighborhood where, many years

later, Rita Gardella O'Dea bought the custom contemporary, cash on the barrelhead, though by this time Paige Gately was no longer a broker. She did, however, receive a finder's fee, which also was in cash. Attorney William Rollins discreetly laid down an envelope and murmured, "A token of Mrs. O'Dea's appreciation."

She got out of the business during the Carter administration, when inflation and high mortgage rates froze the home-building industry and chilled the real estate market, which she could have weathered if her dying husband's medical bills had not forced her to dip into her clients' escrow accounts. Her banker friend, Ed Fellows, shuddered when she revealed the problem."I'm not asking for help, just time," she said, for her notes at his bank were overdue. His eyes turned suspicious and his voice jealous.

"Who's bailing you out?"

"Alfred Bauer," she replied readily and watched him flinch. "I also need a small favor," she went on quietly.

"Have I ever said no to you?"

A month later Ed Fellows appeared before the planning board and vigorously endorsed proposals by Bauer Associates to build a motel in one part of town and a hundred houses in another.

As Andover's population grew, so did its industrial base. Raytheon, Hewlett Packard, Gillette, and Digital Equipment all erected modern plants on the fringes of the town, where vast farmlands continued giving way to tree-shrouded industrial parks and office complexes. New companies coming in were usually in the high-tech field, though oldtime residents were scarcely aware of their existence. Their upper-echelon employees sought housing in the town, but the rank and file were anonymous commuters swerving off interstate highways in the morning and lurching right back on again at day's end. "That's the way we like it," boasted one of the selectmen at a Chamber of Commerce dinner.

Not all the companies, however, were desirable. A plastics manufacturer was suspected of pouring poisonous waste into the Shawsheen River, and a maker of polyurethane foam for cushions and mattresses went broke and left behind a hundred or so barrels of deadly chemicals, which worried the fire chief because some of the chemicals were explosive. But on the whole, few voices protested the town's economic development, which stabilized the tax rate while ballooning property values celestial to begin with. "You don't argue with affluence," joked the selectman at the Chamber dinner, to which Alfred Bauer responded, "Hear, hear." He was a recent resident of the town, but, through the efforts of Paige Gately and Attorney Rollins, he already seemed to know everybody who mattered.

From his home on Southwick Lane, Bauer rang up a Boston number, heard Rita O'Dea's heavy voice on the other end, and said, "Let me speak to your brother. Something to tell him."

"Tony's busy. Tell me."

"I'm living in Andover."

"So?"

"It's where you plant money and watch it grow."

Three

After William Rollins locked up his Mercedes for the night, a ghost followed him up the steps, through the door, and into the dark of his townhouse. He switched on a dull light, removed his coat, and stared into space. "I feel you more strongly than ever," he said clearly and soberly, despite quivers in his legs, as if the floor were bending under him.

He entered the deep shadows of the front room and made his way to the liquor cabinet with no need for a light. He knew where everything was. He poured a bourbon and tossed it down, then dried his lips with the edge of a finger. For a sweet second or so, he felt an emptiness of mind and a softness of mood. He poured himself another drink, larger, meant to last, and in the near-dark he took two steps toward his favorite chair and then stopped short, his breath catching.

"What the hell are you doing in my house?"

The shape in the chair stirred, and moonlight from the window gave the angular face a small glow. The voice that floated up was Sergeant Dawson's: "Waiting for you."

"You have no right."

"I agree."

Rollins's legs quivered again, but he quickly steadied them and licked away the droplets of bourbon that had slopped onto his wrist. "How did you get in?"

Dawson raised a hand and with a jingle displayed a pouch of keys. "I took a chance one might fit."

"Is your key there as well, Sergeant?"

Their voices were dry and muted, without tone. Dawson, though he did not show it, was suffering a headache of hammerstrokes proportion. He said, "She's dead, Counselor. What do you think of that?"

"I'm in shock. Paige Gately told the Bauers, who immediately got in touch with me. I've informed Mrs. O'Dea."

"You've been busy."

"We all had affection for Melody."

"Except yours was less obvious."

"Yes, different from yours." Rollins sank into an overstuffed chair, one he usually avoided, and became a shadow. "Do you want a drink, Sergeant? I think you could use one. Please, help yourself."

Dawson rose, rested solidly on his feet until he got his balance, and made his way stiffly to the liquor cabinet, where he clanked bottles. "I can't see," he complained, and Rollins, with a slow movement, illuminated a table lamp.

"Better?"

Dawson treated himself to a taste of rye, his face drawn, as if in a melancholy. He stayed beside the cabinet, a hand resting on the top. "Would you like to talk about her?"

"In memoriam?"

"It seems appropriate."

Rollins smoothed back the hair at his temples. His bourbon glass was under the lamp. Wearily he removed his tinted spectacles. Without them, his face was stark and disconcerting, arch at the mouth. "A fascinating young woman. She taught me a lot."

"I'm sure she did."

"Doesn't that bother you, Sergeant?"

"I'll let you know when it does."

"She said I used good body English in bed."

"Congratulations."

28

There was a pause as Rollins's face seemed to push out, grow bigger. "I'm lying."

"I figured."

"I suspect you know more about me than you should."

"Probably. I apologize."

An acute silence followed. Dawson finished his rye, and Rollins nursed his bourbon, the vague threat of a curse on his lips. "What do you want, Sergeant? Why are you really here?"

"Tell the Bauers I want to question their son. It doesn't have to be at the station. It can be anywhere. Their house. Mine. Yours. Do you understand what I'm saying?"

"You can't be serious."

"They have until five tomorrow evening, no later."

Rollins smiled unbecomingly, and his voice gave an ominous coating to each word. "War of nerves. It won't work."

"We'll see."

"They'll crush you."

Dawson began wending his way out of the room, a faint drag to his step. At the last moment he stopped and looked back. "Who was it you spoke to? Melody?" He smiled bleakly, without expecting a reply.

"My mother."

Dawson kneaded his hot brow. "I should've guessed."

Police and Fire were under the same roof in a brick building of colonial design, located on Main Street below Elm Square. Dawson got aspirin from the desk sergeant, who said, "Go home." Instead he went into the fire station, borrowed bedding, and slept restlessly on a spare cot. He woke in the early morning with what felt like a cold footprint on his heart. A fireman said to him, "A tough one, huh, Sonny?" He cleaned his jaws with an electric shaver, showered, and returned to the same clothes, straightening with care the weakened lapels of his check jacket. The same fireman, offering him coffee, said, "Who was she? Anyone we know?"

Another fireman said, "Chute's looking for you."

A couple of hours later Dawson sat squarely behind his undersized desk in a basement cubicle of the police station. He smoothed his hair with his hand and cleared his throat. Before him was a brief statement typewritten on Town of Andover stationery. He had prepared it, and the Essex County district attorney's office, through Chief Chute, had approved it. Clipped to his shirt was a button of a microphone and zeroed in on him was a hand-held camera from one of Boston's lesser television channels. The Boston *Herald*, which sought sensation, had dispatched a reporter, but the *Globe* had not. A reporter and photographer were there from the Lawrence *Eagle-Tribune*, but no one was present from the town's weekly tab, which was going to press that day and would wait a week to report the murder.

In a clear, inflectionless voice, Dawson read the statement. He gave the place, estimated time, and probable cause of death. The victim's identity, he said, had not yet been positively established, but she was eighteen to twenty years old, her hair dark reddish brown, her height medium. The body showed evidence of a beating, homicide suspected. An autopsy was being performed at Lawrence General Hospital. He looked up from the statement and said, "That's all I'm prepared to say for now, except that we don't believe she was a resident of the town."

The reporter from the *Herald*, whose large features jammed his small face, said, "That doesn't tell us much, Sarge. What was she doing in the motel?"

Dawson ignored the question.

The reporter said, "I heard something about a car being towed. Mazda. Hers?"

"We're checking."

"Any leads?"

"None I can talk about."

"An arrest expected?"

"That's the whole point, isn't it?" Dawson freed himself of the microphone and was on his feet, slipping an arm into the wrinkled sleeve of a tan topcoat that was unlined and in danger of losing a button. He dodged the video camera, but the *Herald* reporter got a snatch of his sleeve.

"Was she shacked up with somebody? I mean, she must've been, right?"

Dawson said gently, "Let me be the detective."

"How come the DA's got you in charge?"

"I was on top of it. And he has confidence in me."

The reporter threw him an off-center smile. "Can I quote you on that?"

"Please."

Ten minutes later, after a brisk uphill walk through Elm Square, the November wind pulling at him, he entered Lem's Coffee Shop. It was past the early breakfast rush, with most of the regulars gone, but Fran Lovell was there. Her hand came out of a booth. "Sit with me, Sonny." They had known each other since high school, where she had been a superachiever, salutatorian of her class. Now she was an officer at Citizens Bank, with a line from a dead marriage etched into her forehead. Dawson shook off his coat, and she shortened her voice. "If you were mine, I'd dress you better."

The waitress delivered coffee, a steaming cup for him, a refill for Fran, who immediately reached for the sugar, the gesture compulsive, as if it produced the only sweetness in her life. She said, "I heard there was a murder."

"How'd you hear?"

"Billy Lord came in for a doughnut. He said it was a young woman."

Dawson glanced away. On the wall behind the luncheon counter, above individual-size boxes of Kellogg's cereals, was a large oil painting of downtown done by a local artist nearly three decades ago. Smoke from cooking and grease from the grill had long since calmed the colors and infused the scene with an eerie quaintness. It was a time when the town's population was less than fifteen thousand. Now it was twice that. He said, "Do you remember a couple of months ago I brought a girl to your desk? She opened a savings account. Melody Haines."

"I loved the name. Was it her, Sonny?"

He nodded.

She began to cry.

"Don't."

She grabbed a napkin. "Why am I doing this? I hardly knew her."

"Is the account still open?"

"She closed it soon after. She came to me because she knew I'd remember her. How do you forget a face like that?" The sugar shaker was between them. She moved it. "It was your money, wasn't it?"

The edges of his face seemed to sharpen. "What makes you think so?"

"You let yourself in for stuff. You always have."

He returned his gaze to the painting. Despite the countless times he had stared at it through the years, it never failed to nudge him, for fleeting seconds, into a mellower time, when no sorrow lasted long, when every hurt healed within the week, sometimes the hour. "I was trying to help her," he said.

"You don't have to explain, Sonny. Certainly not to me."

"Fran, can I count on you?"

"For what? Discretion? Of course." She lit a cigarette and tipped her head back. She wore her hair long, but it lacked style and care, as if she no longer valued her appearance. "It must be difficult for you," she said.

"A little."

"Did you kill her?"

After a lapse, he said, "Is that a serious question?"

"No. I'm sorry." Her hand started toward his, then crept back. "Who was she? What was she?"

"Not now, Fran. OK?"

"Sure, I understand. I always do." She drew hard on the cigarette and smiled faintly through a hot haze of smoke. "Do you ever flip through the old yearbook, Sonny? All the pictures?"

"Lent the book out," he said absently, "never got it back."

"Christ, I was sweet. And you were something yourself. Girls went for you, did you know that? Of course you knew. You had your pick—and you weren't even on the damn football team. Jocks hated you." She gestured carelessly. "Remind me, Sonny, how many times did we date? A dozen? More?"

He remembered nothing beyond a few sloppy kisses exchanged on a nameless road through woods where houses now stood. She dropped an ash.

"It was once," she said, "that's all. You never called back."

"You were seeing someone else."

"What did it matter at that age?"

He pushed that ashtray toward her. "Why are we talking this way?"

"First time I've had cards in my hand. But don't worry, I'm not going to play any."

He sighed. "What's the matter, Fran? Things lousy at home?"

"No worse than usual. Why didn't you ever marry, Sonny? Did you know something I didn't?"

"You were too quick, I was too slow."

"You went into the army."

"The navy."

"Then the police."

"It was what I wanted."

Cold air stretched in when the door flew open and a yellow-helmeted work crew from Massachusetts Electric trooped in and took seats at the counter. He swallowed coffee. She dashed out her cigarette and picked up her bag. "In some ways we're alike, Sonny."

"What ways?"

"I don't think you'd want to know." She reached for her coat, which was rugged-looking, practical. He rose to help her on with it and afterwards slipped on his own. He paid both checks. Hers included a breakfast. "Walk me to the bank," she said. "Make me feel young again."

He consulted his watch. "I can't."

"That's right. You have a killer to catch."

He held the door for her and followed her out into the cold, where their breaths ran ragged. He said, "She was beaten to death."

"Billy told me." She drew her coat tighter together and prepared to cross the street, a lean figure hidden in wool. "Sonny."

"What?"

"You'll never find another like her."

The exercise room overlooked an indoor swimming pool at the far end of their house. Harriet Bauer, her knees braced over the rail of a slant board, was doing sit-ups. Silently she counted off twenty, then twenty more, her midriff flashing out of her sweat suit each violent time her back struck the board. Alfred Bauer was in the pool. He swam the length several times, once underwater, where he was a glow of pink flesh curving as if through sleep. He pulled himself out, his blue eyes bloodshot and his chest expanded. Harriet Bauer was still at it, still counting, her hair in her eyes and her nostrils flared like those of a horse. He pattered to her with a towel slung around his wet waist. "Enough," he said, but she kept going as if some inner mechanism demanded it. "Harriet!" Finally she fell back, her heart pounding. Her voice wafted up.

"I'm fine."

He dipped down, smelling of the pool, and brushed her hair aside. Then he gazed at her with an intentness that tried to see past her skin. With a sudden grip, his strength formidable, he brought her to her feet. Her loose trousers hung low on her hips, and her stomach was sucked in like a soup plate. Her breath hit hot against his face.

"I could've done a hundred."

"I don't doubt it."

"*More* than a hundred."

"You're riding high," he said.

"That's the point," she said.

He guided her over a gym mat and through a swinging door into a room that housed three wall lockers, a stall of frosted glass, and a portable refrigerator. She slaked her thirst with a blend of fruit juices that came from the health store and wiped her mouth on her gray sleeve. Then she teetered for a moment, still full of nervous energy and shaky strength. She tugged at her top to get it off.

"Need some help?"

"I can manage."

They showered together, a ritual, the soap passing between them, the spray lukewarm. The opaque glass, tinged in iodine, cast them in a ghostly sepia. He pressed shampoo into his palm. "I wish I had hair," he said, lathering hers, old gold when wet. She soaped his chest.

"You have plenty here." A little later she sponged his head, which, lowered, shone like a brass ball.

He said, "Are you worried about Wally?"

"I always worry. He's our baby."

"Maybe he should see the shrink again."

"Turn around." She sponged his shoulders. "I don't think that's wise. God knows what he might tell him."

"It's privileged."

"I wouldn't depend on it."

"The guy's like a priest. Besides, we own him."

She soaped his back, her fingers at times digging in. "But not the cop."

"Don't be so sure," he said with steel in his voice as she embraced him from behind, the water beating upon them. One of her legs muscled its way between the two of his. "How much, Alfred?" Her words rippled through the spray against the heat of his neck. "How much did you love her?"

"Don't talk nonsense."

Her embrace quickened into a sudsy grip, slippery but secure. "I'd never play second fiddle, not even to a memory," she said, her nails digging deep.

"You're hurting."

"Who's stronger?" she asked.

"Don't test me."

"I always win in bed."

"That's where I give an advantage." He started to say something else but stopped when they each heard a footfall outside the stall. A shadow flickered on the rough glass, and the milk white shape of a face could be seen. They thought that their son, who had left less than an hour ago for school, had inexplicably returned. But the voice was a woman's.

"When you're finished," Paige Gately said.

Their bedroom was commodious and richly carpeted. The four-poster bed, bedecked with a satin spread, looked more for show than for sleep. In the depths of the room, where Alfred Bauer was dressing, was a series of wardrobe doors, with mirrors nearby. Bauer put on a thick-striped shirt. His shirts were made to measure, some silk, the rest of quality cotton, his tailor an Italian in Lawrence, the same skillful fellow who made his suits, which were a continental cut. Harriet Bauer, wearing only a bra, stood with a foot on the bed and rubbed a moist towel over the leg she had just shaved. The calf, smarting from the keenness of the blade, was strong and shapely, the thigh sumptuous. Knotting his tie, Alfred Bauer said, "Isn't she something?"

For longer than a moment there was no response from Paige Gately, who had followed them into the bedroom no farther than the matching towels they had let fall. She wore a fitted cashmere coat molded across her hips and held kidskin gloves in one hand. "She could easily get five hundred dollars. Is that what you want me to say?"

Harriet Bauer looked up slowly, precisely. "I used to get a thousand for a weekend."

The gloves twitched. "That was years ago, I understand."

"Yes, Paige. When the dollar meant more."

Alfred Bauer breezed forward, slipping on his jacket and buttoning it. The suit was Cambridge gray, with a bit of silk overarching the breast pocket and complementing his tie. "She was the best, Paige. Take it from me."

"I'm not arguing."

He took Paige Gately's arm, gently.

In the study the smell of charred logs drifted up from the grate. The morning wind made dire sounds at the windows, like computer music, and a tree hovered close enough for twigs to tick on the panes. "Please, sit," he said, but she stayed erect, still bound in her snug coat, her mouth an oval of red in a smooth, ageless face. She spoke low.

"Where's your son?"

"In school, of course."

Her face turned waxen. "Everybody knows he was at the motel yesterday. Certainly Dawson does."

"I'm aware of that, but what does it mean? Nothing."

"He's your worry, Alfred. Yours and Harriet's." Her red mouth seemed to ignite her words. "The less I know the better."

37

"That's understood."

"I don't want him near the Silver Bell again."

"That goes without saying."

"He needs help."

"In one way or another we all do," Bauer said calmly and turned to the cherry book cabinet, a shelf of which was devoted to the assassination of John F. Kennedy, whose politics he had detested, but whose prestige, charm, and power he had admired.

"You're a cool customer, Alfred."

He reached for something on the high top of the cabinet. It was a gold pen, which he clipped to the inside pocket of his jacket. On the pocket, in silver stitching, was his monogram and the date the suit was made. He said, "I have no use for people who panic. What gives me confidence is knowing you never would."

"I'm flesh and blood."

"You're more than that, Paige."

"What about Dawson?"

"What about him?"

"He's not your usual policeman," she said firmly. "He's not even your usual man. He's all emotion when you think he's all business. And he's all business when you least expect it."

Bauer's attention had been fixed on the vibrations of her throat. Now it alternated between the taut brightness of her lips and the careful cut and silvery shimmer of her hair. "Let me assure you," he said with equanimity, "that *is* your usual cop."

"What am I to do?"

"Nothing."

They let several seconds skip by, during which time they calmly regarded each other, nothing in their expressions to suggest collusion or even interest. He walked her to the foyer, watched while she fastened the top button of her coat, and waited while she put on her gloves and flexed her fingers in them.

"I'll tell Harriet you said good-bye."

Then he opened the door for her. The cold sun, a shot through the clouds, shocked their eyes. Shielding hers, she said, almost as an afterthought, "When this is over, I want to talk with you about the Silver Bell."

"You want out?"

"On the contrary."

His smile turned lenient, indulgent, while the rest of him went on guard. "What do you want?"

"Nothing unreasonable."

"You swear?"

"I do."

"Nothing that would displease Rita O'Dea?"

"You have my word," she said.

He had held his smile. "Then I'll breathe easier for the both of us."

She took a tentative step out into the cold, the wind rocking her until she squared herself. He was about to close the door when she turned and stared at him over the drawn collar of her coat. The wind seemed to disperse her voice in every direction. "Tell me, Alfred, will you miss her?"

There was no reaction, not even a breath. His blue eyes stood up to the sun, though not very well. She lifted a gloved hand, as if she might pull his head against her heart.

"Come here."

He stretched forward, certain feelings no longer submerged. His eyes carried a desolating sense of loss. Their kiss was dry, shallow, and ambiguous. "A part of me went with her," he said.

* * *

The drive did not take long, thirty-five minutes from the police station in Andover to the bowfront brownstone in Boston's Back Bay, where Melody Haines had shared an apartment with two women her senior by five and seven years. They were waiting for him, for he had telephoned much earlier, catching them before they left for work. They did not know the whole reason for the visit but anticipated something bad and greeted him grimly. The studio room he stepped into had a clean uncluttered air and a subtle scent of furniture polish. The older of the two, almond-eyed and fresh-skinned, intriguingly tall, said tightly, "Yes, you're the one. You're Sonny."

He nodded. Melody had mentioned them only once, but he remembered everything. This one was Sue, Delaware-born, Amherst-educated, a writer for medical periodicals at Tufts. The other, hanging back under a ball of briar-brown hair, was Natalie, a native of New Hampshire, short and dumpy, blind without her glasses, shy to hostility with those she did not know. She too worked at Tufts.

Sue said, "Your eyes, they're as green as Melody said. But you're old."

"Yes."

"But from Melody's perspective, not so much from mine. I'm not flirting with you, Sonny. I'm simply delaying what I don't want to ask."

Not knowing any other way to put it, he said, "She's dead."

Sue stood fixed while Natalie took a short backward step, her round face swelling under her brittle hair. Sue's face went expressionless and gaunt, which brought out its bones, all of them narrow and keen, patrician in their structure. "Shit," she said. She turned, put her back to him, showed him the endless pale stalk of her neck. "How?"

"It was a homicide."

"What?"

"A homi—"

"Yes, I heard you!" Her voice was high-toned, and she calmed it, gradually faced him again. "Who did it?"

"I'm working on it."

Natalie retched, a hollow sound, and at once pressed a plump hand over her mouth. Sue said, "Easy, kitten." The bedrooms were to the left, one with a door open enough for Dawson to glimpse the glamor of a travel poster and the ruffles of a bedspread.

"I'd like to look through her things. Would you mind?"

"Yes," Sue said with some hoarseness. "At this point I don't know why, but I'd mind very much."

"Later, then." He buried his hands in the pockets of his topcoat and stood woodenly. "As far as I know, she didn't have a family."

"She had no one."

"She had us," Natalie said from her distance, though her voice was hardly heard, her face hidden. Then she pulled back, tears starting.

Dawson said, "Would one of you identify the body? It's a legal thing."

"Why can't you?" Sue countered.

He did not answer.

On the way out of the building Sue kept a close eye on Natalie and whispered steadying words. They were each bundled in quilted jackets and woolen caps. A sleazy-looking young man emerged from the steamy warmth of a sidewalk vent with his hand out. They ignored him. Sue said to Dawson, "Melody would've given him something."

"I know," Dawson said and unlocked his unmarked car.

The traffic was fitful on Storrow Drive and worse at the bottleneck leading to Route 93. Sue, who had been quiet, said, "We know what Melody did. We've always known." He could see the movement of her mouth and the top of Natalie's hair in the rearview mirror as he milked the brake in the gush of merging traffic. No driver gave an

41

inch, not even those in the flimsiest of cars. Sue said, "We tried to warn her."

"And I tried to help her," he said and saw her mouth bend.

"Some help." Then immediately she said, "I'm sorry. I didn't mean to lay that on you."

On Route 93 he swung to the inside lane and let the bulk of traffic tear by. The sun was a welcome blast as the wind cut through cracks in the car. Passing the Medford exit he heard Sue say, "Sit up, Nat." Natalie's groan seemed more a child's than a woman's. Between Stoneham and Reading the roadside was bleak with bushes baring their thorns.

Farther on, traffic thinned, and Dawson slipped lower behind the wheel. A knot in his neck dissolved, though a tenseness in his shoulders remained. Sue sat forward and gripped the back of his seat. "Drive faster, please."

Lawrence General Hospital sat on a hill amid the brickwork of a tiny old industrial city that lay like rubble near the sprawling affluence of Andover. Andover's history stretched back to the Puritans, some of whom burned witches, while Lawrence's past extended only into the last century when Boston money men created it as a business enterprise, erecting stupendous mills and loading them with immigrants, among them Dawson's great-grandparents.

He pulled into a parking space reserved for a doctor, and the three of them plodded through a haze of mortar dust from a nearby reconstruction project and entered the hospital through a side door below ground level. A security guard passed them on, and a white blur of hospital personnel ignored them. As they neared the morgue Natalie grew unsure of her footing and dropped her head to one side as if something had jarred it. At the door she said, "I'll wait here."

"No, I need you," Sue said with authority.

The morgue hummed with a chill, smelled of cold metal, and tasted of chemicals, some sweet. A handsome black woman in a spotless smock came forward over an expanse of floor that looked as if it had just been swabbed. She had been expecting Dawson and drew him well to one side. "For you," she said quietly. It was a copy of the medical examiner's report, which he tucked away without looking at it.

"Anything interesting in it?" he asked.

"There was no sign of recent sexual activity," she said in a half-whisper. "The doctor thought that odd. Her stomach contents suggested her last meal was at Burger King or McDonald's."

"Cause of death?"

"Internal hemorrhaging. Her ribs were in her lungs. It's all in the report. A copy's gone to the district attorney."

"Did he ask for it?"

"Yes," she said. There was a sound from Sue, a smaller one from Natalie. The woman said, "All of you?" He nodded, and she directed them into another room, where the chill was greater and the hum heavier.

The body was covered to the neck with a sheet that resembled canvas. The top of the head was swaddled. Only the face showed. The bruises and swellings had softened, but the skin had gone gray, claylike. Natalie gave a partial look, Sue a full one, her lips drawn tight. Natalie whimpered and pulled back.

Sue, with an emptiness of spirit and tone, said, "Yes, that's our pal."

Their movements were mechanical after that. Dawson said to the woman, "Do you have something for them to sign?" She guided them to a less forbidding section, where an ordinary desk, like a teacher's, was cluttered with papers and held a glass ball, the kind that stormed when shaken. Sue was given a pen.

"I've never signed anybody's life away before," she said, and did so with a flourish, as if making a flower of her name. Natalie's signature was a scratch.

Afterwards he drove them into the neatness of Andover, a gold to the green where arborvitae had sprung to lush proportions. Sue sat glumly beside him, and Natalie lay jackknifed on the backseat, her glasses off, her woolen cap tugged nearly over her eyes. Sue gazed out at rigid arrangements of houses affordable only to the few and said, "How do you manage to live in a town like this?"

"I was born here."

"That's not what I asked."

"I live in a small house. My father bought the land, all woods then, and cleared it on weekends. He and some buddies built the house themselves, his gift to my mother. They're both dead now. The house is their gift to me."

"Poor Sonny."

He shot a hard look at her. "You've never had much to worry about. Silver spoon, wasn't it?"

"Sugar on it. And Daddy still does for me, dividends every quarter. When I'm thirty I'll be rich. Want to marry me?"

"I doubt you'd have me."

"The odds are against it. Poor you again. Poor Melody. She loved you, Sonny."

"It would be nice to think that," he said, pulling sharply into the side lot of the police station and squeezing in between cruisers, one belonging to Officer Billy Lord. He silenced the motor and glanced over his shoulder. "She asleep?"

"Pretending. Sit up, kitten."

There was a stir, and seconds later, with pudgy fingers clasping the top of Sue's seat, Natalie wrenched herself up. Her glasses were back on, her cap was off. She blinked at the sight of the mock-colonial station. "What are we doing

here?" she asked and received no answer. Dawson looked
toward the street. Cars glittered by in the cold sunlight.

"There's the problem of the funeral," he said slowly
and felt the chill of Sue's breath.

"I'll take care of it."

"I'd like to help," he said, but she shook her head,
which was held high, her neck a ramrod. "Where?" he
asked.

"Here, your turf. That way, every year, you can put
flowers on the grave."

"You make it sound like penance."

"Make it what you want."

He turned his gaze to the station. Billy Lord had stepped
out and was scratching himself. Despite the shield on his
jacket and the holster on his hip, he looked more like a
letter carrier than a policeman. Dawson said, "If you don't
mind, somebody else will drive you back to Boston."

"Sure, Sonny."

"In front of others, call me Sergeant."

"Whatever you say. Are you hurrying to get rid of
us?"

In a strained voice, as if retrieving himself from a clutch
of bad thoughts, he said, "I'm hoping for a development."

"Then you don't know who did it." The voice, which
sounded clogged, was Natalie's. She was crying silently,
her face a puddle of tears.

"I didn't say that," Dawson said and tapped the horn
to gain Officer Lord's attention.

A hulk of a man with a baggy face sounded the chimes
with two quick jabs, his signal, and then let himself in.
"Rita, I'm here," he called out in a raspy voice and heard
her heavy tread on an upper level in a room with a cathedral
ceiling. He stood on the white pelt of a sheep and waited

for her. She came down in a caftan of a shade between tangerine and pumpkin, her black hair flowing, a look about her of Halloween.

"I expected you yesterday."

"I was busy."

"Have one," she said, reaching into a Waterford dish of root beer drops.

"No thanks." He never ate hard candy. He imagined the horror of choking on it.

"I got a problem with the kitchen faucet. Damn thing drips."

"I'll look at it," he said and made his way to the kitchen. His name was Ralph Roselli. Once a week, more often if needed, he drove up from Boston to look in on her, to do chores, run errands. In the summer he watered the shrubs, and in the winter, a curious sight in a camel's hair coat and Florsheim shoes, he shoveled snow from the walk. He did all this out of equal measures of loyalty and guilt. He had been her brother's driver and bodyguard, an assassin when called upon, but a mere bystander bereft of choice when small-caliber bullets had been pumped into the back of Tony Gardella's head.

In the luxurious kitchen he tossed his coat over the back of a chair and busied himself at the sink. As a boy he had worked on cars, some stolen, and in the army, when not in the stockade, he had been a demolition specialist, which accounted for the scars that ran up one side of his body. He had stood too close to somebody much less of a specialist than he.

"Needs a washer," he said when Rita O'Dea came into the kitchen. "Next time I'm here I'll bring one."

Her mouth pouted. "That means I got to wait a week."

"I fixed it a little. It ain't so bad." He looked at her fully. Her eyes were puffy. "What's the matter? You sick?"

"I didn't sleep all that great."

46

"Stuff on your mind?"

She gestured with an impetuous hand. "Get the cups and sit down."

Over coffee and buttered biscuits she told him of Attorney William Rollins's late-evening visit and of the news he had borne. Roselli listened quietly, his face a large loose mask of attentiveness, his eyes encased in stupendous pouches. She said, "You didn't know her like I did. It turned my stomach and hurt my heart."

"I remember her. You were teaching her to cook."

"Showing her sauce."

"She didn't look like what she was."

"She was lonely is what she was. Like me. She was younger, I would've adopted her. As it was, I should've made her my companion. I mean, I could've insisted."

Roselli ate part of a biscuit without haste, his eyes fixed on it. When he looked up, she was staring at him. Her voice went heavy.

"Everybody's lonely, Ralph. Even you."

He licked butter from a blunt finger. He seemed to be listening mechanically now, his ear admitting sounds his brain might or might not bother to sort out later.

"Don't tell me you don't wake up in the middle of the night and wonder what's left."

He said, "I can't stay long like last time. You got more you want me to do."

"I got a list."

He dug a tortured spoon out of the garbage disposal, unclogged the hose to the vacuum cleaner, and installed fresh batteries in the smoke alarms. In the laundry room, squatting between soiled bedding and a bottle of bleach, he tightened the drum in the clothes dryer, which had been making an undue noise. Later, as he was passing a window, something outside caught his attention.

"Rita, c'mere."

She was in the kitchen, her hands wet. She brought paper toweling with her and positioned herself beside him. "What's the matter?"

He pointed. "There's a kid out there."

At first her squinting eyes passed over the boy, who stood tall, husky, and quite still, the green of his athletic jacket blending him into the distant shubbery. Then, drying her fingers and puffy wrists, she glimpsed the shock of blond hair and made out the face. "It's all right. That's my godson."

"Just standing there, looks weird."

"He looks cold."

"What's he want?"

"My arms."

Roselli looked at her curiously.

"Go get him, Ralph. Tell him I got biscuits."

Four

William Rollins removed his tinted glasses, and his face looked limp without them. He was in his law office, elbows on his desk. A nag of a headache and an uneasy feeling in his chest made him meditate death. Shoulders drawn, as if preparing himself for death, he wondered whether people waited for you beyond the grave. Was there a welcoming? Would his mother wave so that he would be sure to see her? The details of dying engrossed him to the point that he gave a start when he realized his secretary was gazing in at him.

"What is it?"

"I don't want to interrupt."

"You're not."

She was plump and middle-aged and always seemed somewhat dazed and apologetic. She had been with him several months, almost as long as he had kept other secretaries. He wanted none of them to know too much, which meant that this one's days were numbered.

"Is it all right if I go to lunch?"

"Yes, please do." He fitted his glasses back on, and his face immediately strengthened.

"Is it all right if I take an hour?"

"That's what you're entitled to."

"I usually take only a half hour."

"Go for broke," he said with unwonted sarcasm, but

in a voice so dry it did not reach her. It was something his mother might have said to his father, the words not quite reaching him either. Their images, idealized by the craft of a professional photographer, smiled from a frame on the busiest part of his desk. He said, "Have a good lunch."

From the window he watched her tramp toward Main Street. His office was on Punchard Avenue, right off downtown, on the second floor of an old Victorian dwelling converted to commercial use. When she vanished, he went to the wall safe and worked the combination with thin, agile fingers. Inside the safe his hand plunged directly to a large buff envelope marked *M*. At his desk he emptied it of stock certificates bearing the name of Melody Haines, a few brief letters in her bold and youthful hand, and a number of hundred-dollar bills secured by a red band. Also falling out was a cassette tape. He played it.

He raced it forward, halted it near the middle, and heard her say: *I can't type.*

From him: *It doesn't matter.*

Then a scratchy silence, the tapping of a pencil, finally his voice again.

Your name reminds me of my mother's. Hers was Melissa.

They start off the same, don't they?

Hers ceases with a sigh, yours with a suddenness.

You're a little drunk, aren't you, Mr. Rollins?

Just a little. Static filled a pause. *You never have to be afraid of me. You can trust me.*

You're not someone I normally would.

Her voice was rich and smooth, quite clear, with a hint of vibrato. His had an ascetic quality.

Allow me to help you.

Why? Why should you want to?

You're worth it.

You remind me of him.

Him? Bauer? I hope not.

Her laugh had an edge. *The cop. You're both liars.*

He stopped the cassette player and ejected the tape. Adroitly, with fingers like a seamster's, he ripped up the letters. His telephone shrilled five times and then went quiet, which meant his answering service was handling it. He returned the tape and certificates to the safe. The money, twenty bills totaling two thousand dollars, went into a small envelope, then into his pocket.

His secretary was back within the hour and entered his office with an air of agony. For the first time he observed what she was wearing, a knit dress magnifying the uneven distribution of her weight, a cheap bracelet embedded in her wrist, shoes meant for smaller feet.

"Did you know?' His silence was his answer. "Why didn't you tell me?"

He observed the high color in her face. He knew she had a problem with blood pressure. The pills were on her desk.

"It was on the noon news at Lem's," she said and coughed. The cough rattled, and a part of it stayed in her voice. "No name given, but Chick from the motel was there. He said the name loud so everybody could hear."

"It has nothing to do with you. Or me."

"Nothing to do with the town. That's what Chick said. A stray from Boston, no business here." Her voice shook. "The poor child."

"Yes," he said, "I agree."

"She didn't know anything about office work, wasn't much help. Why'd you hire her? I never understood."

"You weren't meant to."

"No concern of mine, is that what you're saying?" Her color deepened, and her breath shortened. "Maybe I should tell the police I knew her."

"Two weeks you knew her. But if you feel you should, by all means, talk to the police." He picked up papers on a tentative residential sale and began to scan them. She stood rooted.

"You're not afraid of me, are you, sir?"

He picked up a pen and made a notation on one of the papers. The ink was green.

"You're not afraid of anything."

He glanced up. "I fear old age. I fear receding gums and all that business. All right?"

She brought a nervous hand to her face. "I can't believe I'm talking to you this way."

"I can," he said calmly. "I expected it. Now I trust you're finished."

She trembled. "Am I fired?"

Coolly, as if reminded of a small detail, one that never should have got by him, he said, "Now that you mention it."

Harriet Bauer searched her son's room. His closet smelled of sneakers that should have been thrown out and clothes that belonged in the wash. Fishing in pockets, she came up with lint, gum wrappers, and stubs from the Showcase Cinema in Lawrence. The boy went to the movies often, alone. She started to set aside a shoe box she thought empty until the lid slid off, revealing a robin's nest still intact after several years' of storage, the blue trace of a shell haunting the hollow.

The bottom drawers of his desk were stuffed with school papers preserved since kindergarten and report cards arranged not chronologically but scholastically, the best on top. None was bad. Ballpoint pens had been chewed, the plastic splintered. A package of cigarettes he had never opened lay hidden under a diary he had never written in. The pages of a pocket-size telephone book were blank. Numbers he needed or had needed were in his head, including Mrs. Medwick's. She was the high school teacher whose classroom he was barred from entering and whose number he had promised Sergeant Dawson never again to ring.

Inside a dresser drawer, stashed under summer socks, were pictures of himself through babyhood, each exhibiting a cherubic face and beatific smile. The photographs had been unglued from the family album and, with obvious tenderness, placed in plastic windows of his own making, as if those early years had been his happiest, which did not surprise her. He was four when she finally broke him of the bottle and hid his blanket, and he was going on six when she stopped taking him into the tub with her.

She remembered how, picking at her sleeve, he would not leave her side, which got on his father's nerves more than hers. In school he was drawn to girls he dared not speak to unless the bill of his baseball cap shaded his eyes. His only pal was a boy with a skin condition who told funny stories in a cynical way and soon moved away because the family could not afford the town.

At age ten, a pivotal year, he came home with a split lip and chipped tooth from a schoolyard fight in which he had not known enough to duck but had merely flailed his arms more in the manner of a girl than a boy. The only damage he had inflicted was with a bite, which he did not seem ashamed to admit. At her prompting, his father took him by the softness of his shoulder, bruised where he had been held down, and said, "I think it's time you worked out."

They each pushed him beyond his normal pitch, beginning with barbells, a pommel horse, and a medicine ball. She swam with him daily in the pool, lung-bursting laps, which was like a violent return to the tub for him, with a towel as big as a blanket to dry himself in. By the time he was twelve he was plated with what seemed the muscles of an athlete, his strength surpassing hers, which was considerable, except that his merely increased the force of his clumsiness, also considerable.

At age fourteen, with chest and arms bulging, he was still his mother's little man, home-haunted every day he was away at summer camp and sullen when he returned, as if he had been betrayed both there and here, apparently worse there because he would not talk about it. In the dresser's bottom drawer, stuffed behind a sweater he no longer wore, she found the letters she had written to him in care of the camp. Also she found what she was looking for.

It gave off a faint scent of something close to honey-suckle. It was of stretched lace, flimsy and white, sinuous in the silky way it lay, stretched as if maybe he had worn it, though she seriously doubted that. She felt that his darker secrets did not include dolling himself up in Melody Haines's garter belt. The shrink would have told her.

She was on her way down the wide stairs, the garter belt dangling from her hand, when the telephone shrilled. She took the call in the study, with her eye on the grate, the fire reduced to smoldering embers. The voice of Rita O'Dea said, "Your kid's here."

"Christ. He's supposed to be in school."

"The school calls, say he's sick."

Harriet's voice rose. "Tell him to come home."

"He's just leaving. Don't get nervous."

Harriet lifted the silken belt, its delicate tackle twitch-ing, and tossed it underhand into the embers. Flames flut-tered up.

Rita said, "I wanted to feed him, he couldn't eat."

"What did he tell you?"

"We didn't talk about it."

"What did he want?"

"Hugs."

The flames glittered blue and shot up smoke, pitch black, a slender plume. "Hugs are my job."

"He needs all he can get. I have to tell you that?"

Harriet hesitated. "What has Rollins told you?"

"His suspicions . . . and yours."

"I didn't tell him mine."

"Maybe he guessed," Rita said flatly. "The kid hasn't been easy for you."

"Please, if you don't mind!" Harriet's voice, seldom governed by extreme feeling, gave in to it. "He has a name. Walter Rolf Bauer. Walter or Wally will do."

There was dead silence. Then: "I guess you forget who you're talking to," Rita said.

"Not for a second. I'm the one changed shitty diapers. You never did."

"You never asked."

"You never offered. I'm the one walked the fucking floor with him when he had croup; Alfred didn't have time. I'm the one pulled him out of his moods, grabbed him by the hair to keep him from going under. All you did was send gifts."

"Easy, Harriet. You're reverting to form."

"What's that supposed to mean?"

"Means you're under a strain, forgetting who you're talking to. You're lucky I've learned to be patient."

Now the silence came from Harriet, who shuddered inwardly, as if she had needlessly exposed herself and foolishly placed herself in danger. From the grate drifted a faint chemical smell.

"Rita."

"What?"

"I'm sorry."

Chief Chute appeared in his busy white shirt, a miniature American flag stitched to one upper sleeve and a replica of the town seal to the other. A lanyard was looped from one shoulder. The wings of the collar and the epaulettes bore chunks of brass, and a gold shield bulged above the flap of the left breast pocket. Sergeant Dawson pushed aside the pad on which he had listed several names and had encircled them with meaningless designs.

"I don't want to break your train of thought," the chief said.

"It's OK."

The chief closed the door behind him. Despite the militancy of his shirt, he had a mild appearance: soft facial features, fuzzy hair he was losing, a pinkish complexion, and a small amount of neck fat overlapping his collar. He said, "DA hopes he's doing the right thing listening to me. And I hope I'm doing right listening to you."

"What can I say, Chief?"

"Something that will wipe away doubts."

"I've given Bauer till five to get his act together. Then I talk to his kid."

"Till five, huh. Why so generous?"

"Gives me time to get my own act together."

The chief moved nearer to the desk, as if from a sense of something shadowy being left unresolved. "DA doesn't know you, at least not well. He asked me if you ever turn your head on things."

Dawson gave himself a second to react. "Was he talking little things or big things?"

"I don't think he was differentiating. Asked me if you cut corners, said he was just curious. Also asked if you had a personal interest in the case. 'Not to my knowledge.' That's how I answered everything."

"Thank you, Chief."

"Then that *Herald* reporter called back. He wanted to know when we're going to give the victim a name. I couldn't see any good reason to withhold it, so I made him happy. I also called the Lawrence paper to let them know. I'm covering your bases, Sonny."

"Thank you."

The chief drew back, a shadow running across his benign features. "I want to retire in my own time and on

56

my own terms. I guess you know exactly what I'm saying."

"I'd never hurt you, Chief."

"See that you don't," he said in a quiet but unmistakable tone of authority.

Shortly later, lightheaded, Dawson cleared his desk. Nothing in his stomach except candy from a vending machine. On his way up the stairs he glimpsed Billy Lord talking with two other officers near the water cooler. He motioned, and Billy broke away. They mounted the stairs together, Billy with a small cigar fuming from his fingers.

"How did it go?" Dawson asked.

"Hit a lot of traffic, and I got nervous on Storrow Drive. Going off it, I almost got rear-ended. Far as I'm concerned, Boston's for the birds."

"I meant how did it go with them."

Pausing at the top of the stairs, Billy rolled his flat eyes. "The one with the funny hair huddled herself in a corner and picked pills off her sweater. Didn't say a word the whole way in."

"And the other one?"

"She was OK, but she wouldn't let me smoke. She said she didn't care about my lungs but was damn concerned about her own." An ash tumbled between them. "She somebody you know?"

"What do you mean?"

"She kept bringing you up, called you 'Sonny.' "

"Yes, she would," he said dryly.

"Wish I had your luck."

"No, you don't. What are you staring at?"

"Lapels on your jacket. Left one doesn't hang right."

"That's the least of my worries," he said and slipped on his topcoat.

"Don't you get cold in that?"

"Why should I?"

"No lining."

"Never noticed."

"You should, Sonny. Good grooming gets you somewhere."

"Look at yourself, Billy. You're a sack."

"I'm not going anywhere."

"Neither am I." Dawson fastened his coat. "At least not far."

Outside the station, his hair leaped up in a stiff breeze and stayed up until he reached his car. Despite the cold, he drove with a window open. Downtown traffic sputtered and stalled from an early overrun of commuters returning from Boston, symptomatic of a renewed splurge of growth, houses mushrooming up everywhere, bulldozers blitzing through Turner's apple orchard, Sid White's cornfield, Dargoonian's farm. With a strenuous thrust of the wheel, he escaped into the lot of Barcelos Supermarket and, lucky to find a space, parked in the deepest reach. Inside the market he poked about, impeding the progress of other customers. Some had carriages with staggering loads, as if their lives were consumed with eating. At the frozen-food bin he snatched up a meat pie. When his turn finally came at the check-out, the female clerk's luxuriant hair and fresh skin stopped him cold. For an insane instant he thought she was Melody.

"Please don't do that!" he said over his shoulder. Someone's carriage was digging into his back.

"Your change," the young clerk said in a haunting tone.

He left the store and commenced hiking through the lot. The day seemed done in before its time, the cold, unsettled air dense with murmurings. Each shadow was progressively more substantial, as if one might abruptly leap to life. Sensing the approach of a car behind him, he stepped aside to let it pass. Instead it jolted to a stop beside him, somewhat closer than was safe. The face that looked out hung heavy from one bourbon too many.

"Got something for you."

Dawson said, "What is it?"

"Gift certificate. Macartney's. Compliments of Mrs. Gately."

"Errand boy," said Dawson.

"We don't want to keep Mr. Bauer waiting. Get in."

"Only if *I* drive."

"Be my guest."

The door opened wide. Seconds later Dawson was behind the wheel listening to the melancholy purr of the motor and sinking into old leather. He gripped the ball of the gear shift. "First time I've driven a Mercedes."

"My only luxury."

"I think you're forgetting Melody."

"Yes, of course, you're right. She was my other one," Attorney William Rollins said.

Paige Gately sat in the office of the president of Andover Citizens Bank. The office contained no frozen steelwork of the present but had been restored to the gilt woodwork of the past. The desk, filigreed at the edges, was a dark expanse of mahogany polished to a depthless shine. Mrs. Gately sat before it in a chintz-covered chair, with her attractive legs crossed and her kidskin gloves in her lap. Her mouth, freshly painted, was very red. She aimed it at the president, whose name was Ed Fellows, a graduate of Phillips and Harvard and once one of her more ardent suitors.

"You look good," she said simply.

"I feel good," he said. He had returned three days ago from the sunshine of Antigua, and the lines in his brow looked like chalk marks against the deep tan of his face. His eyes hung pale over half glasses, which he removed.

"And Claire?"

"Fine," he said. His wife had been a classmate of Mrs. Gately's at Abbot Academy years before the all-girls school vanished into the campus of Phillips. Claire Fellows—her name was Beland then, her family one of the town's wealthiest, her wedding one of the biggest—had been his second choice.

"And the children? They're doing well of course?"

He nodded. He had two sons who had followed him to Phillips and Harvard and were living in New York. With mild interest, Mrs. Gately had followed their progress in the pages of the Andover *Townsman*. She knew that the older one, whose name she could not remember, was working on Wall Street.

"I suppose," she said, "I'd better not take up too much of your time." Then, in a businesslike voice, her enunciation crisp and precise, a product of Abbot, she spoke swiftly and surely of the assets and liabilities of the Silver Bell Motor Lodge. Everything was in her head, and her face swelled as she went on. The owner, of course, was Alfred Bauer, but she knew to the penny how much Rita O'Dea had put into it and the degree of influence that unpredictable woman exerted.

"Your point."

"I want to buy it."

He withdrew his elbows with a flinch and retreated into the accommodating red leather of his chair, which had been his father's. "My advice is to walk away from it."

"I've worked too hard for that."

"Do they want to sell?"

"Not yet." As she tilted her head, a light played on the short cut of her hair, and the clean, ageless line of her jaw shot into prominence. "But I have my ways."

The set of his mouth was not happy.

She recrossed her legs, her spellful eyes fixed on his. In essential ways he was a copy of her late husband, each of the same soft stuff, each the crushed son of a powerful man whose ghost had lingered. In the quiet conversations at her husband's wake, mourners had forgotten the son and resurrected the father, who had been a selectman for nearly thirty years. Fellows's father had owned the bank.

Fellows said, "Why do you want it?"

"I know something they don't," She was casual. "Inside information."

He was wary. He did not want to ask any more questions.

"A major hotel chain has been looking at the property," he said.

"But now it has an odor. A stigma." It was his first allusion to the murder, the news of which had spread through the bank from Fran Lovell's desk into the tellers' cages and over to his secretary. "It could kill the interest."

"I doubt it."

He started to say something and checked himself. His lips were taut, his eyes noncommittal. Slowly he returned his elbows to the desk and brought his soft brown hands together. "I'd have to see the books."

"Naturally."

"I can't promise anything."

"Of course not," she said. Their voices were mere murmurings, but each word was charged.

"You're playing with fire," he said from a sealed face.

"When an opportunity comes, Ed, you take it."

"They're not your kind. You don't know what they'll do."

She smiled faintly and rose from her chair. "This isn't their territory. It's ours. Our town, Ed."

He also stood up, his pinstriped knee banging the desk. He fetched her coat and unconsciously traced a finger over the cashmere before helping her on with it. He started to touch her hair but pulled back at the last instant. She turned around slowly, screwing a slender hand into one of the gloves and then stretching her fingers.

"I remember when you wore a blazer with the Phillips cachet on the breast pocket. You and Biff. Neither of you knew what to make of me."

"I still don't. You scare me, Paige."

"I knew I would. Sorry."

He watched her turn toward the door, trim and compact, self-contained. He spoke to her back. "Our lives have taken such odd turns."

"True," she said.

Her gloved hand was on the doorknob when he spoke again. "What was her name?"

"Who?"

"That poor girl."

"Melody," she said forcibly. "I thought the world of her."

Harriet Bauer was in the study when her son came home, scarcely a sound from him. "Wally!" she said when he tried to slip unseen up the stairs. He stopped instantly and turned around reluctantly with his hands stuffed in the pockets of his green athletic jacket. She gripped the banister and looked up at him. "You don't skip school unless you tell me. That understood?" His nod was almost indiscernible. "And you don't go to her. You come to *me*."

"She's my aunt."

"Godmother. There's a difference." She gestured. "Come down here."

He did so sluggishly, in jeans that were too tight, too small for his muscular legs, and in sneakers with leather-cupped heels, padded ankle collars, and loose laces. His hair hung over his forehead like Joe Palooka's. She pushed it caringly to one side.

"Let's go out."

"I just came in."

"Wait for me at the door," she commanded.

They went walking through nearby woodland owned by the town. The sun had lost its glare, and the sky, seen through the fretwork of naked branches, was empty except for a single cold-weather bird winging west. Harriet Bauer wore a parka and leg-warmers. Wally tramped beside her with his jacket open and the loose laces of his sneakers snapping from side to side. He kicked at dead leaves. The path they followed was tortuous and narrow, roots erupting at eccentric angles.

She said, "Zip your jacket."

"I'm not cold."

"You will be."

The air smelled of mosses, of a creeping wetness just below the ground, and of stagnant water brimming a hollow. They stopped near a granite boulder where, a few years ago, he had spied on birds with binoculars she had bought him for his birthday. She remembered his particular excitement over the glimpse of a scarlet tanager inside the spring leaves of a maple.

"I found something of Melody's in your room."

His head came up sharply.

"It was tucked away in your dresser."

"You had no right."

"I have every right. Time you got rid of it, so I burned it."

"It wasn't hers," he protested.

"Yes, Wally, it was."

"How do you know?"

"Darling, I bought it for her."

A sound was heard far to their left, beyond birches that appeared poised to spring out of the ground. Someone wearing red was walking a dog along another path.

"Come on," she said, and they pressed on.

He said, "Do you think I did it?"

"It wouldn't matter. You're my flesh."

They heard the dog bark, but the animal and its owner

seemed farther away now. She reached out and made him take her arm, which disturbed his footing. She wished she could wave a wand and make him insensible of threat, invulnerable to retribution.

"Will we go to the funeral?" he asked.

"I don't know," she said, for she had not thought that far ahead.

"I worry about her. I wonder where she is."

She flipped him a curious look.

"Whether she's anywhere," he explained. "Do you believe there's a life afterwards?"

"There's nothing."

"What does Dad say?"

"The same."

The sky was a deepening gray-rose, and shadows made the pitch of the path difficult to follow. A broken branch got in their way. His voice reverted to a tenor. "Then why does Dad bother with church?"

"He's in business. People pigeonhole your character by what you do on Sunday, rest of the week doesn't matter." She slowed their step. "I think we'd better turn back."

He was glad to, as if the surroundings were no longer familiar or friendly. He had a pale, dehydrated look and was tense at the shoulders. When she tried to encourage a tighter grip from his arm, he resisted.

"Don't!" she said. "Don't ever turn from your mother." She made him walk faster. In the dim his hair seemed ghostly at the edges, and his eyes were inked out. She freed his arm when she saw his nose drip. "Wipe it." There was a search. "No hankie?" She gave him a tissue and watched him use it.

"Everybody has a soul," he blurted out.

"Are you telling or asking me?"

"I don't know."

"Nobody knows," she said and heard the dog bark. It was closer now. "Listen, Wally, in time you'll have to talk to the policeman. We can only delay it so long. Can you face it?"

"I don't know."

"Sergeant Dawson. He was good to you before."

"I don't like him." His nose was running again, more tissue needed, which she provided.

"Why not?"

"He looks right into me," he said with trembling lips.

"Then you must learn not to let him."

She pushed him along until they were near the street that led to theirs. Soon they saw the dog, a golden retriever, and the red-jacketed man who was walking it. "It's nobody," she whispered, meaning the man was merely a neighbor of shy habits and uncertain health. They cut across his expansive lawn without speaking to him. "Wally, wait."

He was sprinting ahead of her, avoiding the lights of a passing car, vanishing into extending shadows. He reached the house well before she did, though she could have caught up, probably could have even outrun him. He left the front door open. She shut it quickly and shed her parka. For a minute she stood still, letting her own quiet self feed into the silence. "Where are you?" she called out and began switching on lights.

A sound from the far end of the house diverted her from the stairs. Her tread was soft on the rich carpeting. She peeked into the game room, which was equipped with a pool table, a dart board, and a video game of the sort and size usually played in arcades. She would have been surprised had she found him there, for the video game had long ceased to amuse. With darts, he was lucky to hit the board, and he could not properly crook his finger around the tip of a cue stick. She trekked on, stepping over his jacket and then his sweater and shirt.

He was in the exercise room, bare to the belt and supine on a padded bench with a rigging of steel tubes rising over him. His hair was already full of sweat, his teeth clenched, his nostrils distended. "That's it, baby, work it out!" she cried. "Clear your head!" He was pumping heavy-duty steel, his young chest rocking and the muscles in his arms lurching. A vein flared in his forehead. "Burn it off!"

The barbell swayed in his quivering grip, and fleetingly his face dimmed out, except for his lips, which looked like fiery bursts of blood.

"If the body mirrors the soul, some people are in trouble, but not you."

"Don't, Mom. Don't watch."

"You're beautiful," she said.

They drove through a woody area of West Andover to the technetronic landscape of an industrial park crowded with similar buildings of brick and glass, imposing in size, sterile and serene in design. Slightly beyond all this, near a dip in the road, was a smaller building of office suites, with a shingled signpost. The shingles bore gold lettering, and one read *Bauer Associates*.

"Keep the motor running," Attorney Rollins said after Sergeant Dawson backed the Mercedes into a parking space. "I'll wait here."

"What's the matter, Counselor?"

"I've had a few. He sees that, I'm in trouble."

"I may tell him."

"No, Sergeant, I'm pretty sure you never would."

The lobby of the building was slightly overheated, with vapid music piped in above the unchallengeable large letters of a No Smoking sign. Bauer Associates was gainable through glass doors. The receptionist, a rigid red-haired woman working a word processor, raised eyebrows shaped in circumflexes. Her mouth was an unopen flower bud.

"I'm expected."

"Name?"

"Dawson."

"Sonny?"

"Yes. Who are you?"

"Doesn't matter. Go straight ahead."

He took a couple of steps and looked back. "Eve James."

"Nice of you to remember. It's been a long time."

The furnishings and walls of Alfred Bauer's office were shaded in cool and harmonious pastels. Arty vases sprouted twigs of dry berries. On a map of Andover coded pushpins designated past and present projects, flags on future ones. Braced on a steel stand was an aerial photograph of a site slated for development in the spring. Dawson, poised in a great blot of silence, could almost hear the chainsaws shrieking through maple and oak.

"Sit down, Sergeant."

He pivoted. "I'm fine. Where's your son?"

Bauer was toweling his hands in the doorway of his private washroom, his domical head slightly lowered. "The business with my boy can wait." He sighed. "You and I, Sergeant, share a common loss."

"We share nothing."

Bauer disposed of the towel, his smile no more than a suggestion. His blue eyes, pale against the pink of his face, flickered once. "Still jealous of me. Kind of pointless now, isn't it?"

Dawson stood rock still, conscious of his stance, of the hang of his topcoat.

"There was something special about her, wasn't there, Sergeant? I mean, more than beauty. More than youth. My wife and I tried to define it and couldn't."

"Don't bait me."

Bauer presented more of himself, a vigorous shape in fitted gray, his trace of a smile deadeningly polite. "We can't believe she's gone."

"I can. I saw the body."

ANDREW COBURN

The older man moved with quiet purpose and propped himself on the edge of his desk, a few feet of carpeting separating them. "We'll miss her."

"Your son," Dawson insisted.

"You never had a child, Sergeant. It's a tough business." Light cast from a wall sealed the face with a ghostly tint. "Let it wait. Till after the funeral."

"I can't do that."

"If I thought he did it, I'd break his head."

"No, you wouldn't."

"Then you don't know what she meant to me."

The voice, deep-chested and somber, tampered with Dawson's equilibrium, and against scrutiny of pale eyes he shifted his feet. He was raw-nerved, dry-mouthed, with feelings too near combustion.

"You need to unbend, Sergeant. I can suggest exercises. I can even give you the use of my pool."

"She died of nakedness."

"What?"

"No defenses." Dawson's voice heaved. "She was a *kid*."

"Yes, a kid. Pure lunacy, what we felt for her. You and I, Sonny, got in too deep."

"Don't call me Sonny."

Bauer's smile, gaining substance the longer he held it, twisted subtly. A hand fluttered. "You like the colors here? She picked them. Those vases? Her choices. She cut the twigs in Harold Parker Forest. You might know the spot, near the pond. Private place to swim. Nothing like feeling the forest air on your skin. I picked the pine needles off her ass."

The silence that followed was sharp, each second calculated. Dawson undid an inner button to let in air.

"She wanted me to take her in. Be her daddy forever. Can you believe that, Sergeant?"

"Yes," he replied, freeing another button. Despite the

heat in his head, he spoke calmly and deliberately. "It's why your wife hated her. And it's why she threw your son at her."

Muscles shifted inside Bauer's careful tailoring. "I could easily beat you to a pulp."

"And I could shoot you between the eyes," Dawson said, threading a finger through the trigger guard of his buried revolver.

"I've hurt you, haven't I?" The muscles relaxed. "Now I'll tell you something you don't want to know. It'll hurt you more."

Dawson waited, and Bauer spoke from the depths. "She wanted to die."

Several minutes later, after he had heard enough, he turned toward the door, and something small seemed to explode inside him, the flame all in his head. He reached the door almost without seeing it, though the paneling was shiny enough to reflect the breadth of his face.

"One last word, Sergeant. If you bother my son, I'll grind you up."

The door closed by itself behind him. He moved with a silent tread and paused behind the receptionist. She was staring at the screen of the word processor and stabbing the keyboard with stiletto fingers, the nails scarlet. Her hair was a red bush that ended low on her neck.

"How long have you worked here, Eve?"

She turned slightly, not enough to look at him. "Why does that interest you?"

"Sometime soon I'd like to talk with you."

"I'm in the book. I always have been."

The sky was dark when he stepped outside, and a wind pummeled him. He hurried to the Mercedes, the exhaust from which floated high and ragged. He climbed in stiffly and fitted himself behind the wheel. William Rollins, sitting exactly as he had left him, said, "Was it interesting?"

He shrugged. "Where do you turn on the lights?"
Rollins showed him.

Traffic protracted the drive back. He tried a shortcut through a development of identical houses, oversize garrisons behind split-rail fences, but he got caught behind a loaded dump truck, which had a couple of rear lights out. Neither man spoke until they reached Barcelos Supermarket and came to a stop in the rear of the lot. Rollins quietly stifled a cough, then cleared his throat.

"He told you?"

"He said she didn't care about living. I don't believe it."

"I wish I didn't."

"I have things to ask you. Later."

"Yes, later."

Dawson pushed himself out of the car, grasping the door as the wind hit him. A male clerk in a dark duckbill cap was rounding up stray pushcarts, briskly clanking one into another, the noise grating.

"Sergeant."

"What?"

"Don't forget your supper." Rollins's hand appeared with the frozen meat pie, which was slipping half out of the plastic sack. Rollins released it carefully. "Something else."

"What is it, Counselor? It's cold."

Again the hand stretched forth, this time bearing a plain envelope that was somewhat wrinkled. "Your money. She wanted me to return it to you. I think you'll find it's all there."

Dawson held it in a frail grip and stared. "When did she tell you this?"

"Back in September. She said there was no rush. I'd know when."

The wind whipped it out of his fingers. Rollins scrambled out of the Mercedes and, aided by the clerk, retrieved it for him.

Five

Sergeant Dawson met Melody on a July day hot enough
to kill, the heat rooting beneath his rumpled light-
weight suit, as if Andover were some sweltering southern
backwater and he the sheriff. It was not yet two o'clock.
He wheeled his airless unmarked car to the Silver Bell,
parked near a rear unit, number forty-six, and waited with
a damp elbow out the window. The can of Coke he had
brought with him went warm. Twenty minutes passed before the door to number forty-six opened.

The well-dressed man paused for a split second as if
to make sure he had forgotten nothing. An unseen hand
shut the door behind him. He approached Dawson's car
to reach his own, his full, neat mustache failing to distin-
guish an ordinary face, and in a flash Dawson realized he
knew him, a senior executive at Lee-Rudd, a computerware
plant in one of the industrial parks. A year ago Dawson
had investigated a break at his house on Gooseberry Knoll,
juveniles from Lawrence suspected, no arrests.

"Hello, sir."

The man stopped short, and in the silence that followed he recognized Dawson's humid face and even seemed
to remember the car. He worked himself into an attitude
of pleasant surprise. "Sergeant Dotson, isn't it?"

"Dawson."

"Yes, of course." He squinted in the sun's glare and lifted a restless shoulder. "Anything wrong?"

"You tell me."

The man, watching with pinched eyes as Dawson took a tepid sip of Coke, came to a rapid decision. "Is this necessary?" he asked in his lowest voice.

Dawson ignored the question and dredged up knowledge of the wife, a haughty member of the garden club, a fearless soprano in Christ Church choir, a bouyant homemaker with maid service, her hair cast high into a peach blond hyperbole. He remembered the hysterics over the white rug in the living room, shat upon during the burglary.

"Do you come here often, sir?"

The husband scowled. "It's too hot for this."

"Cool in there?"

"I have a right to privacy. You're invading it."

"How old is she?"

"Christ, I don't know." The words leaped from him. "But old enough, I'm sure."

"How sure? That's why I'm here."

His face wilted behind his mustache. "Don't do this to me."

"How much did you pay her?"

He began to tremble. "Why me?"

"Anonymous tip," Dawson replied readily. "Male voice, not quite a man's. I almost didn't bother with it."

"Sergeant . . . it's not all that you think." He passed a hand over his jaw, a need for composure, a struggle for dignity, which failed to arrive. "I'm under doctor's care. Stress. Tension. You understand."

"I'm not paid to, Mr. McCleaf. You see, I haven't forgotten *your* name, nor am I likely to. So it would be to your benefit if I never see you here again."

Dawson dismissed him with his eyes, but the man was slow to react, and then his step was tentative and shaky.

He forced himself into his black executive car, started it up, and, after sitting perfectly still for a few moments, lowered the tinted window.

"Sergeant."

"Yes?"

"She's a good kid."

"Get out of here, Mr. McCleaf."

Afterwards, the dust settling, Dawson watched a bee wobble in the air as if stunned by the heat. The sky was an unbroken blue, too brilliant for him to appreciate. With a shove he slid out of his car and stood tight-jointed in the sogginess of his suit, his hidden revolver punching out its shape. Slowly he used a handkerchief on the back of his neck. Then his ears picked up. She was coming out.

She had on a striped jersey, jeans with much of the color bleached out, and tennis shoes with bright laces. A delicate fist gripped the strap of the leather bag suspended from her shoulder. She wore minimal makeup and had the air of a careless and confident student of a prestigious university. She headed directly toward him, brown-eyed, full-lipped, low-waisted, with subtlety in her beauty and drama in the long deep swirl of her hair. Her voice was magnetic.

"Do you have the time?"

He gave it to her without consulting his watch and systematically observed the flawless features of her face. "I'm a police officer."

"I think I would have guessed that."

"I'm Sergeant Dawson."

"Without a doubt. Sonny, isn't it?"

The ice cream stand was just outside Andover, with picnic tables shaded by silver maples and the air enriched by mowed fern. A breeze began to billow in, and thunder was heard in the distance, but the sky stayed bright. They faced each other over iced fruit drinks, the table gouged with lovers' initials. "I could have arrested you," he said. "I still can."

She shook her head, politely. "I don't think so."

He had her driver's license. He returned it and watched it disappear into her bag. "You're much too sure of yourself."

"No," she said. "Only of the situation."

They watched a mother at another table clean a child's face with her moistened thumb. Closer by, two boys in bathing suits were examining the shed skin of a grass snake. He said, "Do you like what you're doing?"

"Please, don't lecture me. Anything but that." Her tone was light, but there was tension in the deliberate way she pushed the straw through the froth of her drink. A lock of dark auburn hair lay across her high forehead, which was smooth and vivid. She said, "You look terribly uncomfortable in that suit. Can't you take off the jacket?"

He glanced around and then swiftly removed the jacket. With the same dispatch he freed the holstered revolver from his hip and tucked it out of sight. "Where's your family?" he asked and got a smile.

"Which one? I was in six foster homes."

"No parents?"

"No father, that's for certain. My mother was a free spirit. I was taken from her when I was four, for my own good. She had a lot of friends. I wasn't one of them. I can remember things that happened when I was two. Can you?"

"Is she dead?"

"I was taken to the funeral, age eight. Everybody has a story, wouldn't you say? Does mine interest you?"

"It's for the record."

"For the record, I was not a pretty child. Wish I had pictures to show you."

"Where were the foster homes?" he asked, and she ticked off communities south of Boston, one as far as the

Cape. Her articulation was precise, no slurs, each word clear and rich. "You sound educated."

"That depends on what you mean by educated."

One of the boys in bathing suits approached the table, with eyes bloodshot from swimming. He was at once skinny and round, his rib cage starkly revealed, his belly big. Melody smiled at him, and Dawson said, "Run along."

"Don't you like children?"

"Usually," he said. Her drink was nearly gone. She drew at the ice with her straw and then smiled cynically at his hand.

"No wedding ring. Good. I wouldn't want to be sitting here with a married cop."

"How did you know my name? Someone in the motel tip you off?"

"Is that what you think?"

"It's what I'm asking."

"Everybody knows you, Sonny."

Three youths in scrubby softball uniforms cast long looks at her over dripping ice creams as they shuffled by, their shoes cleating the ground. She gazed up at the sky, which lost its glare in the same instant that the texture of the air changed. A thrilling breeze blew over them.

"It's going to rain," she announced.

"Who steered you to Andover?"

"Do you enjoy quizzing me?"

"Melody," he said, using her name for the first time, "I don't like anything about this. It's not what I'm used to dealing with."

"I gathered that."

He folded back his shirt cuffs, which had picked up sweat and grime, and looked toward the road where a gravel truck rumbled by with an overload, the yellow dust nearly reaching them. "You can do better with yourself."

She had both hands on the table. One twitched. "Tell me about it." A man sitting just out of earshot in an open shirt, absently scratching into belly hair, could not take his eyes off her. They gulped her up, swallowed her whole. "I'm waiting, Sonny."

"You're young. You're more than pretty, you know that. You've got a brain."

"I'm listening, enjoying every word."

A drop of rain fell on his wrist as a grayness shot through the sky. People were leaving, including the boys in bathing suits, the man in the open shirt. The softball players were already gone. "You have the best."

"The best what?" The motion of her lips did not seem to match her words. "Best tits? Best snatch? Ass? I've gotten high marks on all."

He gathered up his jacket and his weapon. She had been sitting with a leg doubled under her. Now she rose to her feet and stood marvelously thin in her low-slung jeans, her hair luxuriant in its fall.

"Shocked?"

"Come on," he said, and they hurried toward the car, though not fast enough. The downpour came between a streak of lightning and a shattering clap of thunder.

They each got drenched, he a little longer, for he had to struggle with the door on her side, hold it open for her, and then give it the proper slam to make it shut, which took two tries. He dodged a puddle and splashed through another in his dash to the other side. Inside, as soon as they cranked up the windows, it turned clammy and close. She dabbed her face with a tissue, the dark of her nipples bleeding through her sodden jersey. He listened to the clamor of the rain against the car and watched the fierce flashes of lightning. Trees eddied in the wind. He glanced at her.

"You all right?"

"Drowned is all. If you want, I'll blow a bubble."

He started up the motor, which protested at first with

a sputter, and worked the wipers to dislodge leaves pinned to the windshield. The heat accumulated, and he picked at the front of his shirt to get it away from his skin.

"Sonny. Look at me a sec."

He did.

"Great eyes."

He ran the defroster, switched on the headlights, and tilted the rearview mirror. With an elbow almost hitting her, he shifted into gear.

"Shouldn't we wait?"

On the road gusts of wind rocked the car, and the rain, too heavy for the wipers, smothered the glass. They crept along, the wipers flailing, the thick tires crunching over fallen branches. Other drivers had pulled to the wayside to wait it out. One had overshot the embankment.

"In case we don't make it," she said, "thanks for the drink."

By the time they crossed back into Andover the rain was falling with less purpose, and when they reached the Silver Bell the sun fired itself through the drizzle and mist. Fording puddles, he made the long turn into the rear lot and braked near the door to her room. She smiled and extended a delicate hand.

"Friends?"

He said, "Don't let me see you in Andover again."

Paige Gately was not in her office nor, it seemed, anywhere else in the motel. The desk clerk's face, full of loose, deep lines, seemed on the point of unraveling. "Swear to God, Sonny, I don't know where she is. Didn't see her when I came in."

"I thought you worked nights."

"Sometimes I do double duty." An idea came to him. "She might've gone home. That's what I bet."

Dawson lifted his eyes from the register, a finger between two pages, and nodded at the telephone. "See if it's so, Chick."

Later he drove to Chestnut Street and gazed up at the high, aloof face of Paige Gately's house, built by a forebear of her husband's, venerable in its clean colonial lines and glassed-in porches. He had been inside once, some years ago, investigating an attempted break. He remembered big airy rooms hard to heat, wide windowsills low enough to sit on, only rich carpets well worth the attention of a thief, paint flaking from one of the ceilings. He rang the front bell and waited in vain.

He found her at the left side of the house inspecting storm damage to flowers. She was poised on youthful-looking legs, with her back to the sun, in a sleeveless linen dress that elongated the trimness of her figure and emphasized the length of her arms. She had been to the hairdresser's for a cut, and her silvery hair, a close-fitting cap, glinted like ice. Her feet were bare.

"I hope this is important," she said.

He glided past the shimmering yellow of day lilies floating over panicles of baby's breath the rain had battered to the ground, and he stopped within a yard of her, his eyes falling to her feet. The nails, which surprised him, were painted. The toes had picked up blades of wet grass. Her voice swelled.

"Why are you so messy?"

He glanced down at himself. "Caught in the rain."

"Not very clever."

"I'd like to know what's going on," he said, and received a blank look. He suspected no explanation was needed, but gave one anyway, quietly and tonelessly, in what had become his professional voice. She listened with civility but with no apparent concern. She shrugged when he finished.

"It's a hazard of the business. What else can I tell you?"

78

"I've been through the register. It may have been more than an isolated case."

"Then I'll have to tell the desk clerks to be more careful, won't I?" She inspected white clusters of carnations and then moved on. He followed, stepping too close to a rose bush with flesh-tearing thorns. He jerked an arm back.

"Tell me about the girl."

"I seldom meet the guests, unless someone has a complaint, which is seldom. She almost sounds like somebody you made up."

"Are there others?"

She turned smartly on the balls of her feet. "I'm an innkeeper, Sergeant, not a madam."

"I wasn't suggesting you were."

"I'm relieved," she said in a tone of patronage. "Any other questions?"

"How much of the Silver Bell is yours?"

She viewed him coldly, silently.

"I don't mean to pry."

"The devil you don't. What makes you think I have money in it?"

"I can't picture you working there for just a salary, unless it's substantial. Which it may well be."

"What's your point?"

"I'm concerned over how much control you have. I know who the principal owner is and who's probably behind him. That's always worried me." He shaded his eyes from the sun. "I wouldn't want anything to get out of hand. No problems, Mrs. Gately."

"The problem is here," she said, touching the tip of her nose. "Yours is one of the longest."

"My job."

"No," she said, "your nature."

A fluffy stray chunk of cloud momentarily muted the sun as they walked toward the front of the house. Her feet slurred over the clipped grass and then left damp tracks on the flags leading to the driveway, which had recently been resealed. The house, bearing new shingles, new drains, rose more stately than ever.

"A word to the wise, Sergeant. There's a certain bit of righteousness about you that isn't attractive."

"You seem to enjoy putting me in my place."

"Everybody has one. Correct me if I'm wrong, but your mother was that nice old lady who prayed audibly in Christ Church so others wouldn't be ignorant of her piety."

"You know perfectly well who she was. She did sewing for you."

"Even the rector got annoyed."

"You hit low, Mrs. Gately."

"It's usually where the truth is."

"I wish I'd gotten some from you."

He moved easily over the slick surface of the drive, which was almost bright enough to record his reflection. His car was parked behind hers. When he looked back, she was standing in a golden haze, her stance rigid.

"Your nose, Sergeant. Just because you're a policeman doesn't mean it can't be cut off."

He drove through downtown, past the academy onto South Main and eventually turned left onto Ballardvale Road, still dense enough with heavy trees to look rural in short stretches. His house was a modest frame fronted by rhododendrons grown to giant size, planted decades ago by his father and nursed by his mother, hard-working up-right people who had died on the same day, his mother first and his father, as if punching a clock, eight hours later. The garage was small and detached, somewhat rickety. Unlike his father, he was not handy with a hammer. He backed into the garage, a policeman's habit, or at least his.

The house was cool, uncluttered, still tidy from the woman who came in once a week to clean and do his laundry. He immediately went into the bathroom, stripped, and showered, lathering himself with soap that was a sample in the mail. Only a sliver remained when he finished. He slicked his dark hair back and weighed himself, the needle never registering a surprise. His lean body had always been good to him, and he could not recall the last time he was sick. Doing a few knee bends, he felt strong, no beginning or end to him.

Girded with a towel, he padded into the kitchen and plucked a bottle of Molson Golden from the refrigerator. He sipped and read at the table. The paper was the *New York Times*, an introductory issue that had been tossed onto his lawn. His house was on a route for samples and offers, pollsters and solicitors. The doorbell rang when he was deep into the obituary of the Wisconsin handyman who had abnormally loved his mother, killed women, looted graves, and inspired the movie *Psycho*. He pushed the paper aside on the second ring.

Through a panel of pebbled glass he saw a feminine shadow and thought it was the woman from the next street, recently divorced, who sometimes came over to make his supper and spend the night. He tightened the towel and opened the door wide. A wry smile confronted him.

"Nice legs, Sonny."

A white shirt had replaced the striped jersey, but she still wore the bleached jeans and dangled the leather bag from her shoulder. He said nothing. He stood like a figure in a frieze, Greek or Roman, and stared at the dull little car she had driven up in, a Mondale-Ferraro sticker on the front bumper.

She said, "You didn't think you could get rid of me that easily, did you?"

Six

Under a pale sun several people gathered at Spring Grove Cemetery for the funeral. The air was chill, but there was no wind. A Unitarian minister from Boston chatted solemnly near the graveside with the two women Melody Haines had roomed with. The tall one, Sue, glanced anxiously at her friend, whose face was a puff of sickness, and then over at the undertaker from Lawrence, whose assistants were arranging carpets of fake grass and belatedly camouflaging the hole with a stretch of cloth that resembled felt from a pool table. The casket was still in the hearse.

Noting her concern, the undertaker said, "Not to worry."

She left her friend with the minister and trod over hard ground to where Sergeant Dawson stood with the collar raised on his topcoat, his hands poked deep into the pockets. "Who are these people?" she murmured. Her arms dangled. "No one seems to care."

"You could be wrong," he replied softly, his gaze drifting discreetly from stiff-necked Paige Gately to Attorney Rollins, whose stance was stoical in the shadow of Rita O'Dea, blown up in a fur coat and matching hat. The Bauers, who arrived without their son, stood redoubtable with their lack of expression. There was not even the blink of an eye.

Sue said, "Who's the woman staring at us?"

He turned his head to look and was surprised. "Her name's Lovell. She works at a bank."

"Did Melody have money there?"

"Briefly."

"Lovell. Lovell. Melody never mentioned her, but that's not surprising."

"Who did she mention?"

"Only you, Sonny."

He watched two of the undertaker's men dig flowers out of the hearse and tote them to the gravesite. The simple bouquet was from him, the tasteful arrangement from Sue and her friend. The lush and exotic concoction, he suspected, was from the Bauers. He said, "Nice of the minister to come here. Did Melody know him?"

"No. He's my friend." She pushed her hair aside. "Nat and I went through Mel's things. There's nothing you'd be interested in."

"You shouldn't have touched anything."

"Clues, Sonny? There were none. No diary, no letters, no mementos. She lived light. No drugs either. She'd been clean for a long time. The autopsy must've shown that." She watched him steady his head, as if retrieving himself from a clutch of bad thoughts. "What's the matter? Something you want to ask me?"

"Not today," he said.

The undertaker and his men drew the casket from the hearse and bore it to the grave, propping it over the hidden hole. The casket had a bronze glitter and a fierce and repellent aura of finality. A sob was heard, which brought Sue up straight.

"My little pal is taking it hard."

He could see that. He could not remember her name. Then it came to him. With frizzy hair hanging out of her wool cap, a coil of it sprung over her spectacles, Natalie looked pathetic one moment and combative the next.

"I shouldn't have left her. Excuse me."

Alone, he took quiet steps toward the others. Attorney Rollins, wearing dark glasses instead of the amber ones, nodded almost imperceptibly. It was more a wince, as though he felt much about him was misunderstood. Rita O'Dea was a luxurious mushroom of fur, her glossy boots only half-zipped because of the heft of her calves. She stared at Dawson out of gorgeous black eyes full of cold interest. Paige Gately gave him a glance, and the Bauers ignored him. He approached Fran Lovell so softly that she did not see him until he stood beside her.

"What are you doing here, Fran?"

"I have a right, don't I?" she replied, reacting as if she had been dug in the skin. Her drab coat belied her position at the bank. She looked more like a teller who, haunted by tallies that did not balance, rarely ventured out of her cage.

"I'm surprised, that's all."

"Good. I'm glad I can still surprise somebody." She furrowed her brow. "Why weren't you one of the bearers?"

"It wouldn't have looked good for the investigation."

"What investigation? What are you doing?"

He regarded her quizzically. "You have a suggestion, Fran?"

"I'm sorry," she said at once, the tone propitiating. "It's just that I forget you're a detective. A good one, I'm sure."

The undertaker and his assistants shrank back from the casket and everyone else inched closer as the minister, Bible in hand, assumed his position. Head lowered, the bald spot in his hair shone like wax. Dawson listened to the words but did not sort them out. Nor did he pay attention when Sue, her voice ringing over Natalie's sobs, read something she had written. His mind was heated with unexpected shapes that bore no quick relation to reality, and he turned his head in a brief confrontation, his green eye pitted against the disarming blue of Bauer's. When the minister tossed dirt spang on the metal casket, it sounded like a minor explosion.

"That was beautiful," Fran Lovell said as people began turning away. Her cheeks were wet. "Can we go to Lem's for coffee? Please?"

"Later," he said. "Do you mind?"

She did, keenly, but he was already slipping away, angling between the heaviness of Rita O'Dea and the rigidity of Paige Gately. He intercepted Sue before she could speak to the minister. She looked at him and said, "It's over. She's gone."

"Yes," he said, his throat sore. "Her car, the Mazda, belongs to the county now. They'll auction it off in time, but I'll try to get you the money from it. Reimbursement for the funeral."

"That's not what's on my mind, nor Natalie's."

He had a pen and a pocket notebook out, some of the pages dog-eared. "I've forgotten your last name."

"Bradley."

He jotted in the notebook. "Nice name. Ordinary in a distinguished way."

"We don't think there'll ever be an arrest."

"There'll be one. You have my word."

Natalie had posted herself near the casket, a flower in her mittened hand. She glared at him.

"What's the matter with her?"

"She doesn't think your word is good enough."

The high school was a block of brick and glass, two stories above ground and one below, a walkway descending to the entrance. To Dawson, it would always be the new high school, for it had been built on a knoll behind the old one a few years after his graduation. The old one had replaced the original, Punchard High, which became a junior high and now, greatly refurbished, was the seat of town government. The smell of the new high school held a trace of the old. To Dawson, it suggested morning mouth and marijuana.

The principal was unavailable, out of the building, conferring with the superintendent of schools, but his assistant was in, a chatty fellow with a face fenced in by black hornrims. Dawson gently interrupted him, mentioned the Bauer boy, and asked to see him.

"What's Wally done now? I can assure you he hasn't bothered Mrs. Medwick again. She'd have told me."

"It's nothing. I just want to talk with him."

"Far as I can tell he's doing OK. 'Course he's quiet, shy, you never know what's going on in his head. I saw him in gym this morning. Wouldn't want him mad at me."

"I'll wait in your office, you don't mind."

"I'll have to pull him out of a class."

"Please."

Dawson stepped into a small office, sat on the edge of a metal desk, and waited. Nearly five minutes passed before the boy appeared, morose in a cable-stitch sweater, a shock of blond hair over one eye, a slouch to the broad shoulders.

"Close the door," Dawson said softly.

The boy did as he was told, with a shuffle, and then stood as if tongueless. His arms hung dead at his side.

"Don't be afraid."

"I'm not."

"That's good, Wally, because there's nothing to be afraid of with me. We've talked before. We know each other."

There was no response. Despite the size of him, the fullness of his chest, the stretch of his sweater at the shoulders, the only aggressive feature was the jut of his chin. The rest of him was muted, equivocal, his muscles merely dimpling what seemed the unshed chrysalis of childhood. Dawson spoke gently.

"I've seen your attendance record. You've had some recent absences."

"I had the flu."

"I'm glad you're better."

Dawson's solicitude seemed to paralyze him. He had a ballpoint pen in his hand, ink on his fingers. When the pen slipped from his grasp and fell to the floor, he merely stared at it.

"Do you still see Dr. Stickney?"

"I don't need to anymore."

"Everything's fine?"

"Yes."

Dawson stared at him in a way at once forebearing and insinuating, as if he could chart his thoughts and understand them all, maybe even trace them to their darkest roots. "I saw your parents at the cemetery. Mrs. Gately was there. Attorney Rollins. Mrs. O'Dea. I was surprised you weren't."

He was silent, a tightness pulling at his face.

"It was a nice service. Subdued. Dignified. She'd have liked it."

The silence lingered.

"Do you want me to pick up the pen for you?"

"I can do it," he said in a burst, as if breaking a spell. He went down fast and came up ghastly from the strain. Something snapped loose within him. "Why don't you say her name? You haven't said it once."

"You say it instead," Dawson urged gently.

"I don't want to."

"Yes, you do." Dawson mouthed it. *Melody. Melody.* Made it into a soundless tune. And watched him recoil.

"I didn't do it."

"Let's talk about it."

The boy's face was full of alarm, sweat on his nose, more on his upper lip. His bottom lip trembled.

"Everybody still wants to help you. Dr. Stickney. Myself. You trust me, don't you?" A bell rang in the room, throughout the school, startling them both. The stampede of feet was ubiquitous, endless rolls of thunder. "The business with Mrs. Medwick. I didn't do you wrong there, did I?"

He chose not to listen.

"I helped you."

He gave Dawson a wild look. He was backing away, pushing the hair from his forehead, his eyes not truly in sync. Neither was his step. "I don't have to talk to you 'less I have a lawyer."

"I know you were at the Silver Bell. I know you made the call. Why'd you do that, Wally? You must've known I'd know."

"You can't prove it."

"I don't have to. You'll tell me."

He stumbled, groped for the door, fumbled for the knob. Dawson did not try to stop him. He had the door open, one foot out. "Do you hate me?"

It was a question Dawson could not answer.

Officer Billy Lord entered Lem's Coffee Shop with a copy of the *Herald* furled under his arm. It was the lunch hour, no stool for him at the counter and no table vacant. He forged his way to the back, where Fran Lovell had a booth to herself and only a cup of coffee in front of her. "Don't mind, do you?" He settled in opposite her, a knee bumping hers.

"Would it matter?" she said with a tinge of asperity. He shifted the knee. "Don't shake the table," she said.

"Ain't you eating?"

"Worry about yourself."

He opened a thumb-worn menu and meditated while a waitress stood with a poised pencil. He orderd a chicken salad on wheat. "Don't toast it." He flattened the newspaper and opened it. "And dessert. Let you know what when I decide."

He rattled pages to the gossip column, but his attention went to the article beneath it. Batting away smoke from Fran Lovell's cigarette, he read swiftly. "You gotta show this to Ed Fellows," he said with a laugh and pressed the paper partly toward her. "Banks in Boston are giving special service to the rich. Ordinary customers gotta stand in line to cash checks, but a guy with big bucks gets the red carpet. They usher him into posh privacy, give him a chair to sit in, and treat him to a glass of wine. If the guy's wife's with him, she can look at the latest *Cosmo*. Or, if she wants, she can use the private powder room. They probably got a little bell on the toilet. She rings it, some assistant vice-president charges in to tear the paper."

"Billy, shut up."

His sandwich arrived, a pickle and potato chips on the side. He nodded at the chips. "Have some." She shook her head and lit a fresh cigarette.

"I was there."

He gave her a blank look.

"The cemetery," she said.

"The girl?"

"Yes."

"Did you know her?"

"A little."

"Sonny's got the case. It's in good hands." He lowered his head to eat. She smoked, and he turned a page, continued to read, chewing with gusto. "Listen to this, Fran. A scientist experimenting with the genes of fruit flies made some with four wings instead of two and some with legs sticking out of their heads. I don't think they should fiddle with things like that, never on people. You know, you could say that guy's got a lot of balls and hurt his feelings. He might have twenty."

"You keep that up, I'll throw coffee in your face."

He shrugged. "You got none left in your cup."

"Tell me about the case," she said, and he returned to his sandwich, picked up the pickle.

"Can't talk about it."

"Why not?"

"Police business."

"That's never stopped you before."

"Sonny's orders."

She butted out her cigarette. "You think Sonny's special. He's not."

Billy Lord gathered up the chips and ate all of them, then used a napkin. "Let me tell you something I read yesterday in the *Globe*, about a doctor in Brookline."

"I'm not interested."

"Just hear me out. Honest to God, it's good."

With a whip of the wrist, she flashed the coffee cup at him, nothing in it but grounds, which spattered the arm of his padded police jacket. She was gone when the waitress came over and asked whether he had decided yet on dessert.

"Cheesecake with strawberries," he said.

When he finished, he groped his way to the cashier, who took his check, rang it up, and said, "What was the matter with Fran?"

"I was making her laugh."

"Couldn't have, Billy. She was crying."

The clerk at Macartney's said, "Good fit, Sonny. Gives you the ivy league look. People will think you teach at Phillips." The jacket was a gray herringbone with leather buttons and suede patches on the elbows. Dawson straightened his shoulders in the three-way glass, and the clerk

gave his back a brush. " 'Course the pants don't go with
it."

"How about tan corduroys? I've got a couple of pairs
at home."

"Sure, Sonny, they'll go."

He tugged the lapels. "I'll wear it." He stepped away
from the mirrors and picked up his topcoat.

"I'll give you a hanger for the old one."

"Might as well heave it."

The clerk did not argue.

On his way out he paused to glance at neckties, then
at sweaters of varying hues, his fingers grazing the wool,
his eyes narrowing at the prices. A voice behind him said,
"Remember me, Sergeant?"

For a second Dawson did not. The man's face was long
and ordinary and lacking something. He stood immobile,
tense, waiting to be recognized and greeted.

"How do you do, Mr. McCleaf."

He touched the top of his mouth. "No mustache."

"So I see."

"My wife thinks I should grow it back."

"She may have something there."

"I saw you come in. I waited." He lowered his voice
considerably. "I was afraid you might call my house."

"Why would I do that, Mr. McCleaf?"

"You know. That girl." He tried to take an easeful
stance and failed. "When I read she'd been . . ." He pulled
at his coat, as if his blood had run cold. "I was in New
York that day, computerware exhibit. Two other fellows
from Lee-Rudd were with me every minute."

"Did they know her too, Mr. McCleaf?"

"No, God, no. What I meant was . . . if you want to
verify . . ."

"Is that what you want me to do?"

He reddened. "No, I meant only if you . . . I only saw
her that one time, Sergeant, so help me. And I appreciate

91

what you did for me. If there's ever anything I . . ." He stopped talking, expended verbally and emotionally, and sank back as if pushed by an invisible hand, Dawson's.

They left the store together.

"Do you want to buy me lunch, Mr. McCleaf?"

He deliberated with pain. "I . . ."

"I guess you'd better not," Dawson said. "We'd both gag."

Wally Bauer cut his last class and drove away from the school in the white Mustang his father had given him the day after he had got his driver's license. He passed two cars on Lowell Street and nearly sideswiped a pickup truck on North Main. The driver blasted his horn at him. When he pulled himself out of the Mustang in the lot of a McDonald's, he blinked his eyes as if he had crawled out of the darkest cave.

He ordered a Big Mac, French fries, a Coke. It was not till he had unsnapped his athletic jacket and settled at a table that the sight and smell of the food repelled him. He forced himself to pick up the bun, lettuce dripping out, and wrapped his mouth around the top of it, his stomach contracting. A few minutes later, a napkin lying destroyed in his lap and another balled in his fist, he tried to take refuge behind a careless smile and the baby-fine hair falling into his face. At the next table a woman stared with bird-seed eyes and spoke to him with a small, pointed mouth. "Don't eat any more. Please."

"I'm all right."

"No, you're not."

Verging on incoherence, he said, "We were sitting there."

"Sorry?"

"Where you are."

"You'd best go home, young man."

Back in the Mustang, he sat behind the wheel with the door open, afraid he might be sick. His stomach stayed hot, but his face cooled in the brisk air. His heart bumped. Eventually the woman who had spoken to him came out of the restaurant. She noticed him at once and approached him with concern. Her voice smashed softly against him.

"Can you drive?"

"Yes," he said, conscious of the highlights of her face and then of the long, vivid nails of her fingers.

"I have two sons, so I know what you're going through."

He let her words ripple over him. He did not hear them, he felt them. Her manner evoked better days, warmer weather, quieter times.

"Whatever you're on, get off it. You have your whole life ahead of you."

He looked at her yearningly and wished she would climb into the car, as if together they might mint ideas for a golden future. She was, all at once, miraculously, his mother, Melody, and Mrs. Medwick.

"Drive carefully," she said and shut his door hard. Then she was gone.

Senses jarred, he drove up the hill to Elm Square, waited in line at the lights, and glanced over at the library, which he associated with shame. He had once been caught with a book under his sweater and had never returned. As he passed haltingly through downtown, he thought he glimpsed Sergeant Dawson's rangy figure in front of Macartney's, which gave him the shivers. He kept an eye in the rearview mirror the rest of the way home, fearing he was being tracked.

No cars were in the garage, which meant he had the house to himself, a blessing. In the bath adjoining his bedroom, he turned on the tap over the oval sink, dashed his hands under the water, and slicked back his hair without looking at himself, instead expelling his breath against the mirror. Cramps put him on the toilet, and for fifteen minutes a fear of the runs kept him glued to the seat. When he rose, all that he flushed away was a single black marble of the sort a cat might eliminate when cornered and terrorized.

In his bedroom he swayed in silence. He did not feel well at all. His head burned, and his throat was intractably sore. He looked at his bed and began shedding his clothes. Tucked up, cozy and private in the covers, safe from the world, he could lie on the tender edge of sleep and dream in spurts, the events in the dreams more vivid than those on the outside.

Before pulling back the covers, he stepped to his cluttered desk, rummaged in a drawer, and drew out the diary he had never written in. His fingers grappled with the blank pages till he came to the right date. *I didn't do it*, he wrote in a quick hand and left the diary where his mother would surely see it.

Dr. David Stickney had offices on North Main Street, in a small red wooden building with white trim. The small sign outside identified him as a licensed psychologist. A boxed advertisement, which Sergeant Dawson had torn from the Yellow Pages, listed services that included treatment for adult and adolescent sexual problems, all health insurance accepted. The waiting room was sedate. Framed documents pertaining to the doctor's credentials adorned a wall. A woman wearing oversized spectacles said, "You may go in."

Dawson expected a leather couch but saw only chintz easy chairs, cream-colored drapes, more documents in frames, these of membership in professional societies. No desk. Dr. Stickney sat behind a small polished table that held only a tape recorder. He did not rise, and Dawson did not sit down.

"I hope you don't plan to turn that thing on."

"I wouldn't dream of it." The doctor displayed a small set of crowded teeth through a neat dark beard. He was tightly tailored in a plaid suit, the cuffs of his shirt fully exposed. The shirt was sky blue, the silk tie lavender. Dawson had the impression of a spider lurking in a flower.

"You live on Sunset Rock Road. Nice houses there."

"I have a comfortable practice."

"I feel I know you quite well, Doctor."

"I feel the same about you. Nearly forty years old, they still call you Sonny."

"Some things stick."

"Rags of childhood. They cling to us all." His tone was cool and ironic, yet professionally pleasant. "Now that we have that out of the way, why don't you sit down?"

Dawson chose a chair that drew him deeper into it than he expected. He undid his coat. He took out his pocket notebook and flipped a page or two, then searched for his pen.

"You're not really going to write in that, are you?"

"I might."

"My father's in a nursing home, Sergeant. When he was eight or nine, he buried a bag of pennies in the garden behind the three-decker he grew up in. Now he's seventy-six years old and wondering if the pennies are still there. And brooding over the probability the garden is gone. I suppose you're wondering what my point is."

"I'm simply waiting for you to make it."

"Melody Haines is gone. You can't dig her up."

"What was she to you?"

"My patient. I treated her."

"Yes, you treated her. A quid-pro-quo arrangement. You sent male patients to her at the Silver Bell for so-called therapy."

"She confided in you almost as much as she did in me. I was her doctor. What were you, Sergeant?" He stroked his beard. "You don't have to answer that."

"You sent the Bauer boy to her."

"If I did, Sergeant, it was with his mother's permission."

"Maybe even her suggestion."

"You're treading into a doctor-patient relationship."

Dawson fluttered pages of his notebook. "What do you think, did he kill Melody?"

"Was he capable? My opinion, Sergeant, is Wally Bauer would've killed his mother first. Not Melody. Melody was his angel."

"Yours too, right, Doctor?"

He replied calmly. "I'm only human, Sergeant. Same as you."

Dawson's face was set in a recalcitrant frown, and his hands lay as stones in his lap. "What you say about the kid, I don't buy it. I think he killed her. He was at the motel. He nearly ran somebody down tearing away in that car of his. Later he made an anonymous call to the station."

"That's information I didn't know. But my opinion still holds. He's not violent."

"He sure as hell scared the schoolteacher, didn't he, Doctor?"

"With what, Sergeant? Words. That's the extent of his aggression."

"You mentioned his mother."

"Ironically."

"He's a big boy, lot of muscle to him. Would you want him mad at you?"

"He has been. A couple of times." Dr. Stickney smiled dryly. "His parents put that body on him. He never knew how to use it, what to do with it. He hides in it. Lives in a world of his own, which isn't necessarily bad."

"It is if you want to talk to him." Dawson lifted a hand with effort, tucked away the notebook. "How long have you been in Andover? Four, five years?"

"Nearly seven. Lovely community. I have a daughter

at Phillips. Perhaps you saw her picture in *The Townsman*. She won a poetry prize."

"Did you know Alfred Bauer before coming here?"

"A curious question. Why do you ask?"

"I think you have a history of using hookers as therapists. I think Bauer supplied them when you practiced in Boston, and he's obviously done it for you here." Dawson gripped the arms of the chair and drew himself to his feet. "And I think you're doing your best to protect his kid."

Dr. Stickney's small teeth glittered inside his beard. "I don't think it's Wally Bauer you came here to talk about. You've already made up your mind about him."

"Then why am I here, Doctor?"

"Melody. You want to know whether she had a death wish. Alfred Bauer told you she did, and I'll confirm it for you. Yes, she wanted to die."

Dawson buttoned his coat. "Sorry. That's something else from you I don't buy."

"Only because you don't want to." Dr. Stickney rose from the table and ran a smoothing hand down his lavender tie. "She had a lot of disappointments in life, Sergeant. You were the final one."

The room, lit only by the pale afternoon sun, had a chill to it. Harriet Bauer drew the covers from her son's head and said, "What are you doing in bed?" His head was deep in a pillow, his eyes closed. "Answer me. I know you're not asleep." She pulled the covers from his shoulders.

"Don't, Mom."

"Are you sick?"

"I hurt."

"Where?"

"Everywhere."

She clamped a hand over his forehead. "Here?"

"Yes."

She touched his smooth pink chest, coddling him in a game as if he were still a child, scarcely more than a baby, in dire need of her indulgence.

"There too," he said.

She drove a tender hand under the sheet. "And your tummy?"

"Yes."

She went into his bathroom and returned with a thermometer, which she coaxed into his mouth, under his tongue. "Be quiet," she ordered and waited the proper time before withdrawing it, an endless thread of saliva trailing it like a ghost of the cord that once bound them. She squinted. He was running a slight temperature. "Get up," she said. "We'll sweat it out."

He tried to return the covers to his shoulders but was thwarted. "I'm scared."

"Not *my* boy. Come on, a few laps in the pool. Together." She forced him out of bed, and he stood shivering, his legs posted awkwardly behind the bulbous pouch of his tangerine briefs. He seemed afraid to breathe, as if something alien would whisk him away.

"Is it over?" he asked with a wheeze.

"The funeral? Hours ago."

"I dreamed about her."

"That's bound to happen. For a while."

"It was real. She talked to me."

"Only in your head." She fetched his robe, which was like a boxer's, electric in color. "Lift your elbow," she said firmly and helped him into it. The letter *W* adorned the left lapel inside a sparkle of stitches. To him, gazing at it with his chin tucked in, it was an *M*.

"I don't want to go in the pool."

"Then go down and pump. Or chin yourself. Work out, baby. It always does you good."

He was wrapped in his robe, the sturdy sash tied tight,

but his shivering increased. He grimaced, as if every emotion in him were tainted. She stroked his fine-spun hair.

"Be strong," she said.

They left the bedroom together and descended the wide stairs, he first, with a steadying hand on the rail. He did not want her to follow him to the exercise room. "I do better by myself," he said, a little color returning to his face.

"Give me a kiss, then."

It was slobbery.

They parted in the foyer. She went into the kitchen, where she had left a sack of groceries from Barcelos on the counter. She was washing down a clump of seedless grapes when the telephone rang. The caller was from the high school. She knew him by his title of assistant principal and by a memory of his black hornrims, which kept sliding down his nose the time she had been in his office, Mrs. Medwick a nervous figure in the background and Sergeant Dawson a rawboned one, all of them gathered against her and her son, who could not bring himself to look at the teacher. "Why, Walter?" the assistant principal asked somberly, and she stepped between them and said, "The shrink will tend to that. That's the deal, isn't it?"

Now, with a grape in her mouth, she said, "Yes, what is it?" Then she listened carefully, without comment but with a growing tremor of alarm as he told of pulling her son out of math class to talk with the sergeant, who was vague about the reasons.

"The same sergeant. You remember."

"Yes," she said coldly. "Thank you for telling me."

"Mrs. Bauer. Is there anything I should know?"

"No," she said. "There's nothing you should know."

Alfred Bauer reserved a private room at Rembrandt's for lunch with Rita O'Dea and William Rollins, with Paige

Gately to join them later. Rita O'Dea slung her mink over a chair, consuming and nearly toppling it. Rollins seated her opposite Bauer and himself at the end of the table, leaving himself enough room to lay out a file folder or two if called upon, though usually everything he needed was in his head. Rita O'Dea opened a leatherbound menu and after a couple of moments slapped it shut. "You order, Alfred. Something yummy." The waiter was baby-faced and dumpling-cheeked. She stared at him with a smile and made him uncomfortable. "Anybody ever tell you you're cute, young man? Look at him blush, Alfred."

Bauer ordered veal. "Won't take long, will it?" The waiter, still red, assured him it would not. Bauer ordered three sherries, but Rollins shook his head. "Make it two," Bauer said.

The drinks arrived presently, followed by three salads. Rollins shifted his chair closer to the table, upsetting the briefcase he had placed beside him on the floor. He lifted his salad fork. "The funeral went well," he said, and Rita O'Dea, a cherry tomato floating inside her mouth, glowered at him.

"I don't want to talk about that stuff, not when I'm eating." She was still wearing her mink hat. She tipped it back a bit.

"Why don't you take it off," Bauer suggested.

"Why, do I look funny?"

"Of course not, you look lovely."

"Alfred always butters me up, have you noticed, Willy? I know exactly what he's doing, but he thinks he fools me. Remember, Alfred, I knew you when you were nothing but a pimp. That was when you first shaved your head and rubbed something on it to make it shine."

There were times he detested her, and this was one of them. Were she not who she was, he would have swiftly and joyfully struck her. Instead he smiled, sipped his sherry, wiped his lips, and said, "Shall we begin?"

"Sure," she said. "I always like to talk about money."

With a signal from Bauer, Rollins gave status reports on construction projects, the future ones including townhouses in Ballardvale, condos on the bank of the Shawsheen, an office complex in South Lawrence, the work subcontracted to companies once wholly or partly owned by her brother and now by her. At times she seemed inattentive, for the waiter had delivered plates of veal strips smothered in a sweet sauce.

"Alfred, this is good."

"I thought you'd like it."

Without dipping into his briefcase, Rollins recited facts and figures, divulged tax breaks he had worked out, and projected profits, which brought a smile to her mobile face. Buttering bread, she looked at Bauer. "What do you think, partner? You happy?"

"You heard William."

"I want to hear you say it."

"I'm happy."

Rollins, as if by afterthought, mentioned a lawsuit over flooded basements and cracks in a few foundations in the Cherry Dale section of town, a site overlapping wetlands, where, he reminded her, bulldozers had sunk in the mud after a spring rain.

"I don't want to hear history," she said. "Tell me about the suit. Is it something Alfred and I have to worry about?"

"I can settle on the sly with the leader of it. I know his lawyer. When he drops out, the others will too."

"That's what I want to hear. Too bad you didn't know my brother, he'd have made you a big man, Willy." She turned again to Bauer. "Any other business?"

Bauer said, "Paige Gately wants to buy the Silver Bell."

"That so? Why?"

"She thinks she can do more with it than we have."

"I don't trust her."

"Do you trust any woman, Rita?"

"You were one, you wouldn't ask. The Silver Bell has a stink to it now, thanks to you. She must have something up her sleeve. What's she offering?"

"No figures yet. She wants to negotiate a fair price."

"Fair price doesn't interest me. She wants to talk money, maybe I'll listen. Or maybe I'll burn it down, her in it, tell her that." She had been using her napkin as a bib. Now she tore it off. "You haven't said anything about my godson. I had a lot of feeling for the girl, but I love him. I don't care if he did it or not, don't let him go down the drain."

"That won't happen."

"No?"

"I'd crush the cop first."

Rollins nervously pushed aside his plate with an obvious wish that he were elsewhere. Rita O'Dea's gaze remained firmly on Bauer. "I never cared much for the way you brought him up. All that body-building crap you and Harriet put him through. It's the muscle in the head that counts."

Bauer, with an effort, held his tongue.

"He needs help, something more than a shrink. That never did him any good. Let him live with me for a while, I'll straighten him out."

"I don't think Harriet would consent to that."

"She's a jealous bitch. My brother told you that years ago."

The waiter reappeared, and Bauer in a curiously heavy voice ordered coffee. Rita O'Dea readjusted her hat. "None for me. I've got soaps to watch." She rose with a swish, her dress riding up on one side, and snatched up her mink. "Help me on with it, young man. Tip him good, Alfred."

After she left, neither man spoke. Rollins reached down and righted his briefcase. When he saw the coffee coming, he turned his cup upside down in the saucer. His hand had a slight tremor. Finally Bauer, without looking at him, said, "You can leave."

Paige Gately arrived a few minutes later, her entrance as quiet as Rollins's withdrawal had been, and sat in the chair he had vacated. She unbuttoned her coat but did not take it off. "Where's Rita?"

Bauer showed a shut face, a part of which seemed frozen. "Be glad she's gone."

"Did you tell her what I want to do?"

Bauer said nothing.

"I deserve an answer."

His eyelids flickered. "At the motel. That day. I want you to tell me everything you know."

"Why ask me? Your wife was there."

He put a hand to his forehead. "Yes. But too late."

"I like your jacket. Nice patches. Good-looking buttons." Chief Chute felt the material. "Where did you get it? Andover Shop?"

"Macartney's."

"Could've fooled me. Sit down, Sonny." Dawson thumped into a hard chair, and the chief settled himself behind his desk, his pink face pleasantly set. "You talked with the boy?"

"Yes."

"Well?"

"I have enough to pull him in. I can probably get him to confess, the state he's in."

"You don't sound happy about it."

"He's so damn vulnerable." Dawson said with a restless gesture, his voice twangy.

"You didn't make him what he is."

"I just don't want to be wrong."

The chief, who had jerked forward in his chair, sank

back. "You carry everything on your shoulders, Sonny. I could never break you of that. I guess that's what made me trust you more than the others." He rubbed the bridge of his nose. "You're probably full of guilt about the girl."

"I should've done more for her."

"No, Sonny, you should've done less."

A silence fell between them. On the chief's desk, in a stand-up frame, was a collage of color photos of his grandchildren. He seemed to be looking at it.

"Go get him, Sonny. Bring him in."

After the call from the assistant principal, Harriet Bauer stood with an unusual stillness, waiting with iron reserve for an inner weariness to pass. Finally she snatched up the phone and rang her husband's office. The receptionist told her that he was at Rembrandt's, a late lunch, business with Mr. Rollins and others.

"Yes, I know that. I thought he might be back by now."

"If it's important, I can call the restaurant."

"Yes, it's important, but it can wait until he gets in. Have him call me."

The receptionist seemed to sense that the conversation was not finished and stayed on the line.

"How's he treating you, Eve?"

There was no reply, none expected.

"Don't take his promises too seriously."

"Will that be all, Mrs. Bauer?"

"Yes, Eve," she said with neither inflection nor malice. "Go back to your Harlequin novel."

The abundant cluster of grapes was still in the sink, and she tore off a clump and picked at it, each grape progressively less sweet, her mood affecting her taste. She remembered herself as a lumbering adolescent with kneecaps red from kneeling and a head sore from praying, an explosive time of her life, waking as if from a drugged sleep inside a fundamentalist farm family with too many members to love, all demanding more than their share, the print of her father's leather-skinned hand scored into her bottom. *Think you're better than us, don't you, missy?* She fled the farm on a Greyhound, good-bye to the hogs and chickens she would miss more than her brothers and sisters. New York frightened her, but Boston did not, and she bared herself in the Back Bay atelier of a second-rate painter who immediately made advances and eventually introduced her into the business. A rising mafioso gave her a smile, and later a blue-eyed, bald businessman told her she was the pick of the litter. Later he compared her to wine. *I want you*, he said, which was no problem, merely a question of money. *Private stock*, he added, which was a little different. To her mind, and by and by his, that meant marriage.

The phone rang as she was putting away the grapes. She heard the receptionist's voice and then her husband's. "Come home," she said.

Quietly she made her way to the exercise room, where she hoped to see the width of her son's chest glittering under a barbell. He was not there, nor in the pool, the surface of which was an unsullied sheet of blue. She was not surprised, for she had considered the possibility he might creep back to his room, either to bury himself in bed or, more likely, to dress quickly and skip out of the house for a walk in the woods or a random drive through the town.

"Wally," she called out when she reached the top of the stairs. She felt he was well beyond the carry of her voice, but she trekked to his room anyway, tapped hard on the door, and pushed it open. Her gaze, cutting into the dim, went immediately to the bed. Her voice softened. "Why didn't you tell me the sergeant talked to you?" She thought he was under the covers because they were rumpled up high in the middle. Then, moving close to the bed, she saw she was wrong. As she started to turn, some tiny sound nicked the silence. It might have come from the intake of somebody's breath, or it might have come from the silence itself. For the first time, her back rigid, she experienced a fear of her son.

"Wally," she murmured, as if he were in whispering distance but had taken on a protective coloring. Her back was to the bathroom. The door was ajar. She gave it a slow push, peered in, and saw nothing. Her fear lessening, she backed out. The door to the walk-in closet was closed. She yanked it open, glimpsed the electric glare of his robe, and froze.

He had hanged himself with the sash.

Seven

"No way I can compete with that, is there?" she said. She stood just outside the front doorway with a small sack of groceries in one arm but would not come in, her gaze traveling deep into the house, all the way to the kitchen. She was from the neighborhood, her face disciplined since her divorce to show little emotion, even in bed. "And certainly too gorgeous for me to hate. I should've backed off when I saw the strange car in the drive. In fact, I should've phoned first."

"It's not in the least what you think."

"You don't have to explain to me, Sonny. I'm not anybody big in your life, never felt I was."

"It's nothing," he said firmly. His hair was still damp from his shower. The towel that had girded his loins was now wrapped around his neck, bunching the collar of the ratty robe he had owned most of his adult life. "Come in and meet her."

"I'm not into that sort of thing." She pressed the groceries upon him. "Here, let her make your supper. My gift to the both of you."

The sack would have dropped between them had he not held on. Her departure was swift, his closing of the door slow. Melody Haines stood in the entryway of the kitchen, clean-lined and fresh-faced, her jeans slung low across her hips. She gave out a sympathetic smile.

"Did I spoil something?"

"There was little to spoil."

"Good. Because she looked like a gloomy person. Not for you, Sonny."

"You're pushing your luck."

She trailed him into the kitchen, stepped past him when he put the groceries down, and poked into them. "I can't cook, but I can try." She held up two small cuts of tenderloin held together under plastic wrap. "I might need some help with this."

"Put it back," he said firmly. His face lengthened. "Why did you come here to my house? A straight answer, please."

"It seemed right."

"That's not an answer."

"But it's straight." She turned and peered through the window over the sink into a backyard flower garden, phlox rearing up in lush bloom, each flake of color a sparkle in the low sunlight. "Who keeps it up, Sonny? You? It's lovely." She faced him. "I'd love to take a walk before it gets dark. Can we do that?"

He stared at her. "Who put you onto me?"

"You don't trust me, do you?"

"I don't understand you."

He felt awkward in his robe and excused himself. Upstairs in his room, he put on a sweat shirt and chinos and frowned into the dresser mirror as if he were trying to puzzle out not her but himself. On his way down the stairs, he heard her lift the receiver from the wall phone in the kitchen and swiftly tap out a number. He had counted the taps and knew it was a toll call.

"Hello, Sue? Mel. Any mail for me? Any calls?" Her voice was swift, distinct, and cheerfully confident, but undershot with a tincture of anxiety. "Miss me? How's Natalie doing? Still moaning and groaning? Tell her to smile." He entered the kitchen slowly, and her eyes seized upon his attire. "You look like an all-American boy," she whispered away from the receiver. Immediately she spoke back into it. "By the way, I've met a marvelous man. Guess what he is. A cop."

"Enough," he said quietly.

"See you when I see you. Love you both."

There was a quiet after she hung up. She stood boldly, yet with a part of her subdued, which made her at once charming and challenging to look at.

"My roommates," she said. "I'll tell you about them sometime."

"Sit down."

She drew a chair and sat at the table, her legs crossed, giving him a view of long, slim ankles and white sneakers with a cerulean trim. He regarded her with reserve.

"Are you on something?"

"Is that what you think?"

"I don't know."

"If I were high, Sonny, I wouldn't need your company."

"Ever been busted?"

"Juvenile record count? If not, no."

He stood with his back to the refrigerator, half listening to the hum. "Tell me about the foster homes."

"Why?" Her tone transmitted indifference. "Not one of them was happy."

"I'm sorry."

"Don't be. I never think about it." Restlessly she uncrossed her legs, stretched, and got to her feet. She seemed drawn to the window over the sink.

"Were you abused?"

"Soiled says it better. That's behind me." At the sink she went up on tiptoes and gazed out, the deep glowing color of her hair covering her back. "A squirrel, have you noticed, scratches and cleans itself just like a cat. I had a cat in one of the homes I lived in. It would never come to me."

"Cats are like that," he said in a patient voice.

"Sometimes, when they tuck in their paws, they sit exactly as chickens do. But they don't lay eggs, only evil thoughts." She half turned. "You're looking at me, aren't you? Do you like what you see?"

"What do you want from me, Miss Haines?"

"Call me Melody. Or Mel. I'd like that."

"My question stands."

She undid an upper button on her shirt. Around her neck was a delicate gold chain, a glitter against her skin. She removed it and let it drip into her other hand. Her smile, tentative at first, became outright. "It's expensive," she said. "Mrs. Bauer gave it to me. Do you know her?"

"I've heard of her husband," he said thinly, and she extended her hand, the chain a drift of gold on her open palm.

"I'll trade this," she said cryptically, "for your green eyes."

His gaze was analytical, his mind was divided, and his decision was slow. "The only trade is information. For that you get my ear."

She turned back to the window and reached into her shirt pocket. He did not see her pop the pill, a stimulant, but he knew she had taken something. It was all at once in her voice. "Ask me anything, Sonny. I'd love to unload."

He grilled the tenderloin. "Sweet of you," she said softly when he served her the biggest cut. She was as hungry as a horse and instantly dug in. He offered to share the single bottle of beer left in the refrigerator, but she said, "I'd rather have milk."

He ate without haste, almost without taste, his eyes fixed on his plate, as she told of a time, not so long ago, when life had a flimsy hold on her, drugs a tighter one. She nearly died from a dirty needle. No more. Now she was clean, she said.

"Hardly," he said, looking up.

"Safe stuff, Sonny. Just to make me smile."

He asked about the Bauers.

"I knew you would," she said and gave herself a mustache of milk, which she expunged with a slow finger. He listened with an amalgam of half-formed feelings as she equated the Bauers with the Three Bears and herself with Goldilocks eating their porridge and napping in their beds, overtouched and overkissed, apple of Papa Bear's eye, mixed blessing to Mama, nursemaid to Baby. He drew back in his chair. She said, "You mustn't think them evil. Nothing was done without my consent."

"Then why did you give it?"

"Can't escape loneliness, Sonny. It's locked into all of us."

"He got you into the business."

"He got me out of it. That was in Boston. One of his clubs."

"You're still a hooker."

"Therapist, Sonny. Much better wages."

"Are there others at the Silver Bell?"

"We don't mingle."

"Are they as young as you?"

"In this work, nineteen is hardly young." She sprang up and began clearing the table, her movements quick and bouyant. She fiddled at the sink and then spun around, her smile farcical. "You don't have a dishwasher. Christ, Sonny, I thought everybody did."

"Leave them."

"No, help me."

She washed, he wiped. Her smile seemed permanent

111

now, as if it summarized her spirit and something of her determination. She peered through the screen in the window. The moon was a bone against the dark sky. "Too late for our walk now," she said and passed him in a dripping plate, which he accepted stiffly, avoiding contact. Her voice hit him in the face. "Don't be afraid to touch me."

"Mrs. Gately," he said roughly. "She another friend of yours?"

"Yes, she's a friend of mine."

"Mrs. O'Dea."

"Generous woman, if she likes you. I do her back." He looked at her strangely. "Massage," she explained cheerfully.

"Attorney William Rollins."

"You know all the players."

"Do I?"

"We need to talk some more, don't we?" She drained the dishwater and dried her hands. "First I have to—" He pointed, told her to turn left, and silently wondered whether any of this was worth it. He also questioned his motives. He did not realize she had left the door open until he stepped out of the kitchen and heard the tinkle. She spoke to him from the toilet, a princess on a throne, or a child in a school chair. "I like your house, Sonny. So much I could do with it."

He edged away quietly, into the living room, with an image he knew would impinge upon his senses for years.

It was much later, nearly midnight, when her voice began thickening. Her eyelids drooped. "No more questions, OK?" She gave a drowsy nod at the couch. "Look, can I?" she said in a tone that blandished him into a reluctant decision. He went for a blanket. The lamp was off when he returned, the only light stealing in from the kitchen, and she was already on the couch, a flower folded up for the night, the side of her face only dimly discernible. She

112

had the length of a finger between her teeth, as if she had a taste for it.

It was another image he would carry.

He rose at the first violent pip of the alarm, his head heavy from less sleep than he was used to. He expected to find her still on the couch, but the blanket was folded. The bathroom was hot and vapory, and the shower curtain was shedding droplets. He locked himself in, leaned over the sink, and found underpants and a bra soaking in it. "This won't do," he mumbled and pulled the plug. Twenty minutes later he emerged dressed for work.

The aroma of coffee rode in from the kitchen, where she looked a wonder in his ratty robe, the gentle slope of a breast visible in the parting. Her face fresh and alive, she made a welcoming sideway gesture with her arm. Breakfast was on the table. "My surprise," she said.

"I thought you couldn't cook."

"Anybody can make eggs."

"Close your robe."

"Sorry."

The eggs were scrambled, slightly undercooked, missing something. He oversalted his, and she poked at hers, bending her head.

"Not perfect, huh, Sonny?"

He lifted his coffee cup and with effort ignored the lightly tanned stretch of her legs, her bare feet tensed near his chair like a ballet dancer's. "Some of what you told me last night was interesting. Would you repeat it to a stenographer? Sign a statement?"

"You mustn't hold me to any of it."

"Then why'd you tell me?"

"I was foolish."

The contours of his face seemed to change, to turn

tired in places, threatening in others. "Someone like Alfred Bauer has no place in this town."

"Nor I. You told me to get out."

"Yet here you are."

"I'm always looking for a home, Sonny. So much I could do for you, but you'll probably never let me."

He ate two mouthfuls of egg and quit. She continued eating hers. "I'm still a cop,' he said. "Doesn't that scare you?"

"I quit being scared when I was twelve. Got tired of it."

She came up in her chair, and he could smell the freshness of her body alive with cool tones where it was impossible for him not to see into the robe, almost down to the hard, flat surface of her stomach.

"I like the town, Sonny. I even like the ZIP . . ..01810. It defies a mirror. Sonny, let me stay." Her slim hand ventured near his on the table. "Can't you be a big brother?"

"That would never work."

"No, but it'd be a start."

He rose. "Get dressed," he told her and waited outside. It was rubbish collection day for his street, and he secured a sack and clumped it near the mouth of the drive. Somebody in a passing station wagon waved, but his eye was on glinting threads of a spider's web strung between two clusters of sunray in full bloom, each flower a sizzle. Already heat was gathering for the high temperatures predicted for the day. The station wagon stopped one house away and backed up. It was the neighbor Norma, who would never again ring his bell bearing groceries.

"Did you bang her, Sonny? Did you bang her real good?"

Chiggers were in the air. He batted them away. No more cuttings from her flower beds and no more weeding of his when the fancy took her.

"Fuck you, Sonny. And fuck your friend."

Melody emerged from the house five minutes later and approached him in the calamity of the rubbish truck's arrival, its metal jaws grinding sacks. She carried her damp undergarments in a plastic bag and looked no more than sixteen in her loose shirt and jeans. She tossed the bag through the open window of her little city-stained car, which had a dent in one fender and a scrape along another. From the depthless quality of her eyes, he knew she had popped another pill.

"I know why you're doing this,' she shouted above the noise. "It's perfectly reasonable."

He waited. She smiled.

"The breakfast was bad."

He and Chief Chute were having lunch at Lem's. Fran Lovell came in with a magazine in her arm and was about to join them until she glimpsed the private looks on their faces. The chief dunked a roll into his bowl of beef stew and said, "You feel for this kid, don't you?"

He was not sure what he felt. Everything she had said to him was written in large letters on his memory—evidence that he felt something. Her beauty, he feared, was too big for her, its effect on others too heavy to handle, placing her always on the brink of something thrilling or devastating and numbering her days. *I'd hate to see her go down the tubes* was what he wanted to say.

The chief said, "OK, you gave her a break, let that be the end of it. What I mean is, don't let yourself get suckered into anything."

Fran Lovell had found somebody from the bank to sit with, if not to talk with. She opened her thick magazine, a special edition of *McCall's*, and riffled glossy pages. His eye caught hers for a silent second.

"Could be talk, you don't want that,' the chief warned, his spoon in his bowl. "Worse thing a cop can do is try to save a hooker. I don't speak from experience, but it's common sense. Anyway, the point's moot. She's gone for good, right?"

It was possible she was gone and just as possible she was not. He pictured her on Alfred Bauer's doorstep, ready to assume whatever shape the man wanted, to cater to the whims of the wife, to tend to the son, to barter for the affection of each, their promises her ticket to the good life.

"Main thing," said the chief, "is you've put a word in the right ear. That should stop the funny business at the Silver Bell. Though I still can't understand why Paige Gately allowed it. I mean, she's proper. She's Olde Andover, an *e* on the end of *old*. 'Course you never really know what makes somebody tick. Look at yourself, Sonny, you're at a peculiar age, almost forty, right? You still ticking the same?"

It was another question to which he was not sure he had an answer. He was not even sure he wanted to come up with one. He stirred his stew, a rich aroma to it, while the chief ate his.

"What if she comes back, Chief? What if I can get her to sign a statement?"

"Why would you want to do that?"

"I could put them all away."

"All except her. Isn't that what you mean, Sonny?"

He did not like being pinned down, his resentment aimed not at Chief Chute but squarely at her for interloping into his life, trading on his sensibilities, enticing his eye. A few minutes later he reached for the check, his turn to pay, the chief's to tip.

"You didn't eat much," the chief noted.

"Seldom do."

"But less than usual this time."

He moved sideways between crowded tables, the chief in front of him, carefully threading the way. "At least speak." The voice was slow to reach him over the clink of flatware.

116

The face was Fran Lovell's, absurd in its reproach, as if she blamed him for wrongs existing only in the dark of her mind. He smiled and waved.

Outside, in the dry high heat of the glaring sun, they paused near a flower barrel brimming with pink and white annuals, gift to the town from a garden club. Down at the traffic signals near the library, a fair-haired youth in cut-off jeans was revving his motorcycle, the same kid that riled his neighbors by roaring through their quiet streets. The chief, shading his eyes, said, "You know what he's doing, don't you? He's fantasizing he's a Hell's Angel. A real biker would toss him over the handlebars and bugger him, don't you think?"

"That your way of telling me I could get burnt?"

"No, Sonny, I was just making a comment, sort of the way Billy Lord would."

He did not follow the chief to the station. He drove to the High Plain Road area, where a rising number of residents were reporting bicycles stolen from their garages, Hispanics from Lawrence suspected, dark-skinned boys seen cruising the vicinity in a soiled and battered van. He backed into a graveled space between the cool of two blue spruces and watched cars rumble by. The rangy well-seasoned woman who lived directly across the road ambled over to chat for a minute, her sun-baked face leaning in on him, her right arm toughened by a tennis racquet. "Hope you get the little bastards, Sergeant, that was the best bike I ever had. Seat fitted my ass like a glove."

The only vans that passed in the two hours he sat there were clean and unscathed and belonged to a plumbing contractor and a termite inspector.

He intended to return to the station, but after crossing the railroad tracks at the foot of Essex Street he swerved right, shot past the old depot, and took the meandering route home. All that awaited him was a bill in the mailbox, a furled newspaper in the drive, and a small unassuming house that suddenly seemed dreary, the way it had when he moved back after his parents had died, a silence running through it like water, filling depths.

He drank bouillon from a cup, read the paper from front to back, watched television until he could not deal with the noise, and then dozed off in the easy chair, waking when he thought he heard a door sigh open, but it was only a breeze agitating the curtains. Later, when it was dark, he stepped out the side door for a look at the stars and stopped in his tracks. Something was working in the warm night air, rippling it where the rhododendron grew massive, scenting it, as if an unseen animal were lurking about. "I know you're there," he said softly. He moved back slowly to the door and waited in the light. Footsteps gradually came out of what he had thought was an emptiness.

"Are you surprised?"

"No," he said.

"Angry?"

He did not answer.

"Sonny." Her face sprang up in all its vividness. "So much in me has never been touched."

"Let's not—" He stopped, looked at her carefully. "Why the hell are you crying?"

"Because I know you're glad to see me."

Eight

No services. The boy's body was cremated Thanksgiving week, the bonemeal scattered by his mother in the woods where they had last walked together. The shock of his death was still in her eyes, and much more was seared into her brain. The rector of Christ Church tried to comfort her, but she would have no part of it, standing as pure force at the front door, ready to drive him back if he attempted entry. Later, when she was in the master bedroom, Dr. Stickney telephoned. "I'm here if you need me."

"I've never needed you," she said and thrust the phone at her husband to hang up.

In the past few days Alfred Bauer had aged ten years, his polished beacon of a head set on a neck of soft clay. In his dry hand was the boy's diary, opened to the only page written on. He spoke. His voice, usually resonant, lacked life.

She said, distantly, "Yes, I've seen it."

"What does it mean?"

"What it says. If you choose to believe it."

"Do you?"

She gazed through him, the dark of her dress stressing the starkness of her skin and the fairness of her hair.

"Please. Do you believe it?" he asked.

"He's gone. So it has no relevance now."

"Do you blame me?" he asked bleakly.

"I blame you. Myself. The cop." Bones never before prominent in her face asserted themselves. Her smile was uncanny. "I blame everybody."

"I never interfered," he said, the tired muscles around his mouth slowing his speech. "You had the final word in bringing him up. I always knew what he meant to you."

"Just as I knew what Melody meant to you."

The silence was brittle, no denial, only a puckering of his features from too much popping inside his head. She turned away, slipped off her shoes, and removed a sweat suit from a dresser drawer, his presence nearly forgotten. Then she spoke.

"I always loved you too much. Never a problem till Melody. She was different, wasn't she?"

"Harriet."

"Yes, dear."

"Did *you* kill her?"

"I was wondering when you'd ask." She scratched at pinch marks left by the elastic top of her pantyhose, which, diminished to a clot, lay next to her dress on the floor. "Like your other question, it no longer has relevance."

"But I want to know."

"I'd rather you think about it."

"I want to protect you."

"Like you did Wally?" She turned to him and stood terribly straight, parts of her painfully arched, belly muscles rippling. Her thighs had a hammered quality, flesh packed in as if from pounding. "Is it too late?" she said, her legs evenly spaced. "Am I too old?"

His bare head tilted in confusion. "For what?"

"To be a whore again."

Sergeant Dawson went jogging in the brisk morning air, a mere mile, but when he got home he could not keep his body quiet. It hummed and throbbed. His mouth was snapped shut, but the air hissed out of his nostrils. His ears rang, and his chest pinged like a hot engine tuning down. Later, when he began feeling more himself and somewhat confident he was not dying, he made a telephone call. He said, "I need to talk to you again."

"I'm not surprised. Is it personal or professional?"

"Does it matter?"

"If it's a question of guilt, I charge a fee. I'm expensive."

"What time?"

"It'll have to be late," Dr. Stickney said. "Make it five o'clock."

It was his day off, but he went into work anyway. Chief Chute spotted him, called him into his office, and said, "I've been talking to the district attorney. He's satisfied the Haines case can be unofficially closed. The boy's suicide is tantamount to a confession."

"I wish there'd been a note. There should've been." He felt a palpitation and ignored it. "Then everything would be clear."

The chief regarded him with avuncular concern. "I know what's going through your head, but you can't let it get you. You had a job to do."

"Did I push him into that closet? That's the question."

"He had too much on his conscience for someone his age, more than any kid could handle. Just looking at him was probably a push. Not your fault, Sonny."

"I went there to bring him in, but I couldn't even cut him down. His mother's arms were locked around him, she was holding him up. Bauer and I couldn't get past her. I don't think she even knew we were there. It was like the three of us were doing this dance around him, stepping on each other's feet and not feeling a thing. It was like a dream."

"Sonny, this isn't doing you any good."

"I knew he was dead. The eyes had hemorrhaged. Do

121

you know who finally cut him down, Chief? She did. Calm as anything, she asked for the knife. I was afraid at first to give it to her, thought she might use it on me. Even Bauer looked scared. With one arm she held the kid up, all that dead weight, and with her other hand worked the knife. Then she told us to get out."

"Let me get you a cup of coffee."

He shook his head. "Amazing woman."

"Sonny."

"Yes?"

"Reporters come around, you let me talk to them, especially the guy from the *Herald*."

He nodded.

"The district attorney will quietly let it out, off the record, that we had the goods on the boy. I mean, we don't want an unsolved homicide hanging over the town, or at least people thinking it's unsolved. People who know anything at all about the case are already putting two and two together." There was a sigh. "I'm glad it's over. I'm more glad for you than for me." The sigh was repeated. "No more personal involvements. I think that's got to be a rule from now on. Sound sensible to you, Sonny?"

He nodded while looking at items on the chief's desk, as if each possessed a significance other than its obvious one.

"One other thing, Sonny. Go home."

He consulted his watch. It was nearly eleven. He drove, without haste, to Dr. Stickney's office. The woman in the outsize spectacles gazed at him from an aloof and cold persona. In her perfect hair was a tortoiseshell comb that seemed as authoritative as the badge clipped to his wallet or the weapon hidden on his hip. "I have you down for five." He picked up a magazine. "The doctor has a client."

"I'll wait."

"Not there," she said when he started to seat himself. She escorted him into a small private room of soothing colors, the pastel artwork on the walls meant to please children. On a table was a sketch pad and crayons.

"Should I draw something?"

"Suit yourself."

He braced himself in a chair like a child who knew exactly how long he must sit. It was twenty minutes but seemed a solid hour. Dr. Stickney appeared quietly and closed the door behind him. When Dawson started to rise, he stayed him with a gesture. "We'll talk here." He drew a chair, and they faced each other across the small table. Stickney's small teeth glittered inside his neat beard. "What haunts you the most, Sergeant? Melody's death or the boy's?"

Dawson's hand trembled. "He didn't leave a note."

"That disturbs you?"

"You usually don't go out that way, not without saying anything."

"Suicide is a message in itself."

"That's what I wanted to hear you say. Do you still think he didn't kill her, Doctor?"

"Sorry, I haven't changed my mind."

"Then why'd he hang himself?"

"A few explanations are possible." Stickney picked up a blue crayon and drew a careful circle on the pad. "One is he was full of fears, some he doubtless came out of the womb with. A warm place the womb. We all want to return to it. You, I, even the chairmen of our biggest corporations. Why not him?"

"That's glib."

Stickney endowed the circle with scribbled hair, female eyes, and a mouth. "Or maybe he simply wanted to join her, a romantic notion he was quite capable of following through on."

"Is that what you think?"

"I'm merely tossing things out for you."

Dawson shivered, more from frustration than from

anything else. "I think you're blowing smoke up my ass."

"Vulgar talk, Sergeant. For some reason I wouldn't have expected it from you." His smile was slight, with the barest hint of sympathy. "But at the moment your mind must be a horror show. You feel responsible. So you want reassurance. More than that, you want absolution."

"The truth is all I want."

"All I have are opinions, and I've given them to you, gratis."

Dawson stared at the pad. For a number of seconds the drawing absorbed him. Then he lifted his chin, his face a crag. "Their relationship wasn't sexual, but the kid's jealousy was."

"She told you that?"

"Yes."

"She told you the truth. He was impotent—except with himself. Only in his imagination was he her lover."

"But his jealousy was real."

"Yes." Stickney raised a hang. He had dainty fingers and traced them over his beard. "The jealousy went deep."

"It could be hateful."

"Indeed."

"Uncontrollable."

"Possibly, given the right circumstances."

"Then why are you fighting me over his guilt?"

"If you're satisfied, Sergeant, that's all that matters."

"I don't like doubts."

"I do." Stickney leaned back. "You see, I deal in them every day."

After a soft knock and a silent turn of the knob, the door sprang open, and the woman in the outsize spectacles peered in. "You have a client waiting, Doctor."

"Yes, thank you. The sergeant has finished his business."

Stickney left the room, and the woman stepped deeper

into it. Dawson remained seated, an odd look in his eye, voices eddying inside his head. The woman approached the table and stared at the pad.

"That's very good, Sergeant."

After Ed Fellows finished talking with Paige Gately on the telephone, Fran Lovell came into his office with a blue file folder, her handwritten notes attached to it, her name imprinted on the notepaper. "Here's the appraisal and the financial statement on the Silver Bell."

"Let's go over it together," Fellows said.

She wound her way to his side of the mahogany desk, detached her notes, opened the folder, laid everything out before him, and then moved back a pace, one hand stuffed in the jacket pocket of her drab skirt suit. The hemline of the skirt was uneven, a thread trailing. Fellows gazed up over his half glasses.

"You were late getting in this morning."

"A little."

"You overslept."

"Yes," she said, and he seemed pleased, then not.

"You don't wear lipstick anymore."

"Sometimes."

"Not often." His tone was wistful. "I remember the day you came to work here, a young married woman. Years fly, don't they, Fran?"

She pointed at the papers, the polish on her fingernail partly chipped off. "Everything should be there, except Mrs. Gately's credit history. You apparently have it."

"Do I? Yes, I'm sure I do, somewhere." He busied himself with the material she had delivered, scanning figures, peeling thin pages, knitting his brow. Then, deliberately, he shifted his attention to her notes. Though her handwriting was large and bold, quite legible, he said with a squint, "I can't make out this word." Her hair drifted forward as she leaned over him. He shortened his voice. "You didn't take a bath this morning, did you?"

"The word," she said, "is *chattel.*"

"Don't move, please. You smell as if you just got out of bed." His voice was little more than a whisper, all his thoughts inside her suit.

"Does my tired body interest you again?" Her expression was glum. She drew herself erect. "It was never healthy what we had. It wasn't even happy."

He turned a faint shade of pink through the faded remains of his tropical tan and, hunching his pinstriped shoulders, commenced reading her notes again. In a voice that was all business, he said, "I gather you don't think much of Mrs. Gately's proposal."

"When has my opinion ever mattered to you?" She backed away, her smile at variance with the hard set of her jaw. "You're such a clown, Ed. Such a terrible clown."

The assistant principal, his face equipped with the immutable hornrims, said, "Tragic. Simply tragic. We know each year some of our students will be highway statistics, but this . . . this, Sergeant, is shocking. We ask ourselves what didn't we do, what didn't we see to prevent it. We're all taking it hard, Mrs. Medwick especially."

"It's Mrs. Medwick I'd like to see."

"He wasn't a popular boy, but at assembly, during the moment of silence, you could hear a pin drop. I'm probably repeating myself, excuse me, but it's so hard to understand. It's my first experience with a student suicide. I pray to God it's not infectious. You know how impressionable and vulnerable adolescents are."

Dawson said, "If I could see Mrs. Medwick for a few minutes."

"She's taking it the hardest. She feels she bears some of the responsibility because of the problem she had with him. I've told her she's being silly, but that doesn't stop the torment, does it?"

"I'll make it brief."

"She's not here, Sergeant. She's taking a couple of days' sick time. Principal thought it best. I did too."

"Thank you." Dawson started to move away.

"You have some torment, too."

"Why do you say that?"

"Your eyes, Sergeant."

Mrs. Medwick lived in the Shawsheen section, on a narrow back street of small neat houses built in the early years of the century when the town's well-being was tied to textiles. Mill workers had lived in them. Now young lawyers, electrical engineers, electronic technicians did— and teachers. Mrs. Medwick's house was halfway down the street, on the left, white with red trim, bordered by juniper, the bowl of the bird bath removed for the winter.

"Yes, come in," she said. She had been looking out the window and had opened the door before he had a chance to use the bell. She led him into the front room, showed him to a chair. "Is it about Walter Bauer?"

"Yes," he said, "if you don't mind."

"Will it take long?"

"No."

"Good." She was dressed in a high-neck blouse and a full skirt, her lips lightly painted, as if she had been undecided about staying out of school. She sat squarely in an opposite chair, her skirt drawn well over her knees. "It was suicide, wasn't it? I mean, there's no doubt, is there?"

"He used the sash of his bathrobe."

"Don't tell me details."

"They were in the paper."

"I wouldn't read it." She pushed the hair from her cheek, a softly shaped face coming into play, troubled around the mouth. She was perhaps thirty-five, no older, with no children and with no husband two weeks out of three. He was a sales rep, with much of his time spent aboard airplanes. "Why did he do it? No, don't tell me." She shook her head. "I don't want to know any of it."

Dawson placed his hands on the armrests of the chair and watched her shift her feet and cross them at the ankles. Her gaze wandered.

"I was always so careful. Women teachers have to be. We're careful of what we say and do, what we wear, otherwise the boys pick up on you. They read something into everything, never a letup. If you have to write low on the blackboard you're afraid to stoop. You know they'll stuff their eyes. Everything's a sexual snicker, though there was never any of that business from Walter. That's what's so strange." Her voice trailed, then forged back. "I have large breasts, I can't help that, but I'm not the prettiest teacher there. Why did he single me out to make those calls."

Dawson, remaining quiet, inclined his head as if to listen better.

"Maybe I seemed vulnerable to him. I don't know. Or maybe I did something I wasn't even aware of, that he built up in his mind." There was a telephone in the room. She looked at it as if expecting it to ring. "Sometimes I pity boys, do you know what I mean?"

Dawson's head drifted back, the smallest beginning of a headache evident. She shifted her legs again, reversing the cross of her ankles.

"No questions. You're just letting me talk." He nodded, and she smiled weakly. "In some way we seem to be comforting each other. Why did I say that, Sergeant? Is there a reason?"

He said, "You must have been kind to him."

"I may have been. He was shy about speaking in front of the class, so I didn't call on him often. I don't know if that was kindness or a mistake. What do you think?"

"I don't know."

"I knew he had no friends, and there were times I

wanted to reach out, pat his head, tell him friends aren't everything, though of course they are at his age."

"But you didn't."

"What?"

"Pat his head."

"No, of course not. I knew better than that. The only time we ever really talked was after class, after the bell. He'd stay in his seat, wait till we were alone, and ask me unnecessary questions about assignments. I think now he liked having me to himself. He told me he had an older sister. But he didn't, did he?"

"In a way he did."

The telephone rang. She did not move. It rang three times and then stopped.

"It's all right. It's my husband telling me he's arrived safely in Cincinnati." She gave out the same weak smile as before. "My husband and I bumped into him once in the supermarket. He seemed so surprised, upset, seeing me with a man. But he must've known I was married. How could he not have? Everybody calls me Mrs. Medwick."

"Is that when the calls began?"

"I don't remember. Doesn't matter now, does it?"

"The calls terrified you."

"Of course. I was alone. And the voice was distorted, the language so ugly, so dirty. I thought it was a man pretending to be a child. But of course it was a child pretending to be a man. Perhaps there's no great difference." She picked at the sleeve of her blouse, straightening the long cuff. "It was easy for you to catch him, wasn't it? Just a simple trace."

"Very easy. Too easy. That's why I didn't think he was dangerous. That was my mistake."

"No, Sergeant. The last few days I've thought about that a great deal. In my heart I know he wouldn't have hurt me. He wouldn't have hurt anybody . . . except himself."

A muscle contracted inside Dawson's face. He found himself staring at her but not entirely seeing her.

"That's only my opinion, but I feel it's not what you wanted to hear."

He hoisted himself from the chair, buttoned his coat, and, aware of a coldness inside him, hiked the collar.

"I haven't comforted you, have I?" she said.

"No," he said and quietly took his leave.

"You'll freeze your arse," Paige Gately said from the center of her living room, which had been grandly redecorated a few years ago. Attorney William Rollins did not stir. He was sitting at a window on a low, wide sill that from November into March was never warm, no matter what the room temperature was. She had given him a liqueur, and he took a small sip, letting the flavor linger on his lips.

"Who's minding the motel?" he asked.

"It minds itself. I pick good workers." Crisp and cool in a dark blazer and white turtleneck, she skinned gold foil from a square of Swiss chocolate. She allowed herself one square a day, which did not disturb her weight. Her metabolism kept her trim. "Sitting there," she said, "you remind me of Biff."

"Are you being unkind?"

"He had his moments," she said. Her face no longer went ugly when she thought of her husband. Her feelings for him had long ago calcified and lay hidden like a dog's buried bone. In her most nostalgic mood he was no more than a faint twinge. "Charming, but an idiot with money."

"Yes, he was," Rollins agreed.

"Speculated away every cent the old man left him. What's the answer when strong men produce weak sons? Genetic irony?"

"People tried to stop him. I was one of them. But Biff wasn't the sort to listen."

"You should have come to me."

"You were unapproachable in those days," he gently reminded her. "Business was beneath you."

She let the chocolate melt in her mouth and stopped herself from taking another. Rollins rose from the windowsill with a shiver. "I warned you," she said sharply and watched him approach slowly with a pale hand wound around the crystal liqueur glass.

"Why don't you sell this house?"

"Never."

"What does it symbolize for you?"

"Everything that's me," she said and, staring at him, could not pick out what had reminded her of her husband. They were so obviously dissimilar that she searched strenuously for a likeness. "You'd be more attractive," she said, "if you cut the hair in your nose. Biff's barber did his."

He colored slightly.

"When I was young, people said I broke balls. That I broke Biff's. Not true. He didn't have any."

Rollins colored more.

She said, "When they buried Melody we were all standing within fifty yards of his headstone. Do you know, I didn't even think of him. It didn't cross my mind he was there."

The mention of Melody's name affected him, as she knew it would. He finished off his liqueur.

"Poor kid," she said. "A girl in her line should've been hard as nails. She wasn't." A pause. "Did Bauer's son kill her? What's your guess, William?"

"I don't have one."

"Now we'll never know for sure, I suppose." She eyed his empty glass. "Do you want another?"

"Too sweet," he murmured.

"Do you want something more manly?"

He shook his head almost imperceptibly.

"Good boy," she said. "Shall we get back to business?"

They stayed standing, facing each other, she with sudden force in her posture and a change in her voice. "Are you with me on this?" she asked, referring to her proposal to buy the Silver Bell. Earlier she had shared with him the secret behind the proposal.

He said, "I wish you hadn't confided in me."

"You're my lawyer."

"Not on this. I'm theirs."

"That's the point. All I want you to do is push the sale through fast. Expedite the paperwork. Time's important. If Rita O'Dea still has doubts, remind her the place has never made the money Bauer bragged it would." She drew him into her eyes, liquid-bright at the moment. "I need you, William. It will be well worth your while."

"They're not the sort you should fool with, Mrs. Gately."

"For Christ's sake, call me Paige."

"They're dangerous."

"The danger's mine, not yours."

"But why put yourself at risk?"

"That's simple," she said with steel in her voice. "I don't ever want to be broke again."

Alfred Bauer rang the doorbell, and the large baggy face of Ralph Roselli looked out at him through a narrow glass panel. Then Roselli opened the door and let him in, but not all the way. "Rita expecting you?"

"It's all right," Rita O'Dea called from the distance. She was in the airy kitchen, seated at the gleaming wooden table in the light of a large window overlooking weather-bent birch and towering pine. On the table was an open box of Italian pastries and a trail of crisp powdered crumbs.

"Ralph brings me these from the North End. Only place you can get them this good." She offered Bauer one. He declined. He took a seat at the opposite side of the table, near where Roselli had been sitting.

Roselli stayed on his feet. "Sorry about your son."

Bauer nodded.

Rita O'Dea said, "How's Harriet doing?"

He shook his head, and for a while nobody said anything, Rita O'Dea a large humid presence under her caftan, eyes brown enough to seem black. Her abundant hair covered her shoulders as it had when she was a young woman and Bauer was worming his way into her and her brother's good graces.

"Somebody should ask how I'm doing," she said. "The kid used to make the Christmas cards he sent me, I still got them all. You want, I'll show them to you."

Bauer, as if a slug were dragging itself across his heart, said, "I want the cop."

She bit into a pastry and got a lot of it on her mouth. "You don't do cops."

"Wally's gone. Somebody has to pay."

"Somebody is," she said. "You." She wiped her lips with the back of her hand. "And Harriet."

Bauer's blue eyes shifted slightly. "I thought maybe Ralph—"

"I'm retired," Roselli said in a dull tone.

"You guys never retire," Bauer said.

"I don't hit anymore."

"If Rita asked, you would."

"Rita ain't asking."

She regarded Bauer in a manner more sympathetic on the one hand and tougher on the other. "You want to count the people I've lost? You got a scorecard? I'll win. You know what I learned, Alfred? Revenge doesn't bring them back—except in a way you don't want. I see my brother's

133

face every night. You know where I see it? In the casket. All these years I still hear my father's voice. You know where it's coming from? The fucking grave."

Bauer closed his eyes and let dark seconds pass.

She said, "I've a husband hiding somewhere, don't know where he is. Feds have given him a new name. What should I do, have Ralph hunt him down, bash his brains in? What will that do for me? Can I be a young bride again? Can I start fresh, hundred pounds lighter than I am?"

Bauer opened his eyes, and she tore off a hunk of pastry and rammed it into her unlikely small mouth.

"We making good money, Alfred? We got things going our way?" Explosive questions uttered in a moderate tone. Her black eyes flashed. "You take out the cop, all that could go. I don't let anybody threaten my livelihood."

"Maybe," he persisted, "there's a way to take him out that wouldn't hurt us." His voice drifted, as if he did not want Roselli to hear. "I promised Harriet."

She said, "Who's the heavy? You or her? I always wondered, didn't want to ask. Didn't want to embarrass you."

"Please," he said. "Don't say no. Think about it."

"Get out of here, Alfred. You're making me morbid. I don't like to be morbid."

Roselli walked him to the door, where, briefly, each man stood stolid. Bauer's arms were slack, his naked face full of fatigue. "What would you do if it had been your kid, Ralph?"

Roselli, whose thoughts always seemed sour, said. "I don't have a kid." He reached past Bauer and opened the door. "What I wouldn't do is cross Rita."

When Roselli returned to her, she was still at the table, the pastry box closed and shoved far to one side, almost off the edge. She loosened the wide top of her caftan, drooped her shoulders, flopped her mass of hair forward, and shut her eyes. "Do my neck," she said, and Roselli's fingers pressed into her flesh, rippled cords, kneaded a muscle. "Go harder," she said in a tone saved for such moments, as if she were a girl again, family fussing over her, boyfriends afraid to touch her because of who she was. Always she had had to make the first move.

Roselli said, "Bauer worry you?"

"It's not him that worries me. It's her." She leaned lower over the table, letting her head loll on what looked like the moist neck of a seal. Roselli rotated his thumbs. She said, "Alfred's always sucked up to me, Harriet never has."

"Years ago, asking you to be the godmother, that was sucking up."

"That was smart. Political. Young as she was, she knew Alfred was nothing without my brother. And nobody was closer to Tony than me." She worked the caftan away from the round slope of her shoulders, and Roselli did more of her, using the heel of his hand, pressuring color into the skin. "Yes," she said, eyes still shut, "Jesus, yes."

Roselli, the front of his trousers swollen, said, "No question now, I guess, the kid did the girl." The back of her bra was embedded into her flesh. He undid the hooks, and the straps flew up like two whips. His hands slid around her, barging into substantial breasts. She lifted her head, eyes fluttering open.

"That's not what I want, Ralph. If I wanted it, I'd tell you."

His silence was his apology. He brought the ends together and refastened the hooks with surprising swiftness for fingers so thick. She sat erect, swished her hair back, and made herself decent, then looked up.

"It could've been Harriet."

Roselli said, "Or Bauer himself."

"Don't think that hasn't crossed my mind." Elbows winged out, she flattened her hands on the table and wrenched herself up. "You didn't know her all that well, did you?"

"Who?"

"The girl. Melody. She did my back better than you."

"Something should have bothered me right away, Billy, I don't know why it didn't. Maybe I was too sure of myself. There wasn't a single print in the motel room. You dusted everywhere, right?"

"Sure I did," Officer Lord said. "Every inch. You saw me."

"That means the person who wiped the place down was cool-headed, calculating, meticulous. In full control, Billy, bloodless. Yet the kid, Wally Bauer, tore away in a panic, nearly running old Chick down in the front lot. You see, one doesn't follow the other. It's a contradiction."

"I don't know, Sonny," Officer Lord said, his flat eyes giving out a moist stare over his coffee cup. They were in Lem's, a window table. Outside was bustling and noisy, the sidewalk thronged with Thanksgiving shoppers. "Maybe you're cutting too fine an edge. Inside the room nobody could see the kid. He must've felt safe. Outside he didn't. Could be as simple as that. 'Course I always try to make things simple."

"I shouldn't have been so sure. So quick."

"Maybe you're being too hard on yourself. Bet you are, Sonny. You tend to do that."

"He was *there*, I know that. Because he made the phone call later, it's on tape. His voice, no doubt about it, despite the distortion. He made a lot of calls, Billy, going back some. Last summer he made one, anonymous like all of them. That's how I met her. She was in that same damn unit. Forty-six."

"Don't tell me too much, Sonny. Probably stuff I shouldn't know."

"What if I had busted her, which is what I should've done, would she still be alive? The kid too?"

"We all make judgments. Even me, every day. Kids raising hell at the bowling alley or McDonald's doesn't mean I'm going to pull them in. Guy gets drunk, disturbs the peace, doesn't mean I got to pinch him. Tell you the truth, Sonny, I never like to lock up anybody. Put a guy in a cell and right away he's less of a man. I mean, something goes out of him soon as you shut the door on him. Same with a woman, but worse. And worse for me, I got to go hunt up a matron to look after her, to take her to the toilet, stuff like that."

Dawson looked out at the traffic, cars backed up at the lights, people scuttling between them. "I wish I'd done better."

"Maybe you should try to take your mind off it. That's what I'd do." Officer Lord clinked his cup in the saucer. "Been meaning to tell you, I like your jacket. New, huh? Real nice threads. You ought to walk slow past Phillips Academy, let people think you teach there. But don't open your mouth, they'll know better." A slight pause. "See, I made you smile. Goddammit, I knew I could."

A radio was playing from somewhere behind the counter, tuned to a memory station, a soft melody, sadly ironic lyrics. Billy Lord cocked an ear.

"You know who that is singing?" he asked and got a nod. "Forty years at least—nobody knows it, not even my wife—I've been in love with Peggy Lee. She sings, I get chills running up my legs. Every so often, you know, I see her on some special thing on television, and she's painted and fat, with this big moon face and funny clothes that make her look like a fortune teller, but, Christ, to me she's still beautiful. I see her with my heart, not my eyes. Listen to her, Sonny, isn't she good?"

Dawson finished his coffee, including some grounds, and wondered whether Billy Lord's words were reverberating meanings he was failing to catch. His headache, though still small, persisted.

"Something else," Billy Lord went on. "I'm still kind of in love with Doris Day. I remember thinking, back then, wasn't possible she could do stuff like you and me. You know, bodily functions. And no way I could imagine that sweet thing ever in heat. Peggy, I sure could—but not Doris."

Dawson scraped his chair back. "Excuse me, Billy."

"Sure I'll excuse you. I'm always excusing somebody, so why the hell shouldn't I excuse you? Where you going?"

Dawson answered without looking back.

"What'd he say?" Billy Lord asked the waitress who was approaching the table with a pencil stuck in her hair.

"The cemetery," she said.

Walking to his car, Dawson did not realize it was raining until he felt the wet against his face. It was a mist turning into a thin drizzle, and he drove with the wipers working at half speed to Spring Grove Cemetery, where headstones seemed to float up in the gray gloom, as if from trickery of the restless dead, Melody among them. The keeper of the cemetery, moving toward his pickup truck, stopped in his tracks when Dawson gave a tap to the horn.

"How you doing, Mr. Wholley," Dawson said from his open window, pulling up close.

"Fine," said Mr. Wholley, an amorphous figure in a visored cap and heavy jacket, the face rough-hewn, with a nose wrongly shaped by an old fracture. "I've got lots of people underfoot but no sass from any of 'em. Nice quiet bunch, some dead 'fore I was born. So any talkin' you might hear, that's me to myself. What can I do for you, Sonny?"

"The Haines grave."

"Girl that was murdered? What about it?"

"Anybody been visiting it?"

"I don't see everybody comes here."

"If you do see somebody, I'd appreciate a call. Maybe you'd note the license plate for me."

"I'm not good on numbers. Don't even know my own."

"A description of the person will do."

"I'm not good at that either." The rain had picked up and was soaking into Mr. Wholley's wool cap. "Whatcha lookin' for, Sonny? Or shouldn't I ask?"

"That's a question I haven't entirely asked myself yet, Mr. Wholley. I'm just letting it kind of lie there in my mind. But I'd appreciate your help."

"I suppose you want me to keep this to myself."

"That would be best."

Mr. Wholley dug out a handkerchief from the deep pocket of his jacket and blew his battered nose, a honk that would have called to attention a company of soldiers. His rheumy eyes gazed off into the wet gloom, over the rising stones and ranks of shrubs. "I'll be lyin' here myself one of these days. You too, Sonny. Peaceful thought, isn't it?"

Dawson slid the gearshift into drive. "You're getting wet. I won't keep you."

"I'll tell her you called."

Dawson knew what he meant.

Mr. Wholley explained anyway. "The girl in the ground."

Harriet Bauer did not answer the door, so Dr. Stickney let himself in and made his way on cat's feet to the study, where he had been told she would be. He found her sitting in a chair near the fire, her shoes kicked off, one foot flung toward the flames. "Hello," he said quietly, and she drew the foot back and looked up at him with a dull lack of surprise.

"I said I didn't need you."

"Your husband thought you might."

"He was wrong."

She spoke calmly, too calmly, and he suspected a roaring inside her handsome skull, around which she had bound her hair tightly, severely. He said, "If you haven't slept, I can prescribe something."

"I've slept a little. I haven't dreamed of Wally yet. Why not?"

He kept his coat on, moved closer to the fire, and chafed his hands, quite sure she was not expecting an answer, though he had a couple of logical ones to give her.

"Did Wally love me? I want to know. I want proof. Tapes. I want to hear his voice saying it."

Dr. Stickney stroked his beard. Nothing in the room seemed friendly, not even the fire. She crossed her legs, the paint on her toenails showing through her stockings.

"Or was I too much for him? Too much mother?"

"We were all too much for him," Dr. Stickney said.

"Did he come out of the womb wrong? Was that it?" Her face was heated, but her voice was cool, as if certain thoughts had to be exorcised with eerie detachment. "Or didn't I wean him right? At sixteen, did he still want tit? Mine? That teacher's?" Her face stretched. "His age, he should've wanted ass. Melody's. You and I talked about it. I was right, wasn't I?"

"We were both right."

"Instead she mothered him."

"Sistered him," he corrected.

"That wasn't the deal."

"Maybe she had no choice."

"Then she wasn't much of a hooker."

He stood fixed by the swelling heat of the fire, his arms tight at his sides, and she rose from the chair. Even without shoes, she was taller than he, a heroic blond presence. She hovered close enough for him to feel the breath of her words.

"Maybe it's good you came," she said. As if to confirm his existence, her hand traced over his beard, her fingers played idly with his mouth; the little finger almost went in. "You're such a neat little fellow. With a head full of other people's secrets. Do you have any of your own?"

He brushed her hand away and for the first time looked at her sharply, censoriously. "Why are we pretending?"

Her face closed.

He said, "We both know it wasn't suicide."

As a rare treat and a way to unwind, Paige Gately made herself a suicidal drink, nearly all gin, and drew a bath that would have been too hot for most people. She added scented soap crystals and oil and disrobed leisurely, exhibiting to wall mirrors a pink bottom that had forfeited nothing to the years. From all angles she was stark geometry, understated, honed, scaled to size, her body never subjected to the throes of surgery or childbearing. Quick glances rendered casual assurance that her essential self remained unconquered. For reassurance, she manipulated a hand mirror and let nothing of her flesh elude her.

She lowered herself into the tub, the water a burning kiss. With her drink within reach on the ledge and her legs pridefully extended, she glowed and swelled and in time let the gin get to her. One odd expression after another swept over her perspiring face as she thought of the Bauer boy, whom she had always considered beyond rescue, the fates pitted against him, and of Melody, for whom she had felt a disquieting and strangely exalting affinity, as if she could have slipped on the girl's scant underpants and, despite the age difference, changed places with her. She remembered dropping a caring hand on Melody's shoulder during a heart-to-heart talk and feeling that, in some measure, she was touching herself.

She refused to brood over what could not be undone.

In overheated content, she sank deeper into the water, hot vapors coiling her hair into tight ringlets. A bead of sweat forged down a cheek, and another dithered at the end of her proud aquiline nose. Presently she closed her eyes, let suds overlap her chin, and contemplated her life without regard to the past, only to the future. Her only fear, a small one, was that she would not be able to rise out of the tub.

Twenty minutes later, slightly woozy on her feet, she plunged into an immense towel and dried herself slowly and surely. In her bedroom she gripped a brass bedpost to steady herself and then slipped on a becoming robe that warmly sheathed her from her throat to her toes. Her legs felt elongated and trembly, but each step she took down the stairs was light and exact, executed with an economy of effort. One hand clenched the banister, the other the gin glass. When the telephone rang, an ironlike jangle, her impulse was to rip the cord away by the roots. Little was left of her drink. She killed it, then put the phone to her ear. The caller was Ed Fellows.

"I thought I'd come over and discuss your proposal."

Her voice was controlled. "Everything's settled. What's there to discuss?"

"Small points."

"They would bore me. You handle them."

"You don't have an attorney. You can't use William Rollins on this."

"The bank attorney will do. That was decided."

There was a lapse. Then: "Let me come over, Paige. Please."

She was firm. "No."

"I can't handle everything myself."

"Try," she suggested while picturing his heavy hand clutching the receiver, the knuckles prominent and bony. She had never liked his hands because of the knuckles, gnawed on when he was nervous. "Don't ask too much of me," she said coolly.

"Why do you do this to me?"

"You do it to yourself."

"I'm coming over," he said.

She said, "I won't let you in."

But she did. He arrived with rain in his hair and on the dark shoulders of his coat, which he removed and draped over a chair. Clearly he had expected only to have his hand held, but at a glance he knew that she had been drinking. He trembled with emotion.

"Your lucky day," she said dryly and was reminded that she did not care for the broad slope of his brow and the tendency of his pale eyes to hover outside the lids, as if a blow to the back of his head had jarred them loose. Only his pinstripes kept him in perspective, but he was taking them off. "My rules," she said.

He struggled with his vest. "Where?" he asked. "Down here? Upstairs? Paige, I can't believe it."

"No stupid stuff," she warned.

"I promise."

Upstairs on the brass bed, a foam-rubber pillow under the small of her back, she suffered his weight, his kiss, and then his harsh entry into her, which required her help; otherwise he would have hurt her.

In his ear she whispered, "Where would you be without me?"

Sergeant Dawson drove home in the rain from the cemetery and backed his car into the garage for the night. In the house he raised the thermostat, heard the boiler rumble into being, and then stuck something frozen into the oven. Within the half hour he received two phone calls. The first was from Officer Lord, who said, "I forgot to ask you. You're between women, right? I mean, you're not seeing anybody special."

"What's it to you, Billy?"

"I mean, if you're alone you got nobody to eat Thanksgiving dinner with. Wife thought you might want to come over here. We eat around two, you want to come."

"Thanks, Billy. The chief already asked me."

"Then you're going there?"

"No, I thought I'd stay home tomorrow. I've things to think about."

"Jeez, Sonny, that's not good. Holiday, you shouldn't be alone. I mean, you know."

• Dawson laughed. "What do you think I'm going to do? Eat my gun?" His voice sobered. "No, Billy."

"I wasn't thinking that, Sonny."

"What were you thinking?"

"I was thinking it would be good to have you here."

The second call came a few minutes later. His heart stopped as soon as he heard the female voice, pitiless to his ear and constricting to his chest. "Life's so short," she said, "almost doesn't seem worth it." The voice had the right rhythm, the proper cadence, even the familiar little catches, which hooked him hard. "You should've married me," she said, "I gave you the chance."

"Who is this?' he asked.

"Don't you know?"

His jaw lifted, as if he deserved the torment.

"Is it raining there, Sonny? It's raining here."

He took the thawed food from the oven and tossed it into the wastebasket. "Why are you doing this?"

"The dead can do as they please."

It was a cruel hoax, heartless and profane, eloquent in its execution and artful enough in its mimicry to conjure up for him all the ambrosial charms of Melody's youth, the heat of her smile, the image of washed hair drying slowly and trajecting its tones, mostly maroon.

He said, "Within limits."

Nine

Alfred Bauer's receptionist, Eve James, approached him through the dim of his unlit office, where he stood as a shadow and waited for her to become a face. Her high heels, shots from a gun when she tread on a hard floor, made no sound on the carpet. He said, "Have you had your lunch?"

"It's after three," she reminded him.

"Yes, so it is," he said, surprised, as if he were outside clock time and functioning with a rhythm determined by his own inner quivers. It was the first time she had really seen him to talk with since the death of his son, and she was uncertain what to say. She touched the soft, expensive sleeve of his suit coat.

"Is there anything I can do?"

He shook his head, and she drew her hand away and stood rigid, her thick cut of red hair brushed carefully back, the style boyish. Her earrings, hoops hanging to the edges of her jaw, shivered when she took a breath. Her circumflex eyebrows were dark against her white skin.

"How is Harriet doing?" she asked, and he frowned.

"Not good." His voice went hoarse. "She spent Thanksgiving in Wally's room. He meant everything to her."

"And to you," she said as he looked toward the window.

"It got dark early."

"It's been dark all day."

He repeated his frown. "Are we alone?"

"You told everybody they could go home."

"But you stayed."

"Haven't I always?" She placed her hands in the shallow pockets of her skirt when he stepped close.

"I haven't had much time for you, have I?"

"I don't complain," she said woodenly. "I've always known where I stand."

"You're irreplaceable."

"No, but I'm loyal." She lifted her nose. "You use too much bay rum. You always have."

He gazed at her hair. "I remember when you wore it long, all over your shoulders."

"I was a different person then."

"What are you now?"

"The best-paid receptionist in the world," she said and moved to one side, resting a hip against the front of his desk. He stayed where he was, something slowly intruding into his consciousness.

"I need your advice," he said.

"You've seldom asked me for that."

"You know the cop. Sergeant Dawson."

"That was a long time ago. High school." She spoke with a growing remoteness. "I was strung out on drugs. I may have been his first piece of ass."

Bauer said, "How can I hurt him?"

The look on her face was doubtful and cautious, somewhat resentful. "I always do for you," she said, "more or less."

His voice an opiate, he said, "It's more for Harriet than for me."

Mr. Wholley, a shapeless figure in his wool cap and bulky jacket, waited at the front gates of the cemetery. He was dredging up his handkerchief, none too clean, when Sergeant Dawson arrived. The car squeaked to a stop. The window was already lowered. "Excuse me, Sonny." Mr. Wholley put the handkerchief to his wrong-shaped nose. "Sometimes it doesn't come out in the proper direction, so I got to be careful." He averted his head, blew hard, and was successful.

Dawson waited without expression.

Mr. Wholley gave a final wipe and said, "You told me to call if somebody came to the girl's grave."

"Yes, I got your message."

"Thing is, he comes here regular. Once a month maybe to see his people. They're in the south section, but that's not where he is today. He's with her." Mr. Wholley tugged at the visor of his cap. "I wouldn't like you telling him I phoned you. I like to please everybody, Sonny, even the living."

"Is he still here?"

"I haven't seen him drive out."

Dawson drove in.

Attorney William Rollins's Mercedes was parked half on the grass near Melody's grave, and he was standing near the marker. He showed no surprise as Dawson slipped out of his car and came near. He adjusted his glasses and said, "Do you miss her too, Sergeant?"

The grave was a mound of earth that would not settle until the spring. Dawson avoided looking at it. "Yes, Counselor, I do."

"Is that why you're here?"

"No."

"I didn't think so." His hands were trembling, his sobriety uncertain. "My parents are buried here, yours too, I suppose. No mother, no father. That's an icy feeling. I've never been able to get rid of it."

"That's the way life is."

"It shouldn't be. It should be pleasant. Pretty. Where's

the damn sun? It should be shining." Dawson took him by the elbow. "I was a smooth, normal birth, Sergeant. My mother told me so. And I never gave her any trouble, but I never quite knew how to make her happy. Nor did my father. All we did was love her." They moved together over the gray grass, Dawson doing the leading. He opened the passenger door of his car and deftly maneuvered Rollins into it, with no resistance until he started to shut the door. "What are you doing?"

"If you got behind the wheel of your car, Counselor, I'd have to arrest you."

"I'm not drunk."

"But I can't be sure."

Rollins laid his head back as they drove out of the cemetery, the narrow road bumpy in places. Dawson turned onto a street overshadowed by spruce and then into a subdivision of imposing new houses with ornate doorways and other architectural pretensions. Rollins said, "My mother would have laughed at these houses and the people living in them. She was a proud and haughty woman, sort of in the mold of Paige Gately, if you know what I mean."

"I think I do," Dawson said.

"She had a perfectly poised face that spent much time in a mirror, a mirror I sometimes held for her. Perhaps it's a blessing she died young. Her beauty was her identity. Had she lost it, she wouldn't have known who she was." Rollins brought his head forward, his glasses slipping a little. "My father was one of those persons who always seemed somewhat dazed, more than a little sad, and vaguely apologetic. I suppose I'm like him. What do you think?"

"If I had to guess hard," Dawson said, his eyes on the road, "I'd say you're right." They were coasting through the area behind Phillips Academy, where the houses were old and gracious and bordered by gigantic shrubbery. "Your father was a lawyer too, wasn't he?"

"A lonely one, Sergeant. He and my mother died together on the Mass Pike, but in death I think they went their separate ways."

Dawson turned right onto South Main. He had been meandering, but now he decided on a direction and drove to Ballardvale Road, to his house. The only green on the ground emanated from a bed of pachysandra. The rhododendron was black and appeared crippled. "Let's go in."

Inside the house Rollins sat at the kitchen table with his coat in his lap, his scarf still around his neck. Dawson dug out a bottle of scotch a downtown merchant had given him a couple of Christmases ago. He dusted the bottle and set out a single glass. Rollins said, "You think I'm drunk. I'm not. The fact is I haven't had a drink, and I don't want one now."

Dawson poured one, anyway. "Just in case," he said and dropped into a chair. Rollins looked up, thin-jawed.

"Why am I here, Sergeant."

"Melody. She won't rest."

"Is she haunting you?"

"A lot of things are. I'm no longer certain the Bauer boy killed her."

"Then you must be going through hell." Rollins placed his hands on the table. They had become quite steady. "You must suspect everybody now."

"Did you kill her, Counselor?"

"I wouldn't know how."

"All it takes is a moment of rage."

"I don't have any."

"Did you love her?"

"Like you, I felt a need to be good to her. Is that love, Sergeant? I hope so. Also I wanted something more from life than gray. She brought color to my office. She was a flower at my dinner table. At my house I made meals for her. At your house she made them for you. That's the difference, isn't it? She thought she had something with you."

"You gave her a job. Why didn't she keep it?"

"She didn't see a future in it."

"You gave her a key to your house."

"Just so she'd always know she was welcome. That was important to her. Isn't that why you gave her one?"

"I took mine back."

"I never would have."

Dawson's face was set in a recalcitrant frown. "Some say she wanted to die. I never got that impression."

"No, I don't think she really wanted to die—just at times she didn't want to live."

"There's a difference?"

"It's in all of us, Sergeant, a cold spot. Call it a chip of ice, bigger in some of us than others. You know it's there when you wake up in the small hours and can't get back to sleep. That's when you know you're all alone in this world, no matter who's beside you. If it's someone who cares for you, it helps. But only a little."

Dawson was quiet.

Rollins said, "Maybe *you* should have that drink."

"That's a thought," Dawson said, loosening his wristwatch, a Timex with slashes for numbers. He laid it gently on the table, face up.

"Are we waiting for something."

"You can never tell."

"I'm a little worried about my car."

"It'll be all right."

"The keys are in it."

"The dead don't drive." Dawson rose from his chair. "Excuse me for a minute," he said and went into the bathroom. He washed his hands, splashed his face, and smoothed his hair back with wet fingers. The top of the sink, near the taps, was scummed with soap and toothpaste, and he cleaned it with a cloth, slowly, deliberately. While rinsing drool from the soap dish, he heard the telephone ring and reentered the kitchen on the third ring. "Get that, will you,"

150

he said and opened the refrigerator, which was smelly from something that had gone bad.

"Please," Dawson said over his shoulder.

The telephone was on the wall. Rollins, slow to act, rose with uncertainty and answered it in a stilted tone. Seconds later he went white. Dawson, closing the refrigerator, observed him carefully.

"Who is it, Counselor?"

"Take it."

"Anybody we know?"

From Rollins came a soft soughing of breath as he extended the receiver as far from him as he could. "It can't be." His spectacles slipped, his eyes filled. "Is she alive? Please tell me."

"If only she was. Hang up, Counselor." Striding past him, Dawson picked up the glass of scotch, downed half of it, and nodded to him. "The rest is for you."

Ed Fellows's office was on the third floor. He rode the elevator down to the bank's concourse, where he greeted customers, chatted briefly with some, paused to joke with an elderly teller who had been with the bank when his father ran it, and then threaded his way to Fran Lovell's desk. "In regard to the Silver Bell," he said, leaning over her shoulder. He sniffed for scent in her hair but found none. "I think we should look over the premises before the sale."

"Why?" She tilted her head. "We've had it inspected and appraised."

"I like to be careful."

"You're the boss," she said, sorting documents on her desk. "Give me a minute."

He waited for her in the parking lot behind the bank. She emerged in her rugged-looking coat, a drab figure until the wind blew her hair back and seemed to add something daring, like a false innocence, to her face. He escorted her to his shiny, ponderous car and opened a heavy door for her, watching her bend at the middle to climb in. When he joined her from the other side, she had tipped the rearview mirror her way and was assaulting her mouth with lipstick. "I might as well try to look presentable," she said harshly, as if the effort conflicted with her better judgment.

"You suit me," he said, laying heavy eyes upon her. She retracted the red bullet of rouge into its casing and placed a single finger on his wrist.

"Don't start anything."

He maneuvered the car out of the lot and onto Main Street, slid along with the traffic, and eased to a stop at the lights where Chestnut Street intersected. His eye went to the decorated display window of a travel agency. "Remember when that was a drugstore, Fran? The fellow made his own chocolate syrup in the back room. The best chocolate from Holland. If you went in on a Monday you were treated to the aroma. I can still smell it, can't you?"

"No, Ed, I have a sinus problem."

"When he went out of business, an oilman from Texas bought the marble soda fountain for his game room. It was a beauty. You remember it, don't you?"

"You're older than I am."

The lights went green, and he turned right and followed Chestnut down to Central Street, which was sedate, tree-lined, steadfast in its beauty, accommodating some of the oldest houses in town, including his own, the grounds exotic with topiary, sculptured bird baths, and, in spring and summer, brilliant flower beds, for which his wife had garnered prizes, though professional gardeners did the work. Passing the house, he smiled with the smugness of a man who felt richly deserving of everything that had been given to him, which included his father's name. He was Junior as a child.

His smile thinned when they skirted a former meadow

now muddled with splits, gambrels, and ranches. "They're creeping up on me, Fran. My father predicted the Hispanics would overrun Lawrence and the blacks would make Boston ugly, but he never predicted this. Do you know what the trash is in Andover? It's the engineers, the computer specialists, all the high-tech people. They're the new factory workers, except they wear clean clothes and live in overpriced houses."

"The bank's making money off them."

"Hand over fist, I don't deny it, but it doesn't mean I have to like them. I don't want them sitting near me in church, but I look around and there they are."

"Take your next right. It's shorter."

"Never was a road there before." He coasted down it. "Years ago real estate brokers protected the town, but now they sell to anybody."

"Don't blame the brokers. Blame the developers. Blame Bauer Associates. That's the biggest. You're all making money." She gave him a wink, which he missed, and then reached into her purse for a cigarette. "But you've always wanted it both ways. Like you had it with me."

"We had good times."

"Does your wife know I exist? If you mentioned my name, it wouldn't mean anything to her, would it?"

"I wish you wouldn't smoke."

"You worried about my health or yours?"

"Both."

She lit up. "Turn left."

He took the turn easily, one large hand on the wheel, and casually mentioned her husband, who had not held a steady job in years and now seldom left the house. "How's he doing, Fran?"

"He's doing fine," she said cynically. "He watches *C-Span* from the moment he gets up to when he drops off. If you want to know what's going on in Washington, he'll tell you. Otherwise he's out of it. Once upon a time I felt sorry for him. Now he's shit under my shoe, probably what I am to you."

Fellows looked hurt. "Be fair, Fran."

"Like life?"

He parked in the front lot of the Silver Bell, and they walked toward the glass entrance, she with a slight stoop. Before they reached the doors he stopped and said, "I'll tell you what. Let's circle the place and give it the once-over. You go that way, and we'll meet here on the other side."

"What's that going to prove?"

"It'll give us a perspective."

"We already have one."

"Do it my way, Fran," he said with quiet force and watched her turn away, her thick coat a cumbersome weight, her hair lifting only a little in a wind that was dying out. He waited until she had put a distance between them and then entered the motel through its glass doors. He received a fast greeting from Chick the desk clerk, who was eating a powdered doughnut out of a sheet of paper.

"Nice to see you, Mr. Fellows." The old man's smile shot out of the faceful of wrinkles, the black mole rising to his cheekbone. "Case you're looking for Mrs. Gately, she's not here. 'Course if it's important I can call her."

"No need," Fellows said, keeping his tone light, a bit put off by the old man's bright eyes. "Mrs. Gately says you work long hours, don't get much sleep. I don't see how you do it. I need my eight hours."

"I catnap, Mr. Fellows. I can sit in my chair and do it. Some people see me, they think I'm dead. I'm surely not."

"I guess business isn't all that great."

"One week it is, next week it might not be. Has its ups and downs like any business." He finished off the doughnut and wiped the sugar from his chin. "You ought to go in the coffeeshop and get a doughnut. We get them fresh from the bakery."

"I might do that," Fellows said. "Actually, I'm here to look around. I guess you know Mrs. Gately is buying the place."

"Yes, sir, I do. She told us all and said none of us have to worry about our jobs. That's a comfort to me, Mr. Fellows. I don't know what I'd do if I couldn't come here."

"You'd make out, Chick."

"No, Mr. Fellows, don't think I would. Well, sir, if you want to look around, go ahead. Place is yours."

"Thank you, Chick." Fellows started to step away but then briskly turned back as if from a sudden thought. "That poor girl who was murdered here. Terrible thing. You were on duty, right?"

"I was coming on duty. You want the truth, Mr. Fellows, I don't like to talk about it. Especially after what's happened to the boy."

"Yes, I can understand that. What room was it?"

"Forty-six. In the rear."

"Anybody in it?"

"No, sir. Nobody."

"I think I might peek in. Got the key handy?"

"No sense to that, sir. Nothing to see. It looks like every other room here."

Fellows smiled. "Call it morbid curiosity. We all have it, don't we?"

"No, sir, not me."

"You're one in a million," Fellows said and held out his hand for the key.

Sergeant Dawson drove William Rollins back to the cemetery, back to his car, which in the fading daylight seemed to have sunk somewhat into the ground. Rollins stared at it but did not get out. He slipped off his glasses, and his eyes looked lost, as if the sockets had grown. He said, "Why did you do that to me? I know you're not a cruel man."

"I had to know."

"You wanted to watch my reaction, study my face."

"Something like that."

"A polygraph would have been kinder."

"This was quicker."

"But not scientific."

"I've never been that kind of cop. Maybe now I'm paying the price. Put your glasses on, Counselor. You make me nervous."

Rollins reached inside his coat, pulled out his slim regimental necktie, and polished his glasses with the tail. He pressed too hard and one of the amber lenses fell out. Carefully he wedged it back into position and snapped it in. "When I heard the voice, I wanted to believe."

"You think I didn't?"

He returned the glasses, shiny and secure, to his face. "It has to be somebody sick."

"Who's healthy, Counselor? Are you?" Dawson leaned past him and pushed the door open. "I don't mean to rush you, but I'm getting sick of graveyards."

Rollins climbed out into the darkness of the day and looked back in before shutting the door. "Can I consider myself in the clear now?"

"More or less," Dawson said.

"Why only more or less?"

"I'm learning to hedge," Dawson said and shoved the car into gear. He might have said more but kept it between his teeth.

He left the cemetery with headlights blazing, laid a heavy foot on the accelerator, and pressed down on curves along a back road as if he carried a special invulnerability. Four minutes later he lurched into breakneck traffic on the southbound side of Interstate 93 and fought his way to the outside lane, where few cars were traveling under seventy.

Within twenty minutes he saw the twinkling of the Boston skyline.

In room forty-six of the Silver Bell Motor Lodge Fran Lovell looked sharply at Ed Fellows and said, "This is what you had in mind all along, isn't it?" He replied quietly, his lie transparent, meant to be. She stood with her coat open but her hands snugged into her pockets. The room had a chill. He had hiked the thermostat, but the heat was slow to come. When he drew near, she made her neck long and let him kiss it. "I suppose I should've guessed," she said.

"Be good to me," he whispered. His Adam's apple jerked. His teeth scraped her skin.

"Don't do that," she said. "My husband has eyes."

He breathed softly, relishing. "Like you used to be," he implored and reached inside her roomy coat. His big knees brushed hers, producing in her the same questionable sensation her unspayed cat did when arching its tail and rubbing against her bare legs.

"I'm not the same person," she said but tossed her hair with girlish frivolity. She let him undo her blouse but impeded his effort with her bra. "They won't be like you remember."

"It won't matter," he proclaimed with magnanimity as heat seemed to surge into the room from all sides, along with a small but pungent smell of dust that threatened to make her sneeze. She pushed away his hands.

"I should use the bathroom first."

"Do it," he said, immediately pulling away and grappling with his own clothes. His fine overcoat, purchased at Brooks Brothers in Boston, was flung to the floor. A Swiss watch glowed from his wrist like a statement of his personal worth.

She was in the bathroom for five minutes, mostly looking in the mirror. Her expression was tense and unsettled, as if she were fourteen again, with her head full of doubts over what boys thought of her and with her face straining out of a dance of springy curls and her young crotch partially shaved to accommodate a bikini.

Now her underpants, patterned as if by a deep frost, were too small for her, and the elastic top had twisted into her flesh. "Christ," she said to the memory of her younger and beloved self. "You had it all and didn't know it."

He heaved his tanned legs to one side, flexed his toes, and viewed her from the prop of an elbow as she emerged naked from the bathroom and marched toward the bed. Breasts swaying low on her chest, buttocks chafing, she felt like a parade.

She sought covers, but he kept them from her, wanting nothing hidden from him. His smile turned stupid. "No funny stuff," she warned. "No acrobatics."

He promised. His hand, a hot iron, pressed between her thighs. "So much of life is *this*, isn't it?"

"For men maybe. Not for me." Her voice took on a crust. "I'm not too old yet to get pregnant, you know."

He kissed her eyes as if to blind her. "Then I'll have to be careful."

But he was not.

Later, with a sheet pulled over her and an arm tossed over the side, she lay as if she had endured a commando raid upon her person. She had bruises on her shoulders and hips, a sore mouth, and an ache throughout. Her voice was thin. "I should feel younger. Why do I feel older?"

"You still got kick to you." He spoke from a dripping face, gathering his breath. "You stayed with me every second of the way."

She had most of the sheet, and he took some of it away for himself. He turned his head from her and closed his eyes as if to doze. She closed hers too. "You'll never know, will you, Ed?"

"What's that, Fran?" He tried to make his voice tender.

"What a woman wants. Or rather what she doesn't want."

He did not reply, and she lay quietly with one leg out of the sheet, her ears supersensitive. She heard every sound in the room, every tick from a pipe, every scratch from the heating system. Then she heard a noise at the door.

Their eyes snapped open.

"Is it locked?" she asked.

"I don't know."

Both leaped from the bed.

The older roommate, Sue, did not seem in the least surprised to see him and let him into the apartment, into the studio room that still smelled of furniture polish, every piece in its place, a dustless environment. "Sit, Sonny," she said, extending a long hand, fingers perfectly poised. She was wearing a fitted skirt suit and low heels. The other one, Natalie, hovered in the background and peered at him through her round glasses. Though the evening was early, suppertime, she was in pink pajamas.

"Why?" Dawson said. His voice suggested a chunk of stone. He had not moved.

"Who are you talking to, Sonny? Nat or me?"

"Both of you," he said. "Her especially."

Sue turned slightly, looked at her friend, and spoke as if to a child, albeit a bright one. "Come here, Nat. The sergeant is asking us something. What it is isn't clear yet, but I'm sure he'll explain."

"The calls," he said harshly, shifting his balance. He had suspected beforehand that something would go wrong and could feel it doing so. It was as if he had been lured here. "There's no point in pretending," he said.

Natalie had crept forward, plumper and rounder than the last time he had seen her, her ball of brown hair frizzier. Nothing seemed credible, Natalie least of all. Her pajamas, all of a piece, suggested to him cups of cocoa, Peter Rabbit books, and Alice in Wonderland.

"I made the calls," she said, the admission coming so readily and innocently that he almost disbelieved it, as if the calls had taken place only in the secrecy of his skull. He wondered whether he was a victim of the same wrong reasoning that had convinced him of the Bauer boy's guilt. He looked at Sue for guidance.

"She's good, Sonny. Very good. Nat, do the queen of England." From Natalie there was only silence, maintained as if by modesty. "OK, do Joan Rivers. Do Nancy Reagan. Nat, do Melody."

Setting herself, Natalie lifted her podgy face and rearranged her breath. Then she spoke in the voice. "Love you, Sonny."

He brought his hands up to pull his coat together. "Enough," he said, but she continued speaking in rich throaty tones bathed in a haunting mellowness. He felt rent. "Tell her to shut up."

Sue pressed a finger to her own lips, and Natalie went quiet, then shivered as if maximum energy had been expended in the mimicry. He stared at them both with incredulity. His original question remained.

"Why?"

"Nat and I miss her, Sonny."

"That's an explanation?"

"Nat wanted to remind you."

He could not bring himself to look at Natalie again, afraid of what he might say or, worse, do. Sue's almond eyes rested calmly upon him. He said to her, "Let's get out of here."

"Where, Sonny?"

"Anywhere."

"Not Nat? Just you and me?"

"Just you and me."

He had parked his car near the building, but they walked by it without a glance. The evening was clear and seasonably chilly. Street traffic was heavy, but they had the sidewalk to themselves. "Do you mind?" she said and took his arm, gearing her step with his, which was easy. Each had a long stride. For the moment he had nothing to say. When they crossed the street, it was her hand that did the guiding against the clutter of cars bearing down on them, cutting them with headlights, whipping them with tails of exhaust. "Down here," she said, and they descended into the warmth of a basement coffeehouse.

She chose a table near a potted plant that cast protective fronds their way. He slipped off his coat and quickly helped her off with her quilted one, which was lighter than he had expected. He slung both coats over an odd chair and ensconced himself across from her. Young people sat two and three at other tables, the girls bright-eyed and vital, the boys roguishly stubbled. They all made him feel old. Their dog-eared paperbacks, stacked near their elbows, made him feel ignorant.

Sue said, "I like your jacket."

"Forget my jacket."

"I'm not sure the shirt is right."

The waitress brought coffee. Sue creamed and stirred hers deliberately, smiling vaguely, doubtfully, a steady pale light emanating from her patrician features. He said, "I don't want any more calls from your friend."

"I don't think you have to worry."

"Was she trying to punish me?"

"I'd rather not answer for her."

"Why not? You two seem pretty close."

Her stare was tolerant. "Is that supposed to mean something?"

"I don't understand the relationship. Are you two . . ." He let the question peter out.

"Are we what? Lesbian?" Her smile stayed vague. "Am I? I don't know, Sonny. Perhaps I haven't decided yet. Is Natalie? I suppose so. So what?"

"Just asking," he said, conscious of her quiet eyes, her long, slender neck, the hint of cleavage inside her starched shirt. The top of her bra was lacy.

"Was Melody that way? No, Sonny, but she was kind, good to Nat, who adored her. Sometimes they cuddled. Like children, not lovers."

He took his coffee black, not his custom, and burned his lips.

"The pajamas you saw Natalie in. Mel bought them for her. A birthday gift. Birthdays were precious to Mel. In the foster homes they usually forgot hers. In some she couldn't open the refrigerator without permission."

He looked away, through the fronds. His skin felt dry.

"They did a job on her," she said, and he looked back at her. "Wasn't unusual for her to go to school bleary-eyed because someone had been at her during the night. But that's ancient history now, isn't it?"

He rattled the cup in the saucer, his hands restless, his shoulders stiff.

"Nat and I can't stop thinking about her. You can understand that, can't you?"

There was laughter from a table of three, spontaneous and carefree. He envied their gaiety, their youth, their future.

"I don't usually read the *Herald*, but Nat gets it for the contests. She always thinks she's going to win something. She saw the story about the boy in Andover hanging himself."

"He was my suspect."

"We wondered."

"I may have been wrong."

"Ah," she said with an air of abstraction. "We were afraid of that when you didn't call."

Love Nest

The trio was leaving, a youth with a dark jaw and two young women in long, open coats and shiny boots. The faces of the women were incurably pretty, as if their tender ages were permanent, their sweet places in life fixed. The lighting gave gold to the hair of one, enriched the redness in the hair of the other, and made a princess of each.

He said, "The boy made anonymous calls too, like your pal."

"Too bad Nat didn't know him. They might've got along."

"Do you want me to tell you about him?"

"No," she said. "Not if he wasn't the one." Her eyes passed over him. "You look tired. Too much in your head?"

"You could say that."

"And you seem scared."

"I want to be right." He felt fatigue wedged into his muscles, along with an unshakable fear. He shifted his feet, and a bone creaked in his leg.

"I'm patient, but I don't know about Nat," she said.

"What's that mean?"

"Nothing, Sonny." She spoke with gentle mockery, her eyes focused now on every part of his face at once. Then she reached across the small table and touched him. "You have nice hands. I wouldn't mind having one on the back of my neck."

From another of the tables came a pop of bubble gum. His ear built it into an explosion. "Yes, I am tired."

She said, "Then I'd better take you home."

Ed Fellows struggled into his pinstripes while Paige Gately watched with a cold eye, her rage tightly reined. The silver in her perfect hair glinted, and her fine aquiline nose lifted, as if a smell in the room offended her. She spoke low. "You push to the limits, don't you?"

He grappled with buttons, his look sheepish, his smile

163

guilty, and she wondered whether any man had a place on earth, a purpose in life, a right to the deep space he filled.

"Are you jealous?" he whispered, wanting her to be, foolishness on his wide face.

Under other circumstances she might have laughed at him, a high-pitched laugh like a whinny. Instead, with a sense of irony, she thought of her husband Biff, juvenile like his name, quick with a smile but slow in the head and rancid in the liver, simian in habits despite the finest schools, and dead long before his time despite the best doctors, who had bled her dry.

"Maybe just a little?" Fellows persisted.

"You're stupid," she replied quietly.

"Don't say that."

"What should I say?"

He gnawed a knuckle, then tied a shoe. "You know my needs."

She looked through him and wondered how much of a man was reducible to flyspeck.

Now both shoes were tied. They were of fine English leather, with perforations and fancy stitching, the same expensive sort, pair after pair, Biff had worn in slush and rain and ruined.

He said, "It was Chick who told you. He phoned you, didn't he? That old bastard!"

"Fix your tie."

"You were always cold. Damn it, always. Always."

She handed him his coat. "Get the hell out of here, Ed."

He shot a glance at the bathroom door. "What about her?"

"Wait for her in your car." She pulled down the collar of his coat, pushed him, and guided him to the door, which she opened quickly and was ready to close on him. He

164

gazed back at her as if he were stepping out of a dream in which she was staying.

"I'm not saying I don't appreciate the other afternoon, but—"

"You're such a fool," she said.

All at once he was contrite, somewhat ashamed. On impulse he grasped her hand, raised it, and kissed the palm. "I owe you so much, don't I?"

Her eyebrows lifted. "Don't ever forget it."

She shut the door solidly behind him and stepped back into the room. Several seconds passed before Fran Lovell emerged from the bathroom, dressed, pale but composed despite the faint tremor of her eyelids. They did not know each other well, only from dealings at the bank, a customer-employee relationship, though through the years each had surmised much about the other, most of it on the mark. Now for the first time their lives touched at a sharp point. With a prim look of censure, Paige Gately spoke first.

"I thought you were smarter."

Fran Lovell lit a cigarette and spoke through the hot haze of smoke. "You don't scare me, Mrs. Gately. You never have."

"It would be better for you if I did. Does your husband know he has horns?"

"I don't need that. Not from you."

"I see. Are you tougher than you look? That would be in your favor."

The younger woman pulled deeply on the cigarette, the effort squinching her face. "What do you want from me, Mrs. Gately?"

They scrutinized each other.

"You were beautiful once, Fran. A shame you let yourself go."

Memories flamed from the ashes. "We come from the same town, Mrs. Gately, but different worlds."

"That's an excuse, and not a very good one." A small smile was shaped. "You know, Fran, I remember the piggy bank I had as a child. I remember the clink the coin made when it went in. Actually I had many such banks, but I never filled one of them. That was not a priority. Now it is."

"Am I supposed to gather something from that?"

"I certainly hope so, for our priorities are not that different." The smile was placid, poised. "Do you like your job, dear? Do you want to keep it? Don't ever pull a stunt like this again, not in *this* motel."

Fran Lovell smashed her cigarette out in an ashtray and slipped on her coat. "You have quite a hold on him, don't you?"

"Yes, dear, and you have a slight one. Don't lose it."

"I get the message."

"I was sure you would."

Fran Lovell made for the door, her posture straight but her steps slow and unnatural. Shoving her hair to one side, she looked back. "We both know what he is, don't we?"

"Yes, dear. He's a pig."

"Sonny's going to stay the night. You don't mind, do you, Nat?"

Natalie was in her bedroom, sitting crosslegged on the bed, eating off a tray, watching television, childlike in the pink pajamas. Her brown eyes went small inside her round spectacles. "Where's he going to sleep?"

"There's only Mel's room, isn't there? Unless we want to stick him on the sofa where he'll be in the way. We don't want that, do we?"

Natalie made a subtle face, and Sue stepped aside in the doorway so that Sergeant Dawson could be glimpsed. Dawson, in earshot, stared their way.

"Look at him, Nat. The poor guy's dead on his feet. I'll be with you in a minute, Sonny."

"Don't pity him," Natalie said.

"He has much on his mind, kitten. Maybe more than you. Do you want me to shut your door?"

"Half."

Stepping back with a smile, Sue closed it a little more than half and returned to Dawson. She pointed with a finger, thumb cocked. "There's the bathroom. Plenty of towels, but don't use the flowery ones. They're Nat's, she's fussy. Feel free to use the fridge."

"I don't want to be a bother."

"We're putting you in Mel's room. That won't make you feel weird, will it?"

He sighed. "I'm some cop. I've never looked through her things."

"You couldn't bring yourself to, and I didn't want you to. Besides, there's nothing of you in there, nothing of me, only things she needed to live day to day. Why don't you go into the bathroom now, get it over with."

"Yes," he said.

"Take a hot bath if you like. If Natalie wasn't here I'd soak with you, but she'd get upset. We have rules. No monkey business here with boyfriends. But you're not a boyfriend, are you? Not mine, not Natalie's." She drifted closer, touched his jaw. "Do you like me? I think you could."

In the bathroom he splashed his face with water, cleaned his teeth with a finger smeared with toothpaste, and slicked his hair back with wet hands. After a rummage in the medicine cabinet, he sprinkled three aspirin onto his palm and licked them into his mouth. Sue smiled when he came out and led him into the room that had been Melody's.

"Everything is more or less as she left it. In the closet are a couple of nice dresses, and in that bureau are a lot of shirts and jeans, which is what she wore the most. She never looked like a hooker, did she? More like the girl next door."

He stared at a small bookcase overstuffed with paperbacks.

"She read a lot. Did she mention it?"

"She didn't have to," he said and glanced at a travel poster on the wall, a panoramic view of a Mediterranean beach bejeweled by a scarlet sun.

"Poster's mine, Sonny. Trip to Greece, paid for by my daddy. Mel never went anywhere like that, didn't have the desire. All she desired was a home."

"She had one. Here."

"No, a real one. Normal."

"This wasn't normal?"

"Traditional is what I meant to say. House with a husband in it. Your house was ready-made. She loved Nat and me, but she'd have loved you more." She moved to the bed, drew down the ruffled spread, plumped the lacy pillow, and turned back the covers. "I'm afraid the sheets haven't been changed, but you won't mind, will you? Only Mel was in them."

He stared down at the bed.

"Get undressed, Sonny. Do you sleep in your shorts or in nothing?" She half turned away from him. "Don't be embarrassed. I won't look."

He unhooked his revolver, unloaded it, and pocketed the slugs. Then he undressed quickly, piling his clothes on a chair, arranging his shoes beneath. She watched in a mirror.

"Mel said you had super legs. She was right."

He killed the light. In bed, his head hit the pillow hard, and for a second or so he felt inexpressibly peaceful.

"Settled in? Good." She slipped forward in the semidark, her features a mix of glimmer and shadow. She sat on the bed's edge and propped an arm over him. "Why did you take the bullets out of your gun?" she asked. He felt the patter of the words against his face.

"I wouldn't want an accident."

"You're not afraid of us, are you?"

"Only of accidents."

Her smile had a cutting edge. "I know you don't trust yourself, but do you trust anybody?"

"I trust my chief. I trust Billy Lord. He's the officer who gave you the ride back. You didn't appreciate the cigar."

"It's an ugly thing to smoke, but it makes a man feel bigger than he is. Who else do you trust?"

"Most of the guys in the department, I guess. The ones who've been around awhile."

"What you mean is, you just trust your own. That's safe. Good thinking." Her smile hovered, still with the edge. Idly she tossed the covers away from his shoulders. "Do you have hair on your chest? Yes, you do." Her free hand traced over it, and with force her fingers raised a strand or two. "Hurt?"

It did.

"My little sister and I did that to my father," she said. "He always said *ouch* and pretended to cry."

"I didn't know you had a sister."

"I didn't. She was imaginary." Cool on his skin, casual in its touch, her hand forged deeper down and found the ridge of an appendectomy scar. "Feels old, so you must've been young."

"Twelve," he said as her hand moved on.

"Some men can't stand to have their navels touched."

He gave a start. "I'm one of them." His eyes shot into hers. "Why are you doing this?"

"I'm interested." Her hand forged over his shorts and arrowed into the opening. "Good growth of hair here. Sort of wiry, like Nat's." Her voice was hollow, stark. For an instant he imagined a knife at this throat, the razor edge

169

beginning to cut the skin. Lightly, clinically, she gripped him. "And a lot of this, isn't there? Are you proud? Most men are."

"Is this what you did with your father?"

"No, Sonny, my sister did. I knew it was wrong."

"Do you still have that sister?"

"Lost her when I was eight or nine. Then she came back in Melody. You're in her bed, Sonny. How does it feel?"

"It's a bed, nothing more," he said, his voice hollow like hers, just as stark. She retracted her hand and returned the covers to his shoulders.

"If anybody could have saved her, it would have been you, not I. I had hope in you, much hope." She rose slowly, as if her disappointments were many, and stood erect. "Go to sleep."

"Do you think I can?"

"Yes."

"I don't think I want to."

"But you will."

He closed his eyes and heard her leave. At a point between sleep and waking, where dreams seem absolutely real, he found himself cheek by jowl in a court corridor with accused murderers, molesters, rapists, the trembling Bauer boy among them, snot on his nose, tears of innocence in his eyes, a noose around his neck though his case had not yet been called. He tried to elbow a path to the boy, but others pushed at him and a rough hand, no one's in particular, shoved him in a different direction.

He woke as if pricked by a needle, his arms and one leg out of the covers, which trailed off him in ghostly fashion. He raised his wrist for a reading on his watch but could not come up with one. The room was darker now, though not so dark that he failed to see the plump figure framed in the doorway, a flare of pink, which did not altogether surprise him, nor the voice that floated in, enough like Melody's to make his skin crawl.

"You rejected me, Sonny. Do you regret it?"

He answered, total truth. "Bitterly."

"I'm fresh, clean. So healthy it's criminal."

"I know that."

"You could have all of me, no folded corners in my life, no markers. Want me to clean? I'll clean. Cook? I'll learn. I'll make you happy."

He said something but nothing intelligible, nothing meant for a living ear, including his own. All at once he felt crowded, hemmed in, as in the dream, and waited to be pushed and shoved.

"Second chance, Sonny?"

The pinkness fell away, lay like a fire on the floor. He heard the quick patter of feet and, rising up on his elbows, glimpsed little tits, a full belly, round knees. He heaved an arm up. "Get out of here."

She scratched him. Crimson threads spread from the breaks in the skin. Then came a movement from another direction, the thump of a knee on the bed. "Are you sure, Sonny? Are you really sure?" She spoke against his bleeding shoulder as if printing the words onto his flesh. The voice was Sue's, the shadowed face perched over the long neck was hers, the almond eyes shining down were hers. The breasts were pale pears boldly displayed. "How often do you get a second chance?"

"Only in fantasy," he mumbled.

She swung an aggressive leg and straddled him, her weight warm and humid and then chafing and burning. "This is for real." The bed pitched. She drove hard, pausing only once to kiss him with blood on her mouth. They finished fast, with matching shudders, as if someone had stomped over their common grave. Her breath fell between them.

"You needed that, didn't you, Sonny boy?"

The voice was no longer affectionate. Lying drained, muscles in both legs twitching, he blinked up at her. She leaped off.

"Get up, you bastard! Get dressed and get out!"

Natalie, forgotten only by him, threw his clothes at him and stood curiously still under her thorny ball of hair, her eyes inside her glasses as empty as Little Orphan Annie's.

"Look what she's got, Sonny."

No need. He guessed.

"I hate him," Natalie said in her own breaking voice, spite in her hand, and he sat up cautiously, gripping his shirt, one of his black socks.

"What do you think, Sonny, is it still unloaded?"

He did not want to guess. He sat mute and immobile, his shirt covering his crotch.

"Would you do it, Nat? Would you really do it?"

Natalie squeezed the trigger as he went rigid. The dry click was deafening to all.

They each dressed, Natalie the quickest with only pajamas to slip on. She assisted Sue with her bra. Sue buttoned her blouse, tossed her hair, and then returned his piece to him.

"Use it on the real killer," she said.

Natalie said, "Or on yourself."

Ten

The Silver Bell Motor Lodge changed hands on an exceptionally bright afternoon, the first day of December, the temperature rising to an unseasonable height. The transaction was conducted in the conference room of Citizens Bank, the sun streaming through the wide windows. Ed Fellows's signature on the bank check was a scrawl. A paraph gave it flare. The figure was substantial, top dollar, payable to Bauer Associates. Only Ed Fellows, Paige Gately, and the lawyers were present. After arranging his copies of the documents into a neat pile, the lawyer from the bank slid the check across the mahogany table to William Rollins and said, "I guess that does it." With a slight tremor Rollins deposited the check into his briefcase. Everybody rose for an exchange of handshakes.

Paige Gately leaned toward Rollins's ear and whispered sweetly, "You son of a bitch, you've had a couple."

He shook his head. "Don't you know when a man is scared?" he whispered back and snapped the lock on his briefcase.

The bank lawyer left. Ed Fellows dusted his hands, as if the deal had been physical, and said, "Well, that's that." William Rollins lingered and drew a stare.

"May I speak with you alone, Paige?"

"Something on your mind?"

"I'd just like to chat for a moment."

"Wait for me in the lobby," she said.

Alone together, Ed Fellows removed his half glasses and allowed his pale eyes to swim free. "Have you heard from the hotel people?"

"I was on the phone with the executive vice-president this morning. Looks good. He wants to talk business." Her smile was arch, artful, confident. "I suggested we get together in a few months. He wants it sooner."

"How was it left?"

"I said I'd get back to him. I don't want to make it too soon for obvious reasons."

"You're a wonder, Paige."

"Are you just discovering that?"

"I've never underestimated you," he said softly. Then he grinned. "And I always knew, some way or another, we'd be partners."

His arm slid around her. She removed it. "You're the junior partner," she said.

She descended to the lobby, where Attorney Rollins was waiting patiently, briefcase in hand, his head a shade tilted as if from a crick in his neck. He said, "Mrs. O'Dea would like a word with you."

"Sounds ominous. Where is she?"

"Phillips Academy. Addison Gallery."

"What in God's name is she doing *there*?"

"Getting culture," Rollins said tonelessly and extended an arm. "I'll drive you."

The sun shone brilliantly on the venerable brick buildings of the academy, the grounds meticulously groomed, the green of the grass almost as rich as in summer, as if landscaping were an extension of the curriculum. Rollins parked the Mercedes across from the chapel, and together he and Paige Gately followed a shrub-shaded path to the impressive stone stairs leading to the gallery.

"I'll wait here and enjoy the weather," he said. "The

174

exhibit's on the second floor. Contemporary British painting and sculpture, on loan from the Buffalo Fine Arts Academy."

"Sounds like you know all about it."

"I viewed it yesterday."

"You haven't told me what she wants, William."

"I don't know," he said. "I honest-to-God don't."

She examined his pale face, then gazed off at the rolling
expanse of the campus. "This is the best prep school in the
country, but it didn't do much for you, did it?" The words
were cruel, but she did not mean them that way. "It didn't
do much for Biff either."

Rollins said, "Don't keep her waiting."

Not too many people were at the exhibit, a few in-
structors from the academy, some students, a townie or
two. Rita O'Dea was easy to find. Wrapped in a flowing
cape, sunglasses pushed into her black hair, where they
glinted like added eyes, she pondered a semiabstract piece
of sculpture entitled *Seated Woman with Arms Extended*. Without looking at Paige Gately, she said, "A tiny head and no
boobs. Looks more like a beetle or a ladybug. What do you
think?"

"I didn't realize you were interested in art."

"I'm fitting in, didn't you know? I finally got around
to joining the Newcomers Club. You know what a new-
comer is in this town? Anybody who wasn't born here. I
went to my first meeting and all they did was jabber about
this exhibit. I figured I'd better take a look so I'd know
what they're talking about. Now I'm here, I think they
were pulling each other's chain."

A head turned.

"You understand any of this stuff?"

"I pretend," Paige Gately said.

They moved on to a piece that was more a carving
than a sculpture. Called *Curved Form*, it was an undulating

U with a hole in its bottom. Rita O'Dea's sizable arms came out of her cape in a gesture of frustration. "Am I supposed to make something of this?"

"It had a certain fluidity," Paige Gately offered carefully.

"What the fuck does that mean?"

A startled security guard stared.

Rita O'Dea suddenly gazed upon Paige Gately's trim figure with an air of envy and anger. Then, vaguely apologetic, she lowered her voice. "My brother all the time used to tell me not to draw attention to myself. Hey, I got a choice? I just step out the door, I got people gawking. You got thin genes, I got the kind make you fat."

Paige Gately did not know her well, but she knew enough to treat her with caution, respect, and a certain amount of flattery. "You have a beautiful face."

"And gorgeous hair. My body had been better to me, I could've been a terrific hooker. I started getting heavy when I was twelve, time I was twenty I was *this*." She spoke with self-mockery and plucked the sunglasses from her hair, snapping the wings in.

They approached a foot-high sculpture on a pedestal called *Family Going for a Walk*, beside which, by the same artist, was a painting of the identical subject. In both works the figures were busily united into a streak as if by sticky clothing.

"This, maybe, I could put in my living room," she said, gesticulating with her glasses at the sculpture. "Let people talk about it . . . if I was giving a party or something. I guess you give a lot of parties."

"No."

"But you go to plenty."

"Not many."

"But you're asked. That's the difference. We come from different worlds, don't we, Mrs. Gately? I'm the wop sister of a dead mafioso and you're an Andover Yankee full of

176

airs. You got class, I got greaseball written on me. I fart, people hear me down the street. You probably do it dainty. That's a difference. I finger myself and howl when I come. What do you do, squeak?"

Paige Gately's face was dead white and partially frozen.

"But under the skin we're not so different. We got the same instincts, Mrs. Gately."

"What's your point?"

"You got something up your sleeve buying the Silver Bell."

"If you feel that way, why did you consent to the sale?"

"Maybe I want to see how smart you are. Or how dumb. Maybe I'm a little bored and can use some fun."

They viewed a large, doleful painting in muted shades of gray and blue depicting the chalky protoplasmic shape of a dog peering over the edge of a gutter through the bars of a catch basin.

"This sucks."

"Yes, it sucks," Paige Gately agreed. The air seemed to vibrate between them.

"Or maybe," Rita O'Dea said, "I don't mind another woman getting ahead, even at my expense. A man, of course, would be different. I'd have to cut his balls off, otherwise people back in Boston would think I'm getting soft."

She smiled, and Paige Gately searched the smile for twists of truth. The red mouth, like the large smooth baby-soft face, was unreadable. The black eyes were dazzling.

"You call me Rita from now on. I'll call you Paige."

"What's all this leading to?"

The sunglasses vanished into a pocket of the cape. "That's for you to figure out."

"I'm afraid I'm slow, Rita."

"No you're not." They were poised now before a big oil painting of a ghastly red-fleshed figure. The figure, fe-

177

male, lay sprawled against flaming colors on a pink sheet in a deep sleep less like death than belated birth. "This, I look at it long enough, would piss me off."

Paige Gately said, "You want a piece of whatever."

"You got it."

The medical examiner conducted a private practice in offices in downtown Lawrence, across from the common, where Sergeant Dawson hunted him down. He was sitting on a bench, taking advantage of the mild weather and brilliant sunshine, his wispy hair lifting a little in the soft breeze. "Nice life," Dawson said, plopping down beside him.

"You think so, Sonny? You want to trade?"

"You have a patient coming in at two. Your secretary said to remind you."

"What do you think of my secretary? Usually I wouldn't hire one that young and pretty. Distracting. But as I get older, I think about sex less and less."

"I think about it more and more," Dawson said.

The doctor laughed, sunlight shifting over his face, illuminating all the hollows. A brightly dressed Hispanic woman was sitting at a nearby bench, her black hair as sleek as a crow. Her children were untidy, noisy, and rambunctious. "Get married, Sonny, that'll cool you down."

A denim-jacketed youth swaggered by, sweeping his hair back with a long black Ace comb that looked like a weapon. Dawson said, "I had my chance, muffed it. But that's not my problem."

A number of city hall workers with scarlet Irish faces paraded by, each greeting the doctor. On the opposite bench an elderly woman hiked up her triple layer of dresses to sun her stunted knees.

"What is your problem? Medical? Maybe I can help you."

"I'm wondering how good a cop I am. If I have a right to be one."

"Career crisis, huh?"

"More than that, Doc. It's a moral one."

"Christ, those are the worst. I hope you're not going to make me listen."

"Did you know the Bauer boy was my suspect in the motel murder?"

"I figured that. I know how shook you were when he hanged himself."

"I put heat on him, Doc. That's how certain I was. His suicide, much as it horrified me, was the clincher. I mean, why else would he do that? Would you have an answer?"

The doctor gazed off at two drunks propping each other up like lovers, their free hands groping for a bench. Closer by, the Hispanic woman opened up a loaf of plain bread and doled out slices to her children. "Different world over here, huh, Sonny? Not like Andover. Biggest fear in Andover is some spic from Lawrence might bust in and steal the stereo. Small chance, right? Any spic trespassing ten feet over the line immediately has a hundred eyes on him."

Dawson brought a hand to his throat, loosened his tie, and opened the top of his shirt. His revolver pressed uncomfortably against his hip like something unwanted.

"Have you heard this one, Sonny? When a woman in Lawrence gets mad at her husband she throws dishes at him. A woman in Andover peels the little alligator off his polo shirt."

Dawson gave a faint nod, then skewed his head around, as if he thought someone were creeping up behind him. It was only a pigeon. The doctor smiled.

"Have you heard this one?"

Dawson's ear was half-tuned to the tireless hum of traffic on Common Street, where the buildings were a gritty monochrome, some in need of repair.

"In Lawrence a woman has her faults. In Andover she's a shade too perfect, result of a facelift."

"What are you telling me, Doc?"

"It's hard for me to get excited over what happens in Andover."

"Then you don't have an answer for me." He started to rise, but the doctor stopped him with a small gesture.

"There was something peculiar. Maybe I should've thought about it more. When I examined the boy's body I found semen stains." The doctor lowered his head and his voice. "I may not have mentioned it in my report."

Something heaved inside Dawson's chest. "What does it mean?"

"It might not have been suicide."

"What else could it have been?"

"An accident."

Rita O'Dea drove herself from the Addison Gallery to the Bauer home on Southwick Lane. Harriet Bauer answered the door on the first sounding of the chimes, failed to hide a trace of displeasure, and said, "Alfred's not here."

"I know that," Rita O'Dea said.

They kissed politely.

A window was partly raised in the sun room, where heavy cream-colored cushions gave substance to the white wicker furniture. Harriet, wearing one of her husband's shirts, the tails flapping, served Rita a blend of fruit juices in a crystal tumbler. Rita took a small swallow, then a deeper one, and licked her lips.

"Not bad. What is it?"

"Coconut, pineapple, and a touch of something else. I forget."

"How are you bearing up?"

The shrug was barely perceptible. The eyes were tired. The windows looked out on a stand of spruce, through which jays swooped, driving away much smaller birds anonymous in their drab dress. Rita spoke in a flat tone from deep in a chair.

"I loved him too, you know."

"I loved him more."

"Of course. You were his mother. But life must go on. I know that better than anybody."

Harriet had not taken a chair but stood like a stray piece of statuary, tight jeans molded to her strong legs. Her fair hair was yanked back, but much of it was escaping the knot. Her eyes were small from a lack of proper sleep. Rita gazed up at her.

"Women should stick together at a time like this."

"I'll survive. I always do."

"You've never liked me, have you, Harriet?"

There was a hesitation. "I've never trusted you."

"You should play everyone by ear. That's something my brother taught me. You knew him well enough, didn't you?"

"I was young."

"How was he? I mean, as a man."

Harriet pretended to remember. "He was the best."

"He was a *magnifico*. When he was alive, everybody kissed my ass. Cops, bankers, politicians. Anything for Tony's sister. That's how big he was." Her eyes started to fill, but she quickly recovered. "Someone, wasn't him, he never talked about that stuff, told me you were a class act. If you'd stayed in the business, you could have written your own ticket."

"Yes, I was good," Harriet said simply.

"Good as Melody?"

There was no answer, none expected. The screech of jays came through the raised window as if the shot of unseasonable weather had jarred their senses. Rita spoke slowly.

"It's not the cop you want, is it?"

Harriet turned her face away, sharply, with a cataclysm of feeling, and drew her lips forcibly over her large teeth.

"No, I didn't think so," Rita said, a suspicion confirmed.

In what seemed a moment of weightlessness, Harriet glided to the open window and raised it more. She went up on her toes and breathed deeply, sunlight irradiating her. Rita regarded her at length.

"You're in tremendous shape. Most ex-hookers let themselves go. Thirty-five, they look fifty. Forty, forget it. Christ, you look like you could crawl into a ring, win on points."

Harriet turned about casually. "I live by my body."

"Not anymore."

"Alfred didn't marry me for my brain."

"But you've got one. My brother said to me, long time ago, watch out for you."

"Your brother was smart."

"He was a genius. He said you got the brain but you don't always use it. He said you were like me that way." Rita loosened her cape and spread her knees. "You told me what Alfred married you for. What'd you marry him for?"

"Same thing."

"You worshipped the ground he walked on, way we saw it."

"Yes."

"Before you came into the picture, when he was trying to get on the good side of my brother, he wined and dined me at Locke-Ober. The bottle of wine cost three-hundred dollars. Got me tipsy. End of the evening, in his car, I gave him a blow job. He ever tell you?"

Harriet was playing with a button on her shirt. She said, "He may have. I don't remember."

"Did you blow my brother?"

She answered without thought or memory. "Probably."

"Fiddling with your shirt that way makes you look a little like Melody. That what you want?"

"Hardly."

"Then you ought to be careful. Every couple of weeks I used to pay Melody a hundred bucks for a massage. She had good hands. You got good hands, Harriet?"

"You know I do."

"Been a long time, hasn't it? I got Ralph doing me now, he's not so good."

"If I ever need a hundred dollars I'll call you."

Rita grimaced. She liked the fruit drink but wanted no more of it. "Here, take it," she said, and Harriet came forward and relieved her of the tumbler. "You finish it."

"Yes, I won't waste it," Harriet said, her dull expression undeviating, something Olympian in her stance.

Rita let her voice drop drastically. "You're going to throw everything away, aren't you?"

"Nothing's clear in my mind."

"I think everything's crystal clear," Rita said, and each gazed at the other with a sort of fascination, as if fully seeing each other for the first time, deep inward looks surgical in nature. Then, with a heavy effort, Rita rose from the chair and pulled at her cape. The floor seemed to quiver under her weight. "I don't think it'd do much good to argue."

Harriet raised the tumbler to her lips. "I don't think you would anyway."

"You act like I don't care."

Harriet gave out a smile both desolate and wise. "Oh, you care all right."

In the foyer Rita added sunglasses to her face and inspected herself in the oak-framed mirror. Something of her image saddened her, and she toyed with the idea that back in time she had been someone else, someone less emphatic but more secure. Harriet waited for her at the open door, toward which she moved with a pinch of regret in her expression, her arms extending out of the cape.

Their embrace was brief but full of feeling, as if they might not see each other again.

Chief Chute said, "I don't have so many detectives I can have one working on a case that's closed."

"It has a life of its own," Dawson said, "almost nothing to do with me."

"The chief and I don't understand talk like that." The speaker was the district attorney, Ned to his friends. He had dense, iron gray hair, a large, virile face with an eagle nose, and the padded bulk of a former college football player. He consumed a chair near Chief Chute's desk. "Or maybe the chief understands. He knows you better."

Dawson sat in a smaller chair with one long leg flung over the other. The chief had summoned him to his office a half hour after the district attorney had entered it.

"Fact is, Sergeant, you never should've been on the case. If I'd known about your involvement with the victim you wouldn't have been. But I can understand the chief doing for you. You're his favorite. I got favorites of my own I stick my neck out for."

Chief Chute stirred uncomfortably at his desk, his soft chin rising above the busy braid of his shirt. "I thought it best to tell the D.A. everything. To protect you, Sonny."

"She was kind of young for you, wasn't she, Sergeant?"

Dawson flushed faintly and bit back what he was going to say, which would not have been politic. The district attorney flashed a smile meant to be man-to-man.

"Was she that good?"

"No," Dawson said. "She was that different."

"I told you, Ned, it wasn't that kind of relationship," the chief interposed quietly.

"That's hard to swallow."

"I was getting information from her," Dawson said.

"That so?"

"You know about Alfred Bauer, his past connection with Tony Gardella. Now it's with Gardella's sister, who lives right here in town now. The two of them owned the Silver Bell Motor Lodge, at least they did until today. Bauer used to import high-priced hookers to the motel, two and three times a week. He worked it through a shrink named Stickney, an old buddy, who provided classy clients for so-called therapy. The clients were mostly from the town's high-tech companies."

The district attorney absently stroked the back of his neck. "So these clients were patients under professional care."

"If you want to be ironic about it."

"Situation like that, I'm not sure it's illegal. I'd have to check. But the chief tells me you put a word in the right ear and Bauer killed the operation. No fuss, no scandal for the town, everything taken care of diplomatically. I'd say that was smart police work. Should've ended there. Instead you involved yourself with the girl."

"She involved herself with me."

"Takes two to tango."

"I wanted Bauer."

"Why, Sergeant? Was it personal?"

"Matter of common sense. People like him and Gardella's sister are too big for the town. A few years from now they'll be putting selectmen into office, that's my opinion."

"What are you, a crusader?" The district attorney snorted indulgently. "OK, you wanted Bauer, but the girl didn't give him to you. Did you seriously think she would?" His smile turned chilly and authoritative. "Looking back, do you think Bauer was ever in the least worried?"

"I don't know," Dawson said in a low tone, and the district attorney gave out another snort, louder and less indulgent. With a glance at the narrow door to Chief Chute's private lavatory, his shoulders straining the open jacket of his suit, he hoisted himself up.

"Mind if I use your toilet, Chief?"

Dawson and Chief Chute shifted their eyes to other places, for he did not bother to close the door. He propped an arm against the facing wall and leaned over the open bowl, his trousers worn so low under the arc of his belly that he nearly did not need to bother with the zipper. He spoke above the forceful clatter of his splash.

"I've been D.A. for twelve years, a lawyer for twenty, and before that I was a cop just like you, Sergeant, sin city of Revere. I learned something all those years. A hooker, from the lowest to the highest, never turns in her pimp. That's her daddy."

He finished with a flourish and a shiver, struck the flushing lever, and stepped to the sink. He spoke over the roar.

"My belief, Sergeant, is deep in your gut you knew this, but you wanted to shack up with her. Who the hell could blame you? I heard she was a knockout. Must've had a heart of gold too. Right?"

Chief Chute, avoiding Dawson's eyes, lowered his fuzzy head and rearranged something on his desk. The district attorney came out blotting his hands in paper toweling.

"What I can't understand is you still fiddling with the case. Far as everybody's concerned, exception of you, it's closed. Even if you did come up with something, chances are I couldn't use it. You'd be suspect. A lawyer would tear you apart, for Christ's sake."

"I did come up with something. Didn't the chief tell you?"

"I told him, Sonny."

"Yeah, he told me, and it's bullshit. Who cares why the Bauer kid put a belt around his neck? Either case, he was sick in the head. You'd rather it not be suicide because you don't want the guilt. I can't worry about that and neither can the chief. He's got a town to look after, I got a whole county."

The district attorney made a sodden ball of the toweling and tossed it into the chief's wastebasket. Then he picked up his coat.

"Something else I learned through the years, Sergeant. Trust your first instinct. Nine times out of ten it's on the mark."

Left alone, Dawson and Chief Chute avoided each other's eyes, their silence uneasy. The chief opened a desk drawer as if in search of something not quite worth finding and rummaged up a fingernail trimmer. "Well, Sonny, I'm glad the D.A. knows everything." He pared a nail. "I feel like a load's been taken off our shoulders, don't you?"

"Your shoulders," Dawson said, rising. "Not mine."

A couple of minutes later he approached the desk sergeant, who was munching a Danish that bore a passing resemblance to a pizza. The front doors of the station were open, letting in sunshine and a breeze. With sticky fingers the desk sergeant held out a yellow slip of paper. "Dispatcher left a message for you. Number, no name."

Dawson stared at the scribbled telephone number. It was local and familiar.

"Beautiful day, huh, Sonny?" the desk sergeant said with icing in his mustache. "But a tease. You know what's coming, right?"

"No," Dawson said, "I wish I did."

He turned left, stepped into the small interrogation

187

room, and made the call from there. The number belonged to Bauer Associates. The voice in his ear belonged to the receptionist, Eve James. He said, "I'm returning Alfred Bauer's call."

She said, "No, Sonny, you're returning mine."

When Fran Lovell emerged from the back door of the bank, the sun had vanished, but the air was still warm, fraudulent in its promise. Walking toward her car with her weighty coat open, she saw Sergeant Dawson waiting for her. She smiled wryly. "Is this a pinch?"

"I'd like to buy you a cup of coffee," he said, and she pulled a face.

"I've got a bunch of errands to do and a kid to pick up. Unless you're planning to ask me to run away with you, I'll take a rain check."

"Could we talk in your car? Just for a minute."

"Sure, why not. If you play it right, you might grab yourself a cheap feel. On second thought, you'd better not. I'm a little sore."

Her car was a small economical model with an overloaded ashtray and coffee-mug rings on the narrow top of the dash. Settled in, she lowered her window and lit a cigarette. Dawson shoved back the passenger seat to prevent his knees from nudging his chin. He said, "Do you remember Eve James from high school?"

"Of course I remember her. I hated her, naturally."

"Why naturally?"

"I was pretty, more than pretty, but she was beautiful. Remember that gorgeous red hair of hers, so thick it must have taken three hours to dry when she washed it?"

"She had her problems."

"Didn't we all. But you're right, she got heavy into drugs, senior year."

"What happened to her after graduation?"

"Her father's company transferred him to Houston or some foolish place like that. Eve stayed, or rather she moved to Boston. Somebody told me she went to work in a health club. She wanted to become a model, but talk was she became something else, if you know what I mean. Christ, how many years ago was that? Don't tell me."

"She's back in town. She works for Bauer Associates."

"I know. I ran into her there on bank business. She was arranging flowers in a vase for her boss's office."

"She's the receptionist."

Fran Lovell laughed. "She's more than that. The dress she was wearing cost at least three hundred dollars."

"I didn't recognize her at first."

"I knew her right away, even with her hair cut so short, but I had to tell her who *I* was, which pissed me off. Have I changed so much?"

"We all have."

"Not you, not her. She's hard in the face, but she's still got the same great shape, which is more than I can say. I tried to get her into conversation, but she wasn't interested in talking over old times. I'm an assistant vice-president in the town's biggest bank, and she looked at me like I'm some old cow. Bitch!" She pitched her cigarette out the window. "Why are you so interested in her?"

"She's asked me out to dinner tonight. Her treat."

Fran Lovell's face stiffened. "Lucky you." She jammed in the ignition key. "Get out. I've got things to do."

"Why are you so mad?"

"I'm not. I'm in a hurry."

"I have another question, not about Eve. About Paige Gately buying the Silver Bell. That was a major league purchase. How'd she get the bank to go along with her?"

"Come on, Sonny. You know she and Ed Fellows have always had a special relationship. Same as I've always had one with him, though mine's not as special."

He gave out a mock look of innocence, and she bristled with impatience and irritation.

"Don't tell me you never wondered how I made it in the bank? I was no big brain in high school, was I? A surprise I graduated."

She started up the car, and he climbed out. Before he could shut the door, she bent her head and looked out at him, her hair falling over half her face.

"You poor fool."

"Why do you say that?"

"Eve James will eat you up."

Rita O'Dea served supper in her spacious eat-in kitchen. The meal was lamb chops, baked squash, and apple sauce. Her guest was Attorney Rollins, who sat tensely at her table, as if he felt he should have been waiting on her. He took small bites. She watched him and smiled. "You've got such dainty hands, Willy. Like I had when I was ten." She deposited a chunk of butter into her shell of squash. "Miss your mama?" she asked, and he went silent. "I'm not making fun of you. I know how it is. I miss my brother. How long's your mother been dead?"

"All my adult life."

"But you had her when it counted. Thank God for something." She salted her food and then placed the shaker near him, but he made no move for it. "Don't you use salt, Willy?"

"I try to avoid it."

"I've been told to."

He said, "Who told you about my mother?"

"The girl told me. We talked a lot when she did my back—I've got a bad one, you know. She said you were a perfect gentleman, treated her like a sister. You even gave her a key to your house."

"It pleased me when she chose to use it."

"Pleased you a lot."

"Yes."

"You a lonely man, Willy?" She paused, filling her mouth. Her gaze was steady. "I already know, but you can tell me. How lonely?"

He used his knife and fork on a thick lamb chop, which had been broiled medium-rare and was full of juice. "There are times I don't want to go home at night, but it passes."

"There are times in this big house, Willy, I want to scream. Loneliness can tear you up inside. But like you I don't let it last long. Instead I think about business. I think about it all the time."

She had poured wine. Now she poured more, her bare arm close to him, the fat in it packed deep. Her full, handsome face hovered.

"People look at you and me, they might think we're soft inside. They don't know us. They don't know I've got my brother's balls. These same people look at Alfred and Harriet, they see something different, but they don't know them either. See what I'm saying?"

He was beginning to, but the look he gave her was at once searching and cautious.

"You and me, Willy, we've dealt with tragedy. We can handle it, but I worry about the Bauers. I don't know if they're made of the same stuff."

Uncertain whether to speak, he continued to eat. The chop gave him trouble, and his knife slipped.

She said, "Something happens, I want to know I can depend on you. I want to know you can step in, keep things moving. The thing that's important, Willy, is every minute of the day I've got to know you're my man."

All of her face claimed his attention, and he nodded emphatically and unequivocally. Her voice, in some phantom way, sounded like his mother's.

191

"I like your name," she said. "You're Yankee, you're Andover. In time maybe we can change the name from Bauer Associates to Rollins. How's that sound?"

It sounded overwhelming, life-changing, heady. It was too much for him to think about at that moment, and he let his confusion linger as if it were something to savor.

"The only thing is, Willy, you've got a black mark against you."

He tightened. "I don't understand."

"The Silver Bell."

"The price was right," he said rapidly.

"It was too right. If I knew that, you should've."

Afraid to look at her, he busied himself with the chop, his knife struggling with the remaining meat. Inside, he was ice.

"Pick it up," she said. "Eat off the bone. Get grease on your face like a man." Her voice had gone unusually low. "It's the way you eat when you're alone, isn't it?"

"Yes." He reached into his plate. "Yes, it is."

"In the old days anybody did me or my brother wrong, Ralph Roselli could go after him in a hundred different ways, each one looking like an accident. But I don't do business that way anymore. Not if I can help it."

He gnawed on the bone, his eyes squeezed shut behind his amber glasses.

She said, "You owe me."

The town, in Sergeant Dawson's estimation, had two reasonable restaurants, but he liked neither. One, Backstreet, he considered too cramped and crowded, and the other, Rembrandt's, he regarded as too roomy and impersonal, with the aura of its past existence, a mortuary, still clinging to it. Eve James suggested the Andover Inn, which he felt was too rich for his blood. "I've already made reservations," she said with cheerful finality. She had frosted paint on her mouth which, pursed, looked like a shiny coin. "Remember, Sonny, it's my treat."

They were in her car, a sporty Mazda much like the one, except for the year and color, that Melody Haines had driven to the Silver Bell. "Nice wheels," he said. "Buy it local?"

"I didn't buy it at all."

"A gift?"

"A bonus."

The inn was elegantly nestled on the grounds of Phillips Academy, just beyond the chapel. The parking lot was full. She drove up onto the grass and was out of the car before he was. "Shall I lock it?" he asked.

"I already did. Just shut it."

Inside the inn, he smoothed his hair back in a worried way and looked down at himself. His tie was regimental and went well with his button-down shirt and herringbone jacket. His trousers were fresh from the cleaners. "You look super," she said wryly.

"You're not so bad yourself."

She had on a silky dress with a scoop neckline and cinched waist. Her bobbed red hair, brushed back in a dense natural wave, emphasized her tight, hard face, which had worn well. She was a little fleshy under the chin, but not enough to matter. The maître d' led them to a table set with fresh flowers, and a waiter's helper, his features cherubic, arrived presently with smoked salmon coronets, cherry tomatoes, and stuffed sections of celery.

"I could make a meal of this," Dawson said.

"But you won't."

"No, I wouldn't want to shame you."

The waiter, brisk and efficient, soon returned with their drink orders, Harvey's Bristol Cream on the rocks, and then moved smartly to tend to a table of elderly ladies dressed in soft pinks, lilacs, and watery blues. The piano player, with eyes that appeared half-shut, was rippling through a medley of nostalgic tunes. Eve lifted her drink.

"Cheers."

"Cheers," he said, and one of the elderly ladies smiled at them as if she thought they were celebrating an anniversary or a reconciliation.

"Suspicious of me, aren't you?" Eve said.

"Very."

"You're wondering why I phoned. Simple enough, Sonny. Old times."

"That's hard to believe."

"It shouldn't be. We're old friends."

He opened the impressive covers of the menu and examined the list of entrées. "I hope you can afford this," he said, and she gave him a clear gaze.

"You know I can."

"You've done well."

"More or less."

"I take it you've been with Bauer for a long time."

Her eyebrows were dark circumflexes, her smile droll. "In one way or another."

"Are you still a hooker?"

"No, Sonny. I'm a good girl now."

Later she smiled up at the dashing wine waiter and selected a moderately priced bottle of Graves, which immediately gained the waiter's approval: a perfect choice, a good year, an excellent buy. He backed off with a bow. "That's what I would've picked," Dawson said.

"You're kidding."

"Of course."

They chose rack of veal for dinner, which was served with anchovy fillets, creamed potatoes, and an exotic vegetable. Usually a fast eater, Dawson took his time, occasionally dabbed his mouth with a linen napkin, sampled the wine, and listened to the piano music. She said, "You've got another question. I can feel it coming."

"Did you know her?"

"Who?"

"Melody."

"I made it a point not to."

"Why?"

"She was Alfred's pet. I used to be. We all get older."

"But he still takes care of you."

"And I wouldn't want to disturb that."

"Yes, I can understand."

"I thought you would. It's one of the things I remember about you." She rested an elbow on the table, and her bare arm seemed to float out of the silky sleeve. The only ring she wore was Andover High School, Class of 1967. "Innocents at play, weren't we, Sonny? Junior year, as I remember. Backseat of your car."

"*Your* car. You didn't like mine. You may have been ashamed of it."

"Wasn't that. Mine had more room."

"Yours was smaller."

"We remember different things, don't we?"

They paused to watch a trolley of rich desserts roll up to the table of elderly ladies, who began agonizing over their choices. At another table somebody's beeper went off, and a man who looked like a doctor rose to his feet. Eve finished eating and placed her knife and fork together, like man and wife, on the plate.

She said, "Remember Hartigan's Drugstore, the ice cream sodas we had? The man in the starched peaked cap who made them? We giggled a lot, couldn't stop ourselves. Remember the spigots popping out syrups? We made everything sexual. Remember the rose-veined marble of the counter? You said it looked like me inside."

"I couldn't have gotten that close."

"We didn't always wait for night to go parking."

"Whatever we thought we had didn't last long."

"At that age nothing should. A sin if it does." She smiled lightly. "But the years have no business going by so fast, do they?"

They skipped dessert. The man whose beeper had sounded had returned to his table and, his wife looking on, was carefully examining his check. In anticipation of theirs, Eve had discreetly laid out a gold Master Card at the edge of the table. She sipped Jamaican coffee through a layer of whipped cream, the rim of the glass sugared, the sparkle adding another dimension to her class ring. For want of something better to say, Dawson asked why she had never married.

"What makes you think I didn't?"

"Did you?"

"No. No time." She dabbed her mouth. "Why didn't you? The real reason."

"I never wanted to be responsible for anybody except myself. Selfish, I guess. Or maybe I was afraid or insecure. Something like that."

"So instead you became a cop, responsible for everybody."

"Yes. But only while on duty."

"Melody went beyond your shift."

"A little," he conceded.

"A lot," she corrected.

He gazed off. "I'll tell you something, Eve," he said, looking back slowly, "I'm always on duty."

"And I'll tell you something," she said. "From what I heard, she'd have stayed a perennial ingenue."

"Why do you say that?"

"She expected miracles. She thought men wanted to marry her, Alfred for one." The waiter collected the card. "You for another," she added.

Later he said, "Thank you for the dinner."

Love Nest

They wound their way out of the dining room at the
same time the elderly ladies were leaving and for a moment
or so mingled among them in what seemed a gust of scent,
mostly hair spray and emanations from the neck. One of
the ladies resembled Eleanor Roosevelt. It was she who had
smiled at them earlier and now smiled again. The wine
waiter bowed, for Eve had tipped him well.

The dark sky was shot through with stars, and the air
was cool and still. "Lovely," she murmured and dangled
the keys. "You drive."

He had to push the seat back. Then, on Main Street,
the car purring with a power he was not used to, he readjusted the rearview mirror. He drove toward Ballardvale
Road. She lowered her window and asked if the breeze
was too much for him. It was, but he shook his head. She
sat sideways in the bucket seat, her dress carelessly riding
up, her eyes on him.

"If you're taking yourself home," she said, "drive slow."
He did, letting other cars pass them, their lights sweeping
over them and chalking their faces. She dropped an arm
over the back of his seat and brushed her fingers against
his nape. "You were my first love, Sonny."

"Are you sure?"

"I am." Her voice came at him in a low pitch, her smile
slanting. "Do you remember where we used to go parking?"

"It's not there anymore. Houses are."

"A shame."

"Your boss built them."

"More shame." Her mouth moved toward his. "Some
other place then. What do you say?"

His eyes shifted into hers, and suddenly she laughed.

"You're not buying it, are you? I told Alfred it was a
long shot."

"He really must hate me."

"He has no choice, does he?"

197

He accelerated and turned sharply onto Ballardvale Road. "What was the game plan?"

"I bruise easily, you surely remember that. And no jury would believe I ripped my dress myself, not this one. It cost six hundred dollars."

"So now you get to keep the dress."

"Silver lining to everything."

He pulled up in front of his driveway, and they both got out. She ambled around to the driver's side, where he held the door open for her, the motor idling. In the starlight her face looked cleansed to the bone, her mouth newly minted.

"Like old times, Sonny, me dropping you off at this funny little house. Strangers must wonder if real people live in it. You're not Andover anymore, you know. Others are. May I?" She rose on her toes, carrying up the mingled scent of her clothes and skin, and for a number of seconds her full lips looped over his. He stepped back with a shiver, and she slipped into the Mazda and grinned out the open window. "You have a lot of willpower. You must be pleased."

"Not entirely," he said. "I have a hard-on you wouldn't believe."

She wrenched the gearshift into drive. "Yes, I would, Sonny. I've seen 'em all."

The Bauers had gone to bed early, Alfred with a book on John F. Kennedy that he was still reading and Harriet with a magazine that she had not opened. She seemed asleep but was not. Her eyes snapped open when the front door chimes sounded. "Are you expecting somebody?" she asked, and he looked with a shade of disappointment at his watch.

"Not this early."

He made the trip down to the front door wearing only his striped pajama bottoms, his chest hair sticking out where he had been scratching. Above his solid shoulders a vein pulsed through the ruined flesh of his neck. He opened the door on Eve James.

"How'd it go?"

"It didn't," she said.

The top of his head hurt, as if from a sudden crack racing over the skull. "Worth talking about?"

"No."

"Come in anyway."

He took her coat, though she had meant to keep it on. While he hung it in the coat closet, she inspected herself in the mirror. She said, "How is she?"

"The same." He seemed to aim his voice over her head. "Had this worked, it might've helped."

"I'm sorry."

"Come up and say hello to her."

They ascended the stairs, his step slower than hers, one foot dragging, an unwilling weight. His belly buckled over the waistband of his pajamas.

"Have you noticed? I'm going to pot."

"No you're not."

"I haven't been working out."

"You will."

They entered the bedroom together. Harriet lay with her fair head against a triple layer of pillows and with both arms and a single foot outside the covers. The magazine rested in the sag of covers between her legs. Viewing Eve with only slight surprise, she said, "What a beautiful dress. Stunning, isn't it, Alfred? Though I doubt I could get into it. I have much bigger bones."

Bauer said, "Eve had to drop off some papers."

"How wonderful of her to work overtime." She patted the bed. "Sit down, Eve. I don't see much of you now. Not like the old days."

Bauer excused himself and went into the bathroom, closing the door behind him. Eve sat on the edge of the spacious bed, crossed her legs, and dropped her hands into her lap. She spoke gently. "How are you doing?"

"Junk going on in my head you wouldn't want to know about," Harriet said with a faint shrug.

"Is there anything I can do?"

"You got any juice with the spirit world? I could use some answers." She wiped the hair from her face, including strands that had been adhering to her cheek. She smiled vaguely. "Are you still afraid of me? You used to be."

"No, I was never afraid of you," Eve said. "Because I knew I was never a threat to you."

"That's true."

They heard the flush of the john, and moments later Bauer emerged from the bathroom and made his way to the distant side of the bed. "I've gained a few pounds," he said, propping pillows and then sitting atop the velvety covers. "In the gut. The worst place." Harriet seemed not to hear, much space between them, the Kennedy book in the middle of it. Her eyes were on Eve. Bauer extinguished the light on his side of the bed as if to diminish himself. "But I'll work it off. No choice in the matter."

Eve felt a dry palm press idly against her wrist. She looked Harriet square in the face and said softly, "Do you want me to stay?"

"It's up to Alfred."

Bauer had not heard the question but knew what it was. "No, dear, it's up to you."

"Then it's up to Eve."

Eve said, "I'm rather tired."

"Yes, we all are." Harriet closed her eyes in the instant. "Get her out of here, Alfred."

Bauer accompanied her down the stairs and to the door and even walked her to her car, gingerly on bare feet, for there were sharp little pebbles on the drive, some glinting up through the dark as if a jeweler had tossed them there.

Trees drooped their gigantic shadows. She said, "You'll freeze."

"It's not cold," he said. "It's almost balmy."

"She's not right, Alfred."

"I know that."

"Will she get better?"

He shook his bald head with a weariness that seemed to come over him all at once. "That I don't know."

"Poor Harriet." She touched the hair on his chest and then slipped her hand into the front of his pajama bottoms. "I wish this was mine. All mine."

"You haven't said that in a long time."

"The time wasn't right," she said, dipping down. Pebbles tore through her stockings into the hard flesh of her knees. His voice grew husky.

"She might be watching."

"She never minded before. Why should she now?"

Eleven

She was staying at his house three and four times a week, showing up at will. She no longer slept on the couch but in a bed set up for her in the room that had been his parents', though now it seemed a child's, a lamp burning through the night, the door left open. When she talked in her sleep, he could hear her. He never went into the room, not even when she called out from a troubled dream, knowing that if he did he very likely would not leave. There was a magical look about her in the morning when she crawled out of bed and made her way down the stairs, her hair gloriously tousled and her bright eyes blinking through a blur. She expected a kiss on the cheek, and he got into the habit of giving her one.

She made breakfasts that were edible. Suppers, however, were a challenge. The only time she cursed was when she overcooked something.

The pneumatic attachment to the screen door in back no longer worked. When let go, it slammed shut with a noise loud enough to wake the dead. "Sorry, my fault," she said, appearing in an old T-shirt and baggy shorts. "I'll fix it," she said, rooting out a screwdriver and pliers from a bottom drawer in the kitchen. Something was electrically wrong with the front doorbell, which rang when no one was there. Eventually she fixed that too, amazing him.

"Who taught you?"

"I don't know, Sonny. I've often wondered." She glanced about, slim hands on slim hips. "Any other little jobs? I want to earn my keep."

Just her being there gave something to him, though he did not tell her so. He suspected she knew.

"Want me to clean? I'll clean."

"I have a woman who comes in once a week," he told her.

"House doesn't look it."

"She's in Maine for the month."

"Fire her. I'll do the job."

"That wouldn't work."

"How do you know?"

She mowed the lawn and brought the smell of grass into the house, along with blades of it on her sneakers. She picked and chewed wild spearmint growing on the sun side of the garage and carried in the scent on her fingers and breath. "I could live here and be happy," she said.

"You only think you could."

"I'd be great for you, Sonny. Don't you know that?"

"I'm old enough to be your father."

"Only if you had married young. And you didn't."

"You're playing house," he said. "In a few months you'd get tired of it."

"I swear I wouldn't." She chewed more spearmint and raised her lips. "Kiss me and see how good I taste." He passed, and she said, "I'm known for my audacity and stubbornness. Character traits, Dr. Stickney says. Do you mind them?"

"In time," he said, "I think I would."

"Dr. Stickney also says you—not you in particular, Sonny, but somebody like you—shouldn't allow yourself sympathy for me because I won't be easy to brush away. He says I'll cling. Pieces of me will stick. I told him that's what I want. Do you know what else I want?" She stretched out a hand, shapely fingers pressed together, thumb extended. "A key."

"Why?"

"I never had one in any of those foster homes. If I was out and nobody was in, I had to wait. Didn't matter what the weather was or how dark it got."

"You have your own place now, your own key. You don't need one here."

"Just in case."

"In case of what?"

"In case I'm out in the cold."

He gave her one. "It's for now," he said, "not forever."

Forever meant nothing to her, for she did not believe in it. She believed the world was going to blow, if not in this decade then the next and if not by the Russians then by Reagan or someone like him. "Deep down isn't that what everybody thinks?"

"I don't know," he said. "I refuse to think that deep down."

"Sue won't either. She says it's best not to."

"Sue?"

"One of my roommates. I've told you about them. And them about you."

"I'm not sure I like that. What do they think of your spending so much time here?"

"They want me to be happy."

"And you're happy here?"

"Absolutely. Sometimes it's almost like we're married, isn't it?"

"No," he said, "not in the least."

Occasionally, sitting with her legs tucked under on the couch, she watched television but found little that amused her or contributed to her sense of reality. Only the better movies held her interest for an appreciable time. Her favorite actor was Jack Nicholson, the kind of man, she mused, who looked as if he did not wash under his arms.

"I hope that's not what turns you on."

"No, but it's real," she said.

He was standing near the couch. He let his eyes sink into her. "How real are you, Melody?"

"I bleed every month. That's real."

He did not mean to ask the next question. It simply flew out of his mouth. "Ever have an abortion?"

"Yes," she said. "When I was twelve."

The final week of August brought a heat wave, temperature approaching one hundred, humidity unbearable, records challenged. With the heat searing through his clothes and soaking his skin, he arrested a bare-chested youth in cut-off jeans who was selling sandwich bags of marijuana behind the bowling alley. The youth said, "If I ran, you couldn't catch me. Would you shoot?"

"I don't have to," Dawson said. "I know your father."

"No you don't. You got me mixed up with my brother."

The youth's girlfriend was with him, her hair butchered in the punk style. She said, "You're supposed to be a right guy."

"I have my moments," Dawson said, "but this isn't one of them." He busted her too, for possession.

Much later in the day he went to the home of a retired marine officer suspected of sideswiping two parked cars in the Shawsheen Plaza and then kissing off a VW camper that was coming the other way. The house, long and low, looked like a regimental barracks. He was confronted first by the bark of a dog and then by the massive plainness of the man's stout wife, who was wearing garden gloves and nervously trimming a rose hedge, sweat drooling down her naked arms. "He's on medication," she said. "Come back tomorrow." Dawson looked beyond her. The man, posted behind a screen door, said, "I didn't hurt anybody. I did more damage to my car than to theirs."

"We'll let the insurance companies handle that. We'll talk about the rest down at the station."

"I can't do that," the man said.

The woman whispered, "He thinks he's confined to quarters. You see, he's punishing himself."

Dawson squared his shoulders and said, "Come out, sir. That's a direct order."

At the station the desk sergeant, who had a headache from the heat and a knot in his stomach from paperwork, said, "Can I ask you a question, Sonny? Day like this, why the hell you makin' pinches? I mean, Christ, this kinda weather, I'd think you'd be takin' it easy."

Dawson said, "I'm proving myself."

"You got nothin' to prove. Everybody loves you. You want, c'mere, I'll give you a kiss."

Billy Lord, who had just checked in with a couple of other officers, said, "How about giving me one instead? Might clear up this cold sore I'm getting. Hope it ain't AIDS."

"It could be," the desk sergeant said. "Where've you had your mouth?"

"On your sister," said Billy, rolling flat eyes. "I got tired of your wife."

Dawson repaired to the basement, to his cubicle office, where the former marine officer was sitting beside the desk in a metal chair, his dry hands resting as dead things in the lap of his thin trousers. His slicked-back black hair, which was dyed, looking like a shoe shine, and a single unending line streaked across his brow like a fine wire keeping his large ears up. He sat erect at the sight of Dawson and said, "Shouldn't I be in a cell?"

"No need for that, sir. Your wife will be here soon with the bondsman."

"She's a good woman, Sergeant. Keeps her area clean." With a trembling hand he pawed into the flap pocket of his damp fitted shirt, white hairs steaming through the spaces between the buttons. "Mind if I smoke?"

Dawson sheltered a flame for the man's unfiltered cigarette and used the opportunity to look into his deep-set eyes. The pupils were enormous. "What kind of medication are you on, sir?"

"Couldn't tell you. Pills are all laid out for me three times a day. Big buggers, some of 'em." He coughed, his face ghostly. "Whole world's on medication, so I don't feel different."

"You don't look good. You want water or something?"

"I'm fine." His loaded eyes heaved forth. "You should wear your uniform, Sergeant. You got the leanness for it. Twenty-six years I was in, had every color woman in the world. That's what I miss the most. The whores. Some you wouldn't give two cents for, but some, Sergeant, you never forget." His shoulders quivered as if he were having a small epiphany.

"I'll get you water," Dawson said to him, but he held up a hand.

"There was one, Sergeant, so sweet and special and young, fourteen at the most, I wanted to adopt her. But the wife wouldn't hear of it." The air went out of him. "Got any like that around here?"

Dawson took an extra breath. "Not in this town, sir. We don't allow it."

Done for the day, he did not go home. Instead he drove through the swelter of the town, the sun hanging low, the heat sticking in, and got onto Interstate 495, where he saw flashes of heat lightning. In less than a half hour he crossed the New Hampshire line and fifteen minutes later reached the coast, a beach in Rye, and wedged his car into an unlikely space off the hot road. The beach, which numbered among the smaller ones, was a bivouac of bright umbrellas, with a youthful crowd swarming the water's edge and a speedboat frothing over distant waves. An ocean breeze drifted up.

He stripped to his chinos, rolling the legs up to his knees, and stashed his weapon and wallet in the trunk of the car. Halfway down the beach, he paused to relish the breeze against his chest. A man in a fisherman's cap and swim trunks, his face and body pleasantly old, smiled with strong teeth and said, "Careful you don't burn."

"Sun's low."

"Don't matter."

He strode closer to the surf along a path between masses of cast-up pebbles as smooth as bird eggs. The sun blistered behind a plodding cloud. A woman with drawn-apart breasts running loose under her zebra-striped bathing suit asked him the time. He was not wearing his watch, but he gave her a good guess. "I didn't think it was so late," she said, gazing at his relative paleness. Her eyes crinkled with concern. "The sun's still strong."

"Yes, I've been warned."

Somewhere on the beach kids were smoking dope. He could smell it, for the breeze had shifted. She sniffed it too. "You can't stop them," she said with careless resignation. "They all do it, my daughter included. If not here, then somewhere else."

She moved off smartly, the stripes of her suit apportioning her body with a vibrancy it did not quite deserve. She took shelter under an umbrella, and he wandered farther down the surf, fewer bathers, a multitude of sea birds, and goosestepped into the water, which was not as warm as he expected. A cold current sliced through his legs and soaked his chinos, outlining his loose change and the keys to his car. When a wave wet him everywhere, he came out and lay on pebbles to dry off, his face to the sun.

He fell asleep for at least ten minutes, though no more
than fifteen. He woke with a start and sat up with an ache.
Bright voices of girls surrounded him, a bevy of nymphets
in the scantest of suits, chattering away as if he were not
there. At times their language was offensive, downright
vulgar. Somebody they did not like was a fucking asshole.
Somebody's mean mother was a cunt. Suddenly a hand
swept at him like a hot ray.

"You're burning," said the woman in the zebra stripes,
which were now providing her soft belly swell with an
illusionary rippling of muscles. Her hand, which had never
actually touched him, floated away. "Mostly your chest,"
she informed him gravely. He looked down at himself, and
when he looked back up she was gone.

The girls had drifted closer to the surf, and some were
venturing into it. Some were talking to a lifeguard, a husky
towheaded youth who idly reached deep into his trunks
and shifted his genitals. One girl had dropped onto the
sand and was lying on a propped elbow with her salt-scaled
legs angled into an attitude of running. Dawson, though
he sensed somebody approaching him from behind, could
not take his eyes off her. She looked nothing like Melody
in the face, but the dark auburn of her luxuriant hair was
the same, and the long loping line of her body was similar.
A voice thudded down at him.

"Look at 'em long enough, they'll drive you crazy." It
was the man in the fisherman's cap. "They'll also put you
in jail if you're not careful."

Dawson rose to his feet, his chinos soggy and clumsy.
He stood taller than the man but only because he was on
a higher rise of pebbles.

"Rule of thumb is pick on somebody your own age.
Gets you in less trouble." The man smiled with his strong
teeth. "Name's Paul," he said and stuck out a hand.

Dawson shook it. "Sonny."

"Cop, ain't you?"

"How'd you know?"

"I was watching when you drove up. I saw what you put in your trunk. I used to carry one myself, thirty-two years, town of Rye. In fact, I was chief. Guess I know about everybody in town, including the summer crowd. That girl lying down there in the bitty bathing suit, her family's been coming here since she was four. She's fifteen now, do you believe it? They bloom fast nowadays."

"Too fast."

"Glad you realize that."

Dawson felt a weary give to his shoulders and a guilt he did not expect. "You're reading me wrong."

"I just don't want you to get yourself in trouble. One cop to another."

With no desire to argue or defend himself, Dawson said, "I'll be leaving now."

"Yes, Sonny. A damn good idea."

No lights were visible in his house, but her little car was in the drive, which surprised him. Her place in Boston, she had told him, had air-conditioning; his did not. He moved quietly out of his car into the dark air, which was breathless and clammy. It was worse inside the house, for the heat of the day had collected. In the kitchen he switched on a light and called her name and heard only insects ticking away outside the window. Stiffly he climbed the stairs and peered past the open door into the room that had become hers. The little night lamp was unlit. He took one step in and stopped. Moonlight shredding in through a tree patterned her. Clad only in her brief underwear, she lay on the bed in the same attitude as the girl on the beach.

"Where were you?" Her tone was accusatory. He took another forward step. The stuffiness of the room was oppressive.

"How can you stand it in here?"

"I waited and waited," she said. "I even worried."

A kind of scowl clenched his face out of proportion. "Are you on something?"

"I swear I'm not. I don't pop anything. I'm clean in every way." One foot was snarled in a sheet that had been kicked away. Stirring, she freed the foot. "Can't you come closer? I can't see your eyes."

He sat on the edge of the bed, his partially dry chinos stiff with sea salt. "This can't go on," he said, and she shivered as if from fever.

"I was afraid you were going to say that." She eased over, onto her back, and propped her head against pillows. "The sound of your steps on the stairs told me."

"You know what I want."

"I would never betray him, Sonny. I would never betray anybody."

He spoke hoarsely. "They used you, the both of them. They even made you available to their son. That was sick."

"I've told you too much, Sonny. Now you're throwing it up at me."

He sat rigidly with his hands on his thighs, his loose and wrinkled shirt mostly unbuttoned. When the air changed subtly, his burnt chest felt it and then his nose detected it. "I don't mean to," he said.

"But you are. I don't see any of them anymore, not even the shrink." She lifted herself slightly, her face framed in her spread of hair. "I'm independent of them all."

"For that you need a job."

"I'll get one."

"A real one."

"I promise."

"Promise yourself, not me," he said. He knew that a breeze was gently kicking up by the changing pattern of moonlight on her tight stomach. The foot she had freed shifted closer to him.

"I'm independent of everyone, except you."

"You're nineteen," he said. "At that age you've got a hundred options. I should be the least of them."

"I don't see it that way." A breeze blew in strong, and leaves outside the window swirled as if to music. There was lightning but no thunder. "It's going to rain, Sonny. Like it did that first time."

He felt the shock of her foot against him almost as if it were a knife. He gripped the slim, hard ankle from the back as the curtain billowed and the first serious drops of rain struck the screen. He meant to cast her foot aside, but instead he gathered it up and traced a thumb over the instep.

"I want it to happen," she said. "More important, we both do."

He folded his hand over her toes. "You're a child."

"A woman, Sonny."

"No. When you're a woman I'll be an old fart. I felt like one today."

"I'm a woman now, Sonny. Have been for years."

"Then I'm the child."

The rain came down in earnest, soaking the curtains and flooding the floor. She lay level now, her head no longer in the pillows but her foot still in his grasp, the heel pressed into his lap. "You can have part of me or all of me. Whatever you want."

He took all of her.

The rain continued through the night, intermittent downpours, lulls of drizzle and mist, occasional lightning, some thunder. The sun rose behind a cloud cover but soon burst clear, with Dawson there to see it from his backyard. The tree near the house gave out its sharpest green and cast a vast shadow. A random breeze pushing through the sodden leaves sounded like people shaking their umbrellas.

212

Phlox grown too tall nodded to him as if in deference. He had planted them. When he lifted his eyes toward the house he knew she was out of bed and tidying up. Sounds carried. He heard the snap of a clean sheet.

He stepped into the garden shed his father had built and began idly poking about. Among the usable things were a short wooden ladder missing a rung, an apple basket rotted out at the bottom, and a rusted shovel lacking a grip. He was not really looking for anything. He simply did not want her to see him just yet.

In fifteen minutes or so she came out with a pair of scissors and crouched over marigolds and mums in full bloom. She made a bouquet. He approached her slowly, dusting his hands as if he had been working. She said, "I didn't hear you get up."

"I didn't want to disturb you."

Each was oddly self-conscious. She rose with the bouquet and dropped a mum. He bent double to pick it up. She pushed the bouquet at him. "For you."

"I should have picked them for you."

"Yes," she said. "Why are you so quiet?"

"I'm always quiet in the morning."

"No you're not."

She was dressed in a loose T-shirt, one of his, nothing beneath. Later, in the house, he asked her to put something else on. "Why?" she asked. "Are we going somewhere?"

"Yes," he said.

She did not want to go to the bank with him, but he insisted. While she waited in the car, he went into one bank, Andover Savings, and drew out money, asking for it in cash and taking it in fifties and hundreds inside a buff envelope. "Hold this for me," he said, back in the car. Then they went to another bank, Andover Citizens, where he softened his footstep, guided her to the desk of someone he knew, and started an account for her. "It's money I

213

won't miss," he told her after it was done, the passbook in her pocket, the sun in their eyes outside the bank. Her lips, pinched together, came apart.

"You're getting rid of me."

"It's money for you to fall back on if you're ever in need."

"Meaning you don't want me to fall back on you. Is that it?" She lowered her eyes and monitored every step they took back to the car, which she entered docilely. "You didn't even ask me if I wanted it," she said as they pulled out of the lot. "You're kissing me off. Why?"

He ran a red light. "It's no longer a professional relationship."

"It never was."

He turned clumsy and nearly struck a mail truck emerging onto Main Street. It was hot in the car, and he mopped his face with his sleeve. She looked away, out her window, then back at him.

"You'll never find anyone like me again."

"I know that," he said, and his heart turned over.

"You love me, Sonny. If you say you don't, you're lying. To me. To yourself. But I don't fit in this town of yours, so how the hell can I fit into your life. Right?"

He looked at her. Her eyes were full.

"Don't worry," she said. "I'm not the kind to cry."

He sped along South Main Street and then slowed for the turn onto Ballardvale Road, where the scented dust of summer drifted in on them. When he angled into the drive and coasted to a stop beside her little car, she extended a fist, something inside it.

"Here," she said.

"What is it?"

"Your key."

Twelve

S ergeant Dawson emerged from Lem's Coffee Shop and spotted the slight spruce figure of Dr. Stickney. Braving a sweep of bruising wind under the unbroken blue of an enormous December sky, he hustled across the street and followed the doctor through the busy sidewalk crowd past Nazarian's Jewelry Store and Thompson's Stationery. Then he trailed him into Citizens Bank, where the doctor proceeded briskly to one of the island counters. When he began preparing a deposit slip, Dawson edged up and said, "Don't you bother to return calls?"

He glanced up casually, dapper in his snug overcoat and confident behind the gloss of his close beard. "I've been busy. Patients come first."

"You must be doing well."

"Extremely. I'm shifting into straight marriage counseling. Very lucrative. So many Andover women are unhappy with their high-powered husbands, and so many of these fellows are coming apart. You know their worst nightmare, Sergeant? One day they'll walk into work, Raytheon, Digital, one of those classy places, and find they're no longer wanted. If that happens, it's not themselves they won't want to face. It's their neighbors."

"It's hard for me to work up sympathy."

"Not for me, Sergeant. It's my livelihood." He returned his attention to the deposit slip, but the pen, dangling a

215

loose chain, quit writing. He tried again, scratching hard, but it had gone dry. "Do you have a pen?"

"Pencil."

"That'll do."

Dawson gave him a stub, and the doctor completed the task in an impeccable hand, the figures neat, tight, and small, like his teeth. Dawson said, "Why didn't you tell me?"

"Tell you what? Whatever it was, I probably didn't want to overload your brain. Sorry, Sergeant. Just a joke. What didn't I tell you?"

"It wasn't suicide."

Dr. Stickney deliberated before responding, then gave himself added time. "Are we talking about the Bauer boy?"

"Nobody else."

"You say it wasn't suicide. What was it?"

"An accident."

"Very good, Sergeant. Are you brilliant, or did somebody put a bug in your ear?"

"What does it matter?"

"It matters very much since the medical examiner ruled suicide."

"Such accidents usually are."

"Yes," said Stickney with a measure of distant formality. "Usually through ignorance or a wish to spare the family." He looked around at the queues leading to the teller windows. "But this is a matter best discussed in camera."

"Nobody can hear us."

After a lapse, Stickney said, "Yes, it could've been an accident, but I don't know that. I didn't see the body."

"But you knew his history, his habits. You knew his bent behavior." Dawson's voice jabbed at him like a knife that had been held in secret. "That couldn't have been the first time he twisted something around his neck."

216

"Everybody has psychological tics, Sergeant. His happened to be pathological and involved risk to himself."

"The less oxygen, the greater the orgasm."

"I see you've been briefed. Ultimate high, sin of Onan. The trick of course is not to hang yourself doing it." Stickney undid the dark buttons of his coat, his manner infinitely calm. "You'd be surprised at the number of teenage boys found dangling in the shower. Not that the practice is rampant, but it's not all that rare among troubled males sexually confident only with themselves."

"Did his parents know he was into this?"

"Let's put it this way, Sergeant. His father didn't."

Dawson looked deeper into the bank, beyond a rail to busy desks. He glimpsed Fran Lovell, but she did not see him. She was preoccupied with a customer and her desktop computer. Her lips, he noticed, were not set in a pretty way.

"Really, Sergeant, does it matter which way he died?"

He glimpsed Ed Fellows chatting deep in the lobby with a dowager of the town, who was perched plump and heavy under a crown of pastel hair, the hues pinkish and blue. Stickney returned the pencil stub.

"Does it change anything?"

"Everything," Dawson said.

"Then I'll give you a theory," Stickney said, still with the utmost calm. "I think he went into his closet for a double purpose. To please himself . . . and, Sergeant, to kill himself."

She was in their son's room, sitting on his stripped bed and sorting school papers. The room was gradually taking on a bankrupt look. So much had been given away, thrown away, burnt. Posters peeled from the walls left their ghostly shapes. Three quart jars of pennies were gone from

217

the shelf, where the stereo still rested, though the television was gone, donated to the Lawrence House of Correction, along with stacks of adventure comic books. The pennies she had scattered in the woods where they had last walked together. The school papers would be harder for her to discard, though she had no doubt she would do it.

Alfred Bauer waited for her to come out.

She said, "Why don't you come in?"

It was not easy for him. The room seemed alien to him, no longer a part of the house, a taboo area fraught with sounds and silences of his son that only his wife could detect.

"Sit down," she said, patting a place on the mattress away from the papers, but he stayed on his feet. "Do you know what I regret?" she said, and he held his breath. "I regret we didn't donate his organs. Then parts of him would still be functioning. Breathing. Living. His heart could've served somebody well."

He was uncomfortable with her voice, which stretched up into something he did not fully recognize. Her head tilted back. Her face was blank and colorless.

"The body was going to be cut up anyway. Somebody should have approached us. Asked us."

"Somebody may have," he offered. "We weren't in shape to hear."

"When he was ten, twelve, I could see into his future. I could see the shape of him at forty, at fifty. I never saw him dead." Her hand brushed over the papers, which included high school examination booklets, grade school drawings, compositions with gold stars. "Do you want to look at any of this before I burn it?"

He shook his head slowly and spoke through dry, awkward lips. "I think we should get away for a while. Florida."

"Is that what you think? Is that what you think we should do?"

"We need the change."

"You look old," she said with the lift of an eye. "All at once you look old. Do I?"

"No," he said.

"Thank God for that. I wouldn't want everything taken from me."

He stooped down, crouched before her, placed his hands on her knees, which were jammed together to hold papers. There was a troubled pause. "At a time like this a man and wife should draw very close."

"Yes, they should," she agreed with the sympathetic start of a smile. "But it doesn't work out that way. And actually our losses are different. Mine is Wally. Yours is Melody."

"Harriet, please."

"I idolized you, Alfred." Her voice had stretched tenuously and was feather-soft, a tickle, and her hand reached out to stroke his bare head, a habit. Her fingers were familiar with every contour. "I loved you more than anything. The others, Eve James, her kind, never mattered. Darling women, but playthings. Melody was different."

Sunlight paced itself into the room, stopping just short of them. Still hunkered down, he felt a strain in his back from muscles losing their resiliency. He had not worked out in days nor plunged into the pool for his customary laps.

Harriet said, "You led her on in a way that was real. She actually thought you might leave me for her. For a time, you toyed with the idea. Do you deny it?"

"I never would've done it."

"You were so jealous when the cop took her over and so relieved when he dumped her. She loved him like she loved you. She couldn't help loving people, could she, Alfred? It was how she kept going, poor thing. You knew that, we both did, because Stickney told us. He said she was searching for saviors and saints. Instead she got us. It wasn't what you'd call an orgy, was it, Alfred, simply an extravagance."

"Why are we talking about her?"

"You hurt me so."

His eyes flickered. "You think you didn't hurt me when you put her and our son together?"

"Wally needed help and you needed hurting. It was really as simple as that." Her smile was dry, placid, ambiguous. Her hand, which lacked warmth, slipped from his head to his shoulder, and her presence seemed to gather around him, to imprison him. She said, "If you hadn't fallen in love with her, I'd still have him."

Claire Fellows, an early bloom and a fast fade in her youth, was quite unremarkable in her middle years: pale, plain, and quiet. She was dressed in muted colors, which tended to blend her into the background when no one was talking to her. Which was the case now. She stood against lush drapes in a private room of the Andover Inn and watched the other ladies mill and chatter over crystal glasses of white wine. The occasion was the annual meeting of the December Club, dedicated to preserving the town's more genteel traditions and instilling proper manners in the children of newcomers, most of whom were unaware of the club's existence. Its first president was Claire Fellows's maternal grandmother, a fact many members had forgotten.

She did not care for the wine, a rather bland Chablis, but sipped it anyway because it made her appear occupied and not in the least mindful that she was being ignored. Then quite suddenly, with a start, she heard her name uttered from the swirl of sounds and leaned expectantly into the voice, hiding her feelings the instant she saw the face.

"How nice," she said. "How lovely."

They kissed, expertly missing each other's mouth.

Paige Gately's scent held a cinnamon quality. The tasteful accessories worn with her fitted navy suit matched the silver glint of her hair, every soft curl magically in place.

"We seldom see each other anymore," Claire moaned.

"I know," Paige said. "A shame."

"We must rectify it. My goodness, how the years pass, and you've been so busy, so industrious. I know because Ed keeps me in touch. I can't imagine why you wanted to buy that motel, especially after what happened there, but I suppose you have some marvelous plans for it. You were always so clever. Remember us at Abbot? I was always rather frightened and silly, and you always had a head on your shoulders. You were always one up on me. You used to tease me something terrible, do you remember?"

Paige did, quite well. She said, "No."

"I was so shy and awkward in class, a miracle I graduated, but things came so easy for you."

Conversations near them grew louder. Three women to their left, one wearing white-textured stockings, were discussing European vacations in relation to the exchange rate of the dollar. Paige, who had brought with her a full wineglass, took a careful sip. "You forget, Claire, I was there on a scholarship. I didn't have your money."

"But for you that wasn't essential. For me it rather was, don't you think? I lacked your toughness and drive. Nothing fazed you, I remember that. Not a very good Chablis, is it?"

"I've had better."

"Those days seem so distant now, so idyllic in my mind. Does it bother you, Paige?"

"Does what bother me?"

"Growing older. I've often wondered if death is final. I sometimes believe it is. Yet nature seems to argue against it. My flowers vanish in the fall but pop right up again in the spring. So what about us? Do we die or just hide for a while?"

"We die."

"You speak with such certainty, it's so like you." Claire sighed deeply as if her admiration were boundless, their girlhood friendship never in doubt. "Odd," she said, "you don't remember teasing me. You were jolly good at it. Others thought you were jealous because I was prettier than you, but I always thought you were prettier."

Paige smiled. "I'm sure you were right."

"You always got whatever you went after. Like the highest grades. Every exam you had those little crib sheets up your sleeve. I bet you thought I didn't know."

Paige smiled again, her reserve inviolate.

"Remember when you decided you wanted Biff and not Ed. I was so relieved. So grateful to you. Of course it hasn't been an easy marriage, but no marriage is. And you had your problems with dear Biff, so handsome, wasn't he?"

"A doll."

"What did he die of? I was never quite certain."

"Everything." Paige tapped the brilliant stem of her glass with a glossy nail and shifted her eyes elsewhere.

"Are you looking for someone to rescue you?"

"Don't be silly. I was admiring Mrs. Bledsoe's white stockings."

"They are nice, but I don't have the legs for them. You do." There was a significant pause, a kind of gathering of breath and resolve. "May I make a minor criticism, Paige? I don't like your perfume."

"Men seem to."

"Yes, I know."

They went silent, each listening to the other's breathing. Paige's was steady and calm. Claire's was not. She sloshed about what little Chablis remained in her glass.

"Are you going to throw that at me?"

Claire's eyelids fluttered, and her wan face flared with

color and heat. "I very much want to. God, how I want to!" She weaved slightly. "But I don't dare."

"Of course you don't. Nothing changes."

Mrs. Bledsoe, the club's outgoing president, a perfect rightness about her, strode toward them with eyes full of concern. "Is anything the matter?"

"Everything's fine," Paige said, smiling nicely. "Mrs. Fellows is simply having one of her hot flashes."

The season's first snowfall came during the night, the accumulation a couple of inches. In the morning Ralph Roselli in a black overcoat and Florsheim shoes was shoveling the graded walk leading down from Rita O'Dea's house. A car was parked on the street, engine idling, a solitary face behind the windshield. Roselli had not seen the car before, but instinct told him everything. When he reached the bottom of the walk, he leaned the shovel against the massive post of the mailbox and shuffled over to the car, driver's side, where the window was halfway lowered. He spoke through the space. "Something you want?"

"Beautiful neighborhood," the driver said. "One of the loveliest in town. When I was a kid, nothing was here. Just woods."

"You ain't a kid anymore."

"The fellow who developed this area had a little bit of taste, not much, but enough. Not like the guys doing it today."

"You get all kinds."

"You don't live here, do you?"

"I visit."

"Do I know you?"

"As much as I know you," Roselli said.

The front door of Rita O'Dea's house opened, and her great head of black hair could be seen. Her voice echoed down through the crisp blue air. "Who is it, Ralph?"

"The cop."

"I thought so. Tell him to come up."

"You hear her?"

"Hard not to." Sergeant Dawson shoved his door open and thrust a leg out. "You know, I've always been more concerned about her than about Alfred Bauer."

Roselli said, "You got good priorities."

Inside the house, trailing Roselli, Dawson cast an admiring eye on an opulent variety of furniture and hanging ferns. The room he was ushered into was bright from a wall that was all window, through which the outdoors flowed in as if donated by the town. He avoided stepping on a white animal pelt. He did not want to get it dirty, though Roselli tracked over it without a trace. He heard a thump. Rita O'Dea had just dropped into a cushioned chair. She had on one of her more colorful caftans, beaded and braided. "We know each other, don't we?" she said. "Just that we've never been introduced."

"I'm Sergeant Dawson."

"I'm Rita. How about I call you Sonny? Take his coat, Ralph."

"I'll keep it on."

"You want coffee, pastry, or something? The pastry's from the North End."

"No thank you."

Roselli said to her, "You want, I'll stay. Otherwise I'll go get snow tires put on your car."

"I'm safe with Sonny. He's an officer of the law."

Roselli left. She gestured, and Dawson dropped into a chair near her, his coat open. He could see himself in the gigantic window, where he was part of the snowscape, a stain in the glass. She smiled.

"You here for a reason?"

"I was in the neighborhood."

"That's as good a reason as any," she said. "I always meant to send you a thank-you note, but I never got around to it. I'm talking about Melody, time you could've busted her. 'Course if I was you, a man, I'd have given her a break too."

"That was a mistake," he said quietly.

"I wouldn't brood about it. She was one of those girls too beautiful for the world. Actually, you look at me close, that was my problem. Difference is I put on weight. Protection. Now, all these years gone, it don't matter."

Dawson was silent.

She said, "A man can't stand that, you know. A woman being too beautiful. Like an insult to him. Same thing if she's got too much of a brain."

He stayed silent.

She said, with a feast of feeling, " 'Course I had extra protection. A brother. That's better than a husband. Better than a knife. Did you know my brother?"

"I never had the pleasure. Naturally I heard of him."

"You'd have liked him. He was a man's man."

Dawson again glanced at himself in the glare of the window. He made out a white cat picking its way carefully through the wet and gradually becoming one with the snow, a trick he decided only nature could perform so delicately.

"I feel we can talk, Sonny. Do you mind me calling you Sonny? I can call you Sergeant, you really want me to."

"Sonny's good."

"I like to talk."

"I like to listen," he said.

"Sign of a smart man. I knew I was reading you right. I'm going to tell you something you might've had your doubts about. I wanted the Silver Bell run straight. Dumb of me to let Bauer do different."

Dawson stared at her skeptically. "I don't know you well, but I can't picture you doing something you don't want to do."

She laughed, swishing back her mass of hair. "Maybe

I'm a romantic. In the back of my mind I knew he didn't want to put girls in there just for business reasons. He wanted an excuse to keep Melody near him. Pardon my language, Sonny, but he had a bigger hard-on for her than you did. Dangerous business if you're married to a woman like Harriet. You know Harriet?"

Dawson gave a faint nod. "I've met her."

"I was a kid, Sonny, my brother took me to operas. I didn't want to go, he made me. He didn't want me to be a dumbbell. He took me to a play once, Greek thing. Medea. You know who she was?"

Dawson gave no sign he knew or did not know.

"Harriet could play the part." She shifted in her chair, sinking back, the white of her legs appearing through the slits of her caftan in smooth rich slices, like cake. "The only woman I've had to handle with kid gloves."

Dawson felt a coldness, as if the outdoors were truly coming in. "What's the message?"

"Time will tell."

The coldness crept deep. "You lied to me. You weren't being a romantic. You've got a brain like your brother's. You make things happen."

"Sometimes," she said softly, "I just let things happen."

"You want it all."

"I always did. It's how I got fat, Tony used to tell me."

He shivered. "What I don't understand is why you've told me these things."

"Goes back to what I was telling you. I came here to live clean, quiet, be respectable. I'm joining the December Club. Mrs. Gately don't know it yet, she's sponsoring me. I got to make a note of that, remind myself to tell her." She heaved out a smile while shifting again in her chair. Her legs were as white as milk. "You see, Sonny, sad to say, I belong in this town now more than you do. I got the bigger investment."

"Terms of money only."

"What else counts?" she said, and there was a long silence from him, an odd expression on his face. "You tired, Sonny? You angry about anything? You shouldn't be. I'm a fair woman takes care of her friends. One of these days I'm going to need somebody new to look after me. Poor Ralph, you know, isn't going to live forever." She patted herself under the left breast. "Bad ticker."

"Then he shouldn't be shoveling."

"Someone has to do it."

"Who is he, or what is he?"

"He was my brother's bodyguard."

"Some bodyguard."

"He had no choice. Sometimes you don't." Her face all of a sudden went hard, as if she kept a deep accounting of wrongs perpetrated against her. Then, matter-of-factly, she said, "Hit came from high above, like God did it."

"You offering me a job?"

"No," she said, "but it's something for us to think about."

"I don't shovel."

"Maybe you wouldn't have to."

He pulled himself to his feet, his legs tired where least expected, in the back of the calves, as if he had been running. His jaw felt heavy.

"I'm scared to death to get on jetliners. Maybe you could do that for me. Run errands. You carry a piece. I could use that too. Play your cards right, you could become invaluable."

"I don't like your humor, Mrs. O'Dea. I don't much like you either."

"I grow on people," she said, watching him close his coat and move toward the glass wall as if he could step through it. "If you're leaving, that's the wrong way. Makes you look like you're coming in." Her smile, large and indulgent, swelled up at him in the glass. "Something I meant

227

to ask you. Last August I guess it was, maybe September, Melody wanted to know if I'd teach her to cook. Said it was for you. Next time I saw her she said she didn't want to learn anymore. How do you figure that?"

He turned from the window, lips peeled back as if to sing. "Who killed her?"

"Why you asking me?"

"Somebody must know."

"That's something even time might not tell you."

Thirteen

Her absence acted harshly on him. He missed her presence across the supper table while hating the brooding stillness of the house and the way each evening darkness fell upon it as if from the swing of an ax. He missed the way she had entered a room and brightened it, enlivened it, and sometimes he missed her as he did the Saturday suppers of his childhood, the mere notion of which could cause him to lust for a lavish plate of homemade kidney beans flavored in juices and salt pork, brown bread on the side. Yet, a week later when she phoned in an excited voice to tell of her job, he was cool, his manner not unlike that of a cynical parole officer. He said, "I didn't realize you had office skills."

"I don't, Sonny, but I'm learning. Mrs. Foss, she's the secretary, is training me. She's a grump, doesn't know what to make of me, but I'm winning her over. Yesterday we had lunch together at Lem's. I looked for you."

He felt a surge of jealousy. "Rollins is Bauer's lawyer. Is that how you got the job?"

"I swear it isn't. Mrs. Gately recommended me."

"Same thing."

"I thought you wanted me to get a job. A real one. This is real."

"I didn't mean in Andover."

"Where, Sonny, the North Pole? Would that be far enough away from you?"

"It's not that," he said. "It's just that you're doing it wrong. All wrong."

"Then tell me how to do it."

"A clean break."

"This is as clean as I can make it, Sonny."

After he hung up, he went into the bathroom and shaved, though he had nowhere to go, nothing in mind. He considered phoning the neighbor Norma but decided against it, recalling her anger the last time he had seen her, the foulness hurled at him from the open window of her car. He thought of other women he had known, but they were married now or remarried, most no longer in town. He wiped the mirror clean with a towel. His hair looked dead, and he feared a comb would not rouse it. Under the shower, he washed it and for the first time in a long time wondered seriously and deeply about the number of years left to him on earth. Drying himself, he figured it did not matter as long as the number stayed shadowed. That way there would always seem time for everything.

The telephone rang. It was Melody again.

"It doesn't make a difference what kind of job I have, does it? I mean, it wouldn't change anything between us, would it?"

He wondered where she was calling from, for her voice seemed far away, interference on the line, now and then a pip.

"Sonny."

"Yes, I'm listening."

"If I hadn't been a whore, would you have me?" Then she laughed. "But if I hadn't been one, we wouldn't have met. And I wouldn't have liked that."

He decided she was in Boston, for he heard occasional sounds in the background, roommates, the sudden rise of music.

"Sonny, have you read *Rain*?"

"What?"

"It's a story in a book Sue lent me. Or maybe it was Nat. I forget who wrote it. I'm not good on authors' names, are you?"

"No," he said.

"It's about us, Sonny, or it could be. I don't want it to be."

"I've never read it."

"You should," she said. "You definitely should, but you won't. Would you like me to come see you?"

"It's late," he said, and the words felt alien on his mouth, as if a stranger had stuck them there.

"You're right of course. You're always right."

He slept fitfully that night, waking in the middle of it with what he felt was a cold footprint on his heart. Early in the morning, not much after dawn, crows screeched as if they were clawing somebody to death. He crawled out of bed and stumbled to the window to make sure it was not so.

She called him again a couple of weeks later to tell him that the leaves were turning, that the trees around William Rollins's house were scarlet and gold. One maple in particular, she said, looked like a firestorm. He said, "What are you doing at his house?"

"I have a key, Sonny."

He went stone quiet, his mind as near a blank as he could make it.

"It's not what you think," she said quickly. "It's like it was with us—except for that one time." He wanted no details, but she went on. He could not stop her, her voice rising as if she were talking to somebody a little deaf. "He's looking for a mother, Sonny, but I'm too young. So he says a sister will do."

"Is that what you want?"

"You know it isn't."

"He sounds sick."

"He isn't. He's a good man. He wears a nightshirt of soft cotton. Ticking. He looks so old-fashioned in it. For years he's wondered about himself. I tell him it's all for nothing. Needless, I mean. We all need people in different ways. Except for you, Sonny. At least that's what you like people to believe."

A week passed, and he did not hear from her. At the station he shut the door of his cubicle, rang up Attorney Rollins's office, and asked for her. The secretary, Mrs. Foss, said that Miss Haines no longer worked there, which took him aback.

"Where is she?"

"I don't know. Who is this?"

"A friend."

"I can't help you."

"It's important."

"Would you like to speak with Attorney Rollins?"

He disconnected. That evening he drove by Rollins's house several times, slowly, hesitating near the drive where a small light bit out some of the darkness. Her car was not there. Once, through a lit window, he glimpsed Rollins with a drink in hand. He considered calling the Boston number but did not.

One night he dreamed of her. Her eyes were two dark secrets in a perfectly pale face. She did not look like herself but like a girl he had had a crush on in eighth grade, Lucy somebody, her father a farmer when the town had farms.

Portions of Ballardvale Road flamed with sumac and fire bush. Leaves covered his garden, and he raked them up. Each night turned colder, the moon brighter. Then, when he had half-succeeded in forgetting her, she phoned. The hour was late, and he felt an enormous distance between them. "I just washed my hair," she said.

"That's why you called?"

232

"No, to see how you're doing."

"You left your job," he said.

"Some time ago."

"Why?"

"Wasn't for me."

His spirits flared and his face brightened from hearing her voice. He visualized the luster of her washed hair. He tried to sound offhand. "So what are you doing now?"

"You could say I'm counseling."

"What does that mean?"

"Exactly?"

"Exactly."

"I'm being good to Alfred's son."

He stiffened in the instant. "You're always being good to somebody."

"It's not like you think."

"It never is," he said, enduring a stomach spasm. "I already know too much about the kid, so don't tell me any more." But he knew she would, at her own pace, as if it were his duty to listen, his obligation to understand. Once he tried to interrupt her, but she kept on, her voice touching him in the vitals, on the raw. Finally she finished, and he felt a languor come over him. "They're using you," he said.

"Harriet, not Alfred. But that's OK."

"Doesn't it make you feel dirty?"

"Were we dirty, Sonny?" A pain broke loose inside him and roamed at will. She said, "Love and kindness can't be dirty, can they?" He had no answer, for it was the wrong question.

He said, "Are you back in the business?"

"No."

"It sounds like it."

"I can't help how it sounds."

He thought back to when he was a child sitting with

233

his parents in a pew in Christ Church, no complications, seldom a shadow, all the faces of the congregation plump and simple, rosy and pure. Or so it had seemed.

"Sonny, I've come to a decision. I think you'll be proud of me."

"What is it?"

"I won't bother you again. I promise."

She returned to William Rollins's house to retrieve some things she had left behind. She tossed an unused flask of hand lotion and a half-read paperback mystery into her denim shoulder bag. Rollins accompanied her into the guest room and pushed open the accordion doors of the closet where he had hung her rain slicker among his mother's dresses, which his eyes caressed. Here and there he rattled the wooden hangers as if to stir life into the finer garments. "I wish you'd look through them, there might be something you want." He seemed all at once too large for his voice. The words trickled out of him. "She was your size, you know. Exactly."

She did not bother to point out his memory lapse. One evening a few weeks ago, at his urging, she had tried on two of the dresses, each too full in the bosom and too high in the waist. He, however, had slipped easily into one of his father's suits, a near-perfect fit, four pennies in one of the pockets, along with a single ticket stub from an Andover movie theater that no longer existed.

He said, "She was like you with your rich skin. She never had to put paint on her face or tint on her eyelids. A little lipstick was plenty. She never used perfume, only plain soap and water, and whatever man she was meeting would know she was going to smell good all over. My father said she had the gift of eternal youth, and whenever she had a bad day he joked that the gods were jealously taking revenge. He never questioned her, even when he

234

had indisputable cause. There wasn't a bone in her body he couldn't have broken if he'd put his mind to it. Instead, he worshiped her."

He stopped talking to rest his fingers against a throbbing throat muscle, and she used the time to extricate the slicker from its hanger and drape it over her arm.

"I'm running off at the mouth, aren't I?" he said. His face was flushed. "It's the first time I've felt embarrassed with you."

"You needn't be."

"I know that," he said. "I've always known it."

He walked with her down the stairs and opened the front door and followed her out. She lowered her head as her hair flew back heavily in the wind. The Mondale sticker on her little car reflected its colors on her hair.

Rollins said, "He won't win, you know. He doesn't have a chance. Most people are like me and the sergeant. We'll all vote for the other fellow." His eyes were abstracted, as if there were little correspondence between what he was saying and what he was thinking. "Fantasies, you see, are what we live on, the sergeant no less than I. And Alfred Bauer more than most."

She opened the car door and tossed the slicker inside. When she turned back to him, he smiled slightly, his Adam's apple shifting over the loosened knot of his necktie.

"You must be careful. So much of my mother is in you."

"Is that bad?"

"Yes," he said. "You're a fantasy people can touch." His smile turned mordant, unforgiving. "I've often wondered about that accident. Whether my father could have avoided the truck."

She set herself to leave, a hip leaning into the car. He reached out quickly, snared one of her hands, and gripped the fingers as if to crush them.

"You're free to come back anytime, any hour."

"I probably won't."

"I know," he said and frowned. "What will you do?"

"What I always do," she said, and withdrew her hand the instant he began to hurt it.

Fourteen

At the Silver Bell Motor Lodge, Chick the desk clerk said, "You can't see her. She's got high-powered people with her. Big business deal."

"What's it about?"

"Hush-hush, Sonny. My mouth is sealed."

"You're very loyal to her, aren't you?"

"Sure I am. Why shouldn't I be? She's a fine lady."

"But what would you do if you couldn't work here anymore?"

"Drop down and die. Everybody's got to do it sometime." His wrinkled face cracked into a smile. "I don't get much sleep, so I got a lot to catch up on. Every time I yawn I think how good it's going to be."

"You make it sound wonderful."

"You're dead lots longer than you're alive, so you got to see the bright side."

"Not when you're nineteen. That's how old she was."

"That's not fair, Sonny. I mean, not fair to me. You're acting like . . ."

"Like what, Chick?"

"Like I don't know."

"If there were things I didn't know and you did, you'd tell me, wouldn't you?"

"Everything."

"I don't believe you, Chick, but it's nothing personal.

237

I just don't believe anybody." Dawson reached into the depths of his coat and produced a coffee cup half out of its paper wrapping. "Give this to Mrs. Gately when she's done with her business and tell her I'll be waiting for her in room forty-six."

"Forty-six? Sure, Sonny. I'll give you the key."

"You don't seem surprised."

Chick drew in his lower lip as if to ponder his reply. "Each new day, Sonny, that surprises me. I can't think of nothing else that does."

"Nor I, Chick," Dawson said and took the key.

He drove his car around to the rear of the motel. In the room he opened the drapes and tossed his coat on the bed, where it fell in a way that disturbed him, the flop of the arms invoking too keen an image. He was about to remove it when the phone rang, Chick on the line.

"I tried to listen at the door, Sonny, see how long she'd be, but I couldn't hear anything. Could be an hour, maybe more."

"Doesn't matter," he said.

"How about I have someone bring you a sandwich or something, pot of coffee you want it?"

"Nothing," he said.

"You sure?"

"Positive."

"Sonny, I thought all this was kind of cleared up. I mean, you know, the boy."

"No, I don't know, Chick. Do you?"

"I told you I didn't."

"Then why are you bothering me?"

"Because I saw her last night. I mean, who she said she was, just fooling."

"Who did you see?"

"On television. Tina Turner. It didn't look nothing like her, Sonny, but it made me sad."

Dawson replaced the receiver, left the coat where it

was, and sank into a chair facing the window. It was late in the day, and the sky had the rosy color of gasoline. He watched the wind pick up and push through a towering stand of firs. Through the window, it sounded like the ruffle of a drum. He closed his eyes.

Paige Gately woke him with a touch on the arm and then stepped back on fashionable high heels, her neat silvery hair garnering light from the lamp she had switched on. Her lips suggested the flare of a match. With sluggish effort, Dawson drew himself erect in the chair. "I was dreaming," he said.

"How pleasant."

"Not really." He stretched a leg to get rid of a small cramp. "How did your business meeting go?"

"That's not your concern."

"Did you get the cup?"

"Not my pattern."

"I hoped it'd be close."

"A famous man once said close only counts in horseshoes and grenades. Is that your new jacket?"

He fingered one of the buttons. "Yes, do you like it?"

"It almost suits you," she said and moved imperturbably toward the bed, brushing aside his rumpled coat, sweeping away a dangling sleeve, and sitting hard on the edge. He watched her cross her legs.

"That's where she was killed."

"I don't need to be reminded, Sergeant. If it hadn't happened here, it would have happened somewhere else. She was ill-starred. She came out of the wrong womb. Blame that big bastard in the sky."

"You're a cool one, Mrs. Gately."

"Do you think I had no feeling for her? I'm the one got her the job with Rollins, and I'm the one got her off drugs. I suppose you think you did it."

"I wouldn't know." His tone was curiously light, his smile vacant. "I do know I let her down."

"I'm sure you did, but I doubt you ever promised her anything."

"Not with words."

"Then you'll have to live with that."

"Is that what you're doing?"

Her throat tightened. "Why are you here, Sergeant? Why am I here?"

"To help."

"Nothing I can do for you."

They faced each other more with an ear than an eye, as if they were listening to each other through a thin wall, their voices mere murmurs but each word charged. "The least I can do is bring in her killer."

She said, "Get yourself a shovel."

"Can I be sure it was him?"

She rose from the bed's edge and ever so slightly leaned toward him on her high heels. "Does it matter anymore? Would it bring her back? If it did, she'd stink of the grave and hate you for it. As it stands now, she died loving you. We talked a lot, so you have my word."

"Why do I feel you know everything?"

"I *seem* to know everything. It's how I get ahead."

"Is that how you got the Silver Bell?"

She did not answer. Making fists, she stretched her arms obliquely and arched her back. "I've had a long day, Sergeant. I'm leaving."

"I'm staying," he said, and she brought her arms down fast as if alerted by an inner signal.

"You worry me," she said.

"I should," he replied, his green eyes luminescent like a cat's.

"This is private property. You're not a paying guest."

"Have Chick register me. And tell him I'll have that sandwich now."

She hesitated, unsure and unsettled. "Anything else?"

"Yes," he said. "Get in touch with Alfred Bauer. Tell him I want to see him."

"Tell him yourself."

"No, *you* tell him," he said and pointed to the telephone. "Do it now."

Something in his face, the eyes, made her decide to accommodate him. Two steps took her to the bedside table, where she picked up the receiver, struck a button for the outside line, and looked back at him. "Have you ever killed anybody, Sergeant?"

"No."

"Have you ever drawn your revolver?"

"Only to qualify."

"Then I'll tell Alfred he has nothing to fear."

Dawson laid his head back and closed his eyes. "You'd be lying."

Chick gave her a broad smile from behind the desk and said, "I got good news for you, Mrs. Gately. A big group of Japanese engineers checked in. They're here visiting Raytheon. Rolling Green's all full, so they came here."

"That's wonderful," she said with scant attention and added automatically, "Alert the restaurant."

"Already did. I wouldn't forget something like that," he said, hurt that she had thought otherwise. She continued on toward her office. "Mrs. Gately."

"Yes," she said with irritation, stopping in her tracks.

"Mr. Fellows is in there waiting. I guess it's OK he went in. He said it'd be. I mean, I didn't do nothing wrong, did I?"

"You never do, Chick."

She entered the office, closing the door slowly and firmly behind her. Ed Fellows was pouring coffee for himself, his back to her. "You have a cup here doesn't match," he said. She went to her desk and sat down, a weariness invading her all at once. She forced off one shoe and then the other. Fellows breezed forth with his coffee, drew up a chair, and fell carefully into it. On the desk was the crystal dish of pink cupcakes and glazed cookies she had laid out for her earlier visitors. Fellows picked up a cookie and bit off half. He eyed her searchingly. "I don't like the look on your face."

"It didn't go right. They chopped their offer by fifteen percent."

"Son of a bitch," he said, chewing fast. "They're playing a game."

"No game," she said. "They're considering another site, but they're still interested in this one. Only at their price."

"I should've been here."

"Wouldn't have helped."

"You at least should have had Rollins here."

"Don't tell me what I should have done, Ed."

"We'll get them back," he said, eating the rest of the cookie. "We'll dicker."

"Won't do any good." Her voice was unhurried, unmodulated. "It was take it or leave it. They weren't kidding."

"What did you do?"

"I took it."

He did some fast figuring in his head, eyes rolling, thick fingers twitching. "We still make a profit."

"Not what I planned."

He smiled to make the best of it. "You know what they say about the best-laid plans."

"I don't need to be reminded," she said with the irony of someone struck down by an unknown hand. "There were three of them, and one didn't look any more than twenty-five, though he was probably thirty. Hotshots in

Brooks Brothers suits. They won't keep much of the help. They took one look at Chick and gagged."

"Not your problem." Fellows brushed crumbs from his pinstripes and reached again into the dish, this time choosing a cupcake. In his big hand it looked like a fluffy Easter chick, much care needed not to crush it. "You have to be philosophical about these things."

"Have I ever not been?" she said, more to herself than to him. Then in a louder voice: "You usually send me something nice from Nazarian's for Christmas."

"Yes, I do."

"This year make it money." She pushed back in her chair and swung her stockinged feet up onto the desk. "You have coffee. Where's mine?"

He rose on the instant, frosting on his mouth, and lumbered to the service set. He chose the cup that did not match. His head bent over his chore, he said, "Was anything wrong before? Chick said you had to go to one of the rooms."

She wondered how much to tell him and then said simply, "A problem with a guest."

Chick delivered the sandwich and a pot of coffee himself and said, "You'd've got it sooner if she'd said something. You hadn't called, I wouldn't've known." He dragged a low table close to Dawson's knees and set the tray on it, fluffed out a napkin, poured the coffee.

Dawson said, "Who's minding the store?"

"A kid from the kitchen. He's a Puerto Rican from Lawrence, but that don't make no difference to me. I mean, long as he's clean and honest."

"Mrs. Gately gone home?"

"No, Sonny. She's in her office with Mr. Fellows."

"Ed Fellows? Does he come here often?"

"Not much. Just on business. He's her banker, her money man, but I guess you know that."

"You'd be surprised at the things I don't know."

"I know what you mean. People think because I work at a motel I know all kinds of things. I just mind my business is what I do." He backed off. "You want anything else, phone's right there."

The sandwich was spiced ham and cheese on rye with lettuce, tomato, and mayonnaise. Dawson ate it all. He drank the cupful of coffee and then a half cup more. He felt stiff from the neck down when he went into the bathroom, where he first used the john and then bent over the sink to gargle and to wash his face. Straightening, he smoothed his hair back with wet palms. He tried to read his face in the glass, but it had little to say. Before resettling in the chair, he drew the drapes against the evening dark. He was not asleep but his eyes were shut when a draft of cold air briefly washed over him. Alfred Bauer's entry into the room, accompanied by the telltale redolence of bay rum, was nearly soundless.

Dawson rubbed his eyes before opening them. "I don't know if it's still hot," he said, "but there's coffee in the pot."

"Seldom touch it," Bauer replied. He started to remove his coat but then decided against it. "Chilly in here."

"Feels warm to me."

Bauer anchored himself in a chair six feet away, near the silent television set. The velvety collar of his dark coat crept up on him. A protective lotion gave his bald head a shine, but his face was dry and paste-colored.

"Have you been in this room before, Mr. Bauer?"

"Don't give me any shit," he replied without rancor or force. His usually rich voice was hoarse and hollow. Dawson scrutinized him.

"You're the fellow was going to grind me up. Looks like somebody's done it to you."

244

"Don't breathe easy, Sergeant. I'm biding my time."

"It's good to know where we stand."

"We've always known," he said, still without rancor but with a bit more drive. Then he smiled. "Do you know what I was thinking about, driving here? My first piece. Do you remember yours, Sergeant? Eve James, wasn't it? Mine came late, in the army, somebody's wife. I opened her, entered her, thoroughly enjoyed her. Then afterwards, when she was dressing, she stared through me as if I didn't exist. Always struck me as inhuman. Melody was never like that."

Dawson had no comment, no reaction other than a compression of the lips.

Bauer said, "Mel and I had something in common, you probably didn't know that. We both got off to bad starts. Lousy parents. My father was a prosperous lawyer but a violent man, and my mother unfortunately had an eye for men. He killed her and then himself, forgot about me. I was brought up in a private institution for male orphans with trust funds. In upstate New Hampshire, not a bad place. Overlooked a lake and the green side of a mountain. From my bedroom window I could watch the sun glance off the water. The buildings were brick, the floors marble. I was there eight years, though it seemed forever, every day the same. I was never mistreated, but never shown affection either. I was just there. Do you know what I mean, Sergeant?"

"I'm not sure I'm interested."

"A man you suspect of murder you ought to let talk. The only good thing at that place, Sergeant, was its physical culture program. The director was a woman. She was in her sixties, but when she got in her tights you'd have thought she was twenty. She drummed it into us every day, nothing more important than your God-given body. I worshipped that woman, but I don't think she ever knew my name."

"All you had to do was tell her."

245

"At that age it wasn't that easy. I didn't go on to college. I could have, but I didn't. Instead I served three years in the army. Never left the States. I was an enlisted aide to a two-star general. I was trained for the position at Fort Lee, Virginia. I learned to prepare and serve drinks and tend to family pets, and to open and close doors after people."

"They also teach you how to pimp?"

"I learned it on my own, for the general, a man with a voracious appetite. I also learned hookers have bigger hearts than other women, long as you treat them right. I always did. I even married one, which I never tried to hide. I'm proud of it."

"What happens if you treat them wrong?"

"Then you don't know what to expect."

"Is that your situation now?"

"You're a shrewd fellow, Sergeant, but always a little off the mark. You'd never succeed in my business."

"You haven't always been so successful. You got your picture in the *Herald* when those health clubs and massage parlors of yours went into bankruptcy."

"I waltzed away with a bundle."

"But you got busted for promoting prostitution."

"All charges were dismissed after long court delays. The Gardella organization gives you juice."

"He's gone."

"His sister isn't."

Dawson felt it was his turn to smile. "Is that good or bad?"

Bauer conceded the point and returned the smile. "Let's just say it's not the same."

"How did you get your hooks into Rollins?"

"A town this size, it's a formula, scientific. You find out the lawyers born and bred here, bound to know people in the right places. Then, long as he's not stupid, you pick the one with the smallest practice. Small practice means he should be doing better but he's got a little something wrong with him, some psychological quirk probably. Doesn't matter what it is, it's a weakness. You put him on a fat retainer and he's yours for whatever you want. You become the big thing in his little life."

"Rollins introduced you to Paige Gately."

"Brought me to her house. Grand old place, plaster falling off the ceiling. I read her in a minute. I told her I needed weight with the planning board, and she said she had a friend. I left the rest to Rollins."

"Who was her friend?"

"You figure it out. Shouldn't be hard."

Dawson reached out and laid cautious fingers on the outside of the coffee pot. "Sure you won't have any?" he said and poured himself a cup, slopping a little.

"Nervous, Sergeant?"

The coffee was no longer steaming but was warm enough to drink black. He took a sizable swallow. "What if I told you I'm wired?"

"I'd laugh in your face. It's not what you got me here for, and I've got nothing to hide from you. The moment you took Melody into your house, you canceled yourself out. You're nothing. I look at you and I laugh. I'm doing it now. No, Sergeant, you're not wired. I got nothing for you. All I got is a dead son and a wife who's not the same anymore. And here I am looking at the guy who had a hand in it. What do you think is going through my mind?"

Dawson, feeling strangely at ease, said nothing.

"I wanted to, I could take you out with my bare hands. I know you're carrying a piece. I could make you eat it."

"For my sake, I hope you don't try."

"I don't have to. You see, this town is mine. I have a future in it. You don't. That's going to grind you down, and something else is going to grind you more. You don't know in your head who wasted Melody. If my son didn't do it you figure I did, and if I didn't do it you figure it was

Harriet. I have the worst news in the world for you, Sergeant. You're never going to know."

He was alone again in the room, the silence deadly, as if he were the only one in the whole motel. He lifted his coat from the bed and turned back the covers on one side, the white of the pillow and sheets dazzling. He hung his coat in the open closet and switched on the television, though not loud enough to hear. With his back to the screen, he took a deep sip of cool coffee to retrieve himself from a clutch of bad thoughts. Then he picked up the phone and rang the desk. "Give me a wake-up call at seven, Chick."

"You staying the night?"

"No problem in that, is there?"

"No, none at all, but you don't have to stay in that room. I can get you another, I'll bring the key right over."

"This will do fine," he said, loosening his tie. There was a long pause from the other end.

"What are you looking for in there, Sonny? Answers?"

"No answers here, Chick. Not even echoes."

"Then why you staying there?"

"I'm too tired to move. It's as simple as that."

He removed his jacket and his holstered revolver and tossed them on the chair Bauer had occupied. Outside it began sleeting. He heard it on the window and parted the drapes a little to look out at it. On the mute television screen youths with godlike looks and girls with active and adventurous legs frolicked on a brilliant beach, the sun a blaze of gold heralding a Coca-Cola commercial. The telephone rang. It was Mrs. Gately.

"The room is fifty-five dollars. With room service and tax, the bill comes to sixty-eight-fifty. I don't want you to be surprised when you get it in the morning."

"Thank you for the warning."

"I don't need to worry, do I?"

"About what, Mrs. Gately?"

"I wouldn't want to think you might blow your brains out."

"I wouldn't dream of it."

"Then have a good night's sleep, Sergeant."

The sleet turned to snow and gradually back to sleet and by morning was a freezing rain. Harriet Bauer was up early tramping through the woods, each twig and blade of grass a crystal, each step she took a crunch. Under her hooded rain slicker she had on her husband's bulky Norwegian sweater. Massive mittens kept her hands warm. A man walking his dog greeted her, but she passed him without seeing him. Then she stopped in her tracks and looked back at him with a small, worldly look. "Why don't you call me later this week," she said.

He was a slight man in his seventies. He said, "I beg your pardon?"

"Beg it all you want," she said, "it won't get you anywhere." She continued on with a firmer tread, a louder crunch, at times a detonation. She passed the man again on her way back but this time ignored him, as if she had never before laid eyes on him or his dog, a retriever that sniffed briefly at her legs.

When she approached the house she saw her husband staring down at her with sleep-swollen eyes from a bedroom window, his mouth set with concern, his chest bare. Inside the house she pulled off her mittens and shed the slicker. He came down the stairs on bare feet, a towel equipped with snaps fastened around his middle. Lipstick was smeared into his bare chest. When he had come home last night she had greeted him in an open negligee, a ruffled

garter belt, and briefs with a lacy front and ribbon ties, and
for the first time since their son's death she had pleasured
him with an expertise acquired twenty years ago.

"I was worried," he said.

"Why was that?"

"You get up earlier and earlier."

"I have to. December days are short."

He stepped near her and, as if he could sense her
thoughts traveling away from him, took hold of her hands
and rubbed them.

"You don't have to do that," she said. "They're not
cold." She sat on a chair and began taking her boots off.

He said, "Would you like me to stay home today?"

"Don't do it for me."

"You're sure?"

She placed her boots inside the chair, neatly. "Yes."

"I'm going to do a few laps in the pool. Will you join
me?"

She shrugged, her face closing up on him.

"Think about it."

"I will," she said.

Late that morning she placed her son's stereo speakers
in the open windows of his room and fired rock music into
the quiet of Southwick Lane. The vibrations reached Porter
Road in one direction and Hidden Road in another. At least
two neighbors telephoned complaints to the police station.
A young officer named Hawes, less than a year on the
force, was dispatched to the neighborhood. He heard the
thump of music well before he reached the cul-de-sac. It
sounded as if it emanated from the trees.

He rang the front doorbell of the Bauer residence but
received no response, hardly a surprise. Who could hear?
Since he had no right to enter the premises, he returned

to the cruiser and activated the flashing roof lights. Moments later the music ceased. He was back at the front door when it opened and Harriet Bauer peered out.

He said, "You can't play your stereo that loud, ma'am. It's disturbing everybody."

She regarded him quizzically while giving a small tug to her loose gym costume, which was stained under the arms and across the midriff. "You're not the one I want to see."

"I'm sorry, ma'am?" He cocked his head, his cap slightly too large for it.

"The detective," she said coolly.

It had stopped raining, but the air was raw. The officer's voice floated out ragged. "Which one's that? We got a few."

She thought for a moment. "The sergeant."

"Sergeant Dawson?"

Her sudden smile showed a mouthful of handsome teeth and cherry red gums. "That's the one," she murmured.

"If you want to get in touch with him, ma'am, there surely is an easier way of doing it. Just pick up the phone."

"I thought my way would be quicker. I was wrong." She smiled once more, innocently. "You'll give him the message."

"Yeah, sure. If I see him."

Officer Billy Lord, not yet on duty, settled himself with occupying force in a chair in Sergeant Dawson's cubicle office. Dawson, his appearance rumpled, was drinking coffee at his desk. Officer Lord lit up a small cigar and said, "Did you hear about my cat?"

"Which one, Billy? You've got three."

"I got four. It's the black one I'm talking about. He

was out tomming last night and got in one hell of a fight. I know he won because he came home with three eyes, one between his claws."

"Jesus, Billy. Don't tell me that stuff."

"My wife went into hysterics. She kicked him out of the house."

"Get him fixed."

"Can't do that, Sonny. He's got a right to his balls, the way I figure it."

Dawson batted the air and averted his face. "I'd appreciate it if you wouldn't blow your smoke my way."

"It's not me, Sonny. It's the air currents. Look, no matter how I hold it the smoke goes where it has to. It's like when you squeeze off a raunchy one. Somebody could be talking to you and be none the wiser. Downwind, of course, the person might keel over. Christ, you could go to jail."

"Billy, shut up."

"People are always telling me to shut up. I've noticed that."

"Listen to them."

There was a scratching on the glass of the cubicle. Officer Hawes poked his head in, his manner hesitant and diffident. His cap was in his hand. "I wonder if I might talk to you, Sergeant. Private. Alone."

"Something personal?"

"I don't know."

Dawson waved him in, and Billy Lord said, "Don't worry about me, Hawes, I'll hide my head."

Hawes looked at Dawson, and Dawson said, "Go ahead, what is it?" The young officer gave a quick account of events at the Southwick Lane residence, passing his cap from one hand to the other, running a finger over the visor. Then he blushed.

"I thought she might be a special friend of yours."

"She's special," Dawson said, "but she's no friend. When did this happen?"

"Little before noon."

Dawson looked at his watch. It was after three.

"I'd have told you sooner," the officer said, "but you weren't around."

"I've been here all day."

"Then I guess I wasn't. I was busy on—"

Dawson dismissed him with his eyes and watched him leave. His bottom desk drawer was open. He closed it with his shoe. His stomach felt savage, and he rubbed it. Too much coffee. "She's been on my mind. She must've read it."

"She don't sound sensible to me," Billy Lord said. "I was you, I'd be careful."

Dawson neatened his desk, slipping reports under a newspaper, tossing his plastic-coated coffee cup into the wastebasket. "I'm always careful."

"I don't know about that. My observation is you're not always too clever with women. They seem to get the best of you."

Dawson rose from his desk, straightened his tie, and slipped on his coat. "I don't know about that, Billy. I really don't."

Billy Lord stirred in his chair, making it squeak. He half grinned as Dawson slipped by him. "What d'you say, Sonny? You want a backup?"

"I'm a big boy now," Dawson said.

Despite the cold, the door had been left partly open for him. He rang the bell as he stepped inside and got an earful of chimes, along with a stark look at himself in the oak-edged mirror. He called out her name and then, closing the door behind him, followed her voice. Wonderful house.

Thickest carpets he had ever walked on, not a sound from his soles. "Wrong way," she said with a catch in her breath. "In here." It was the study, warm from a leaping fire, perhaps too warm. He saw her face, broad with sweat under the red band. She stood in her deeply stained gym costume with her legs spaced wide, as if she had been wrenching her trunk, touching her toes. He could tell something was ticking inside her skull. "You took your time," she said.

"I got your message late."

"No harm."

"I wish you'd gotten it to me a lot sooner."

"Let me take your coat," she said and advanced on him with a husky stride. Her hands reached out to help him. He did not want his back to her, but it was so arranged. As the sleeves of his coat slid away, she felt his arms through the herringbone of his jacket. "You have strength in those arms, Sergeant. I imagine you can take care of yourself."

"So far."

She stepped away with his coat and draped it over the back of a leather chair. "That's my husband favorite chair. It's where he reads his Kennedy books. He's a Republican to the core, loves Ronald Reagan, but for style and class he has always admired Kennedy. Americans are finally learning to worship their dead, don't you think?"

"Is your husband home?"

"Why? Would that worry you?" The fire from the grate threw heat against her face. "I worship the memory of my son. I was awake during the birth. I felt him squeeze his way out."

"It wasn't suicide, was it?"

She ignored the question, gave no indication she even heard it. "Whose memory do you worship? Melody's? She was never a proper whore, you know. She never had my moves, but perhaps she didn't need them. People just naturally gave to her. Among other things, Alfred gave her a Mazda. What did you give her, Sergeant?"

"Not much."

"That was bad business on her part. I married Alfred and got everything." She removed the sweat band from her head and pointed to her left. "Something I want you to look at. It's on the bookcase. Lovely piece of furniture, isn't it? Alfred says it has the lines of a woman."

He took three silent steps to the bookcase of cherrywood and glass and lifted a photograph off the top. It was a large black-and-white glossy of a young woman in a trenchcoat and beret, blond and beautiful. He said, "Is it you?"

"When I was an artist's model. That's what I was wearing when I met Alfred. Outside a brownstone in Back Bay. Nothing on under the coat. He told me I looked like a big Brigitte Bardot. I come from a family of strapping women." Her voice swam at him. "I'm glad it's not in color. Black-and-whites, Sergeant, give a sense of timelessness. I can look at that picture and know everything my body was doing then and what was in my mind."

Dawson returned the photo to the bookcase, feeling the heat of the fire through his trousers. She touched her hair and gave it a push back.

"I wasn't a hooker for long, not much more than a year, but Alfred said I was the best. Tony Gardella said I was *numero uno*. Top dollar is what I got." Her sleeves were pushed up, every movement of her arms muscled. Her fingers were tangled in the drawstring of her sweat pants. "What do you think I'd get now? What would you pay?"

"I'm not in the market," he said, his eye jolted by a sudden glut of thigh. She slid her hand into her pubic hair, which was little more than a dusting, and brought up strands through her fingers.

"I know all the tricks, Sergeant. Though I might as well admit it, I have mileage." Her smile was toothy, dazzling, yet wistful. "I'm not nineteen."

The pungent aroma of Ben-Gay stuffed his nose, and he moved slightly, his back to the fire, which almost seemed to draw him into it, like arms. The heat put force into his voice. "Where's your husband?"

"Alfred?" Her voice shot up. "Alfred, where are you?"

"He's here?"

"He must be in the gym, Sergeant."

It was a long walk, endless carpets. He knew he was close to it when he heard the hum of a dehumidifier and breathed in the sharp smell of chlorine. His head began to hurt when he pushed through the doors, one of them nearly hitting him because he did not move fast enough. Exercise mats were scattered about, and he tripped over one on his way to the tiled edge of the pool where Bauer waited. Bauer stared at him out of blue eyes pinpointed with hemorrhages, his open head unbalanced on a neck of loose skin. Crouching, Dawson felt for a pulse, knowing there was none. The weapon, a barbell, lay close by. Then his blood ran cold at the sound of Harriet Bauer behind him.

"Would you call my lawyer? William Rollins." Her voice was careless. "Would you do that much for me?"

There were several telephones in the house and one nearby on the wall near the shower room, but he did not see it. All he could think of was the one back in the study. "You'd better come with me," he said.

"I'll be there."

"Put something on."

The trip back to the study seemed longer, as if the carpeting were slowing him down, pulling at his shoes. In his dreams travel was smoother and reality sharper than this. In the study he stepped over her sweat pants, plucked up the phone, and punched buttons. "This is Dawson," he said moments later. "Notify the state police there's been a homicide at 10 Southwick Lane. I'm on the premises. If Billy Lord's around, tell him to get over here. Also notify the chief."

He went back to the gym, but she was no longer there, only her husband. He called out in a voice that startled him but received no answer.

Billy Lord arrived before the state police did, almost smashing into Dawson's car in the circular drive. His bull-frog body labored to the front door, which Dawson held open. "Jesus, Sonny, what happened?" he asked, his flat eyes expanding.

"Come in," Dawson said and succinctly, in no more than a dozen words, told him what he knew and what he thought he knew.

"Sonny, what's that you're holding?"

"Her pants."

Billy Lord's eyes went bigger.

"I want her to put them on."

"Where is she?"

"We have to look," Dawson said. They moved quietly into the spacious dining area, which sparkled with crystal and china, and into the elongated kitchen, where a cuckoo clock cheerily announced the hour. Then, stopping abruptly, Dawson felt himself go sick. He gripped the back of a cane chair for support. "She's nowhere downstairs," he said with absolute certainty. "She's up."

They mounted the wide stairs. At the top Billy Lord used fumbling fingers to unlatch the holster of his service revolver. Dawson stayed his hand. "We won't need that." The wail of a siren could be heard, state police arriving.

"Let's wait for them," Billy Lord said. Dawson's stomach bucked, then gradually behaved.

"We won't need to do that either."

"Where is she, Sonny?"

"Her son's closet."

257

Fifteen

He hung on her voice. Listening to it hard was like palming a lotion over his hot skin after a workout. She told him to sit down, and he chose the chair nearest the bed, where she sat on the tight-made edge. In repose, his face regressed in age. He looked ten. "How did you know I was here?" she asked, and he pushed his fists into the pockets of his athletic jacket and answered with a moodiness she was used to.

"I always know."

"But how?" she asked, and a pointless minute passed. He cast his eyes down in his sneakers, the lace loose on one and coming loose on the other. She said, "Do you drive through the lot and look for my car?"

"Yes."

"But I have a new one."

"I know." His lifted face darkened. "My dad gave it to you."

"Does that make you mad?" she asked gently and knew the answer without his giving it. In the sunlight flooding through the window, the drapes yanked back to their tightest furls, his fine-spun hair was more white than blond, spectral like a baby's. "I didn't ask for it," she said. "I didn't even want it."

"But you took it."

"Have you ever said no to your father?"

258

"He's not *your* father."

"It was a joke, Wally." She knew well enough what was disturbing him and tried to talk around it, lightly and quickly. "Your dad didn't like the Mondale sticker on my car. He wanted me to put a Reagan one on or at least take the Mondale one off. I wouldn't, so he bought me a new car with nothing on it except the dealer's decal. He called it a compromise."

"Do you and my dad still . . ." His voice trailed off in agony, and the large lobes of his ears colored.

"We're just good friends now," she said softly and got a doubtful look. "Do you want me to swear to it?"

"You don't have to. Not if it's true." His eyes, which easily went dewy, glistened. "I wish we were the only ones in the world. Then nobody could . . ."

"You make too much of me."

"I love you," he said simply and frankly, and she immediately patted a space on the bed's edge. Hands emerging from his pockets, he hoisted himself out of the chair and obediently sat beside her, though with noticeable room between them. He wedged his hands between his knees.

"Today you love me, which is good," she said. "In time it'll be somebody else, and that'll be better."

"Never," he protested.

"Some sweet chick in school, you wait."

He hung his head to one side, and locked his hands tighter between his knees. "I still don't date."

"But you will."

"I don't know."

"Nothing has to be rushed." She reached over and stroked his hair, smoothing parts that were wisping up as if to float away. "Isn't that what Dr. Stickney keeps telling you?"

"I don't like him. He acts like he knows you better than I do."

"Maybe he only thinks he does."

"*Every*body knows you better than I do." There was a sulk in his voice, and she slid close to him, placing an arm around him, uprooting his hands. At once his nose nuzzled into the charcoal wool of her sweater, like a kitten remembering its mother. He dawdled a finger over the *M* monogrammed above the breast. "I still have it," he whispered against her.

"What do you have?" Her head dropped forward over his. "Are you going to tell me or make me guess?"

"The garter belt my mom gave you."

"You snitched it?" She laughed. "I wondered what happened to it."

"I didn't want you wearing it for anybody else," he said, and she could feel the blood in his face. "Only for me. When I'm ready."

His breath cutting through her sweater irritated her skin, and she said, "You'd better sit up now." His head rose slowly, a flush still in his face, his ears bright.

"Can we lie on the bed and talk?"

"Not today."

"But something might . . . work. I can feel it."

"Another time," she said firmly, and something combative and glum passed over his face and drained it.

"You've got somebody coming."

"Later."

"Who?"

"You know better than to ask."

"I've a right to know."

"No, you don't," she said, wishing there was a way to spare him. Her voice mellowed. "It's a kind of favor for somebody else. A friend has a friend who needs help."

"What are you going to do for him?"

"Nothing more than I do with you. Just talk."

"You promise? You swear on your honor?"

"Do you want me to?"

260

"Yes."

"OK, I swear on my honor." She jetted up, tossed her hair, and looked at her watch. "You hungry, Wally? I'm starving! How would you like me to buy you a Big Mac?"

He rose reluctantly, then grinned. "With fries?"

She said, "Tie your sneakers."

"You don't mind, do you?" he said and drew the drapes with a certain flourish, as if shutting out an audience from a stage. He raised a wrist and viewed his watch. "I only have an hour. I wish I had all afternoon." He lobbed her a lazy smile impaired by two martinis he had had at lunch with a customer of minor importance. "Melody, isn't it? Pretty name. Fits." It was her last little time on earth, and she stretched an arm to extinguish one of the lamps burning harshly on each side of the bed. "Don't," he said, gravitating closer. "I wouldn't want you in shadow. Nineteen, aren't you?"

"Yes."

"Lovely," he said. She did not like him. He sensed it and ignored it while removing his shoes, which smelled smartly of polish and the good leather beneath. His movements slowing, he shed his suit and sought a hanger for it, then one for his shirt. "Might as well be neat. I notice you are, everything stacked so nice on the chair."

She smiled politely. He did not like her manner but adored her looks. Rubbing a bare shoulder, he abruptly frowned because she was staring at his stomach, not at all the ripple of muscle it was when he rowed and played squash at Andover and Harvard. "Something you don't like?"

"Why don't you relax," she suggested.

"I was about to say the same thing to you," he said and his eye went on the alert for derision, though there was none. He skinned off his black hose but kept on his loose boxer

261

shorts, buying time to soothe his self-esteem, which he felt had been tampered with. He placed a solid pallid knee on the bed. She was under the covers, and he lifted them with a slow hand. Looking at her, he drew in his mouth. He wanted to stare to his heart's content and told her to close her eyes, which was something Harriet Bauer had advised her never to do, a cardinal rule. Never turn your back on a John was another. He wants to blow bubbles up your ass, make sure you're looking over your shoulder.

"You're not being very helpful," he said, heaving a sigh. "Do you know who I am?"

"I have an idea," she admitted.

"Then you know you're in good hands."

She knew only that she was chilly and sought to retrieve the covers, but he had swept them beyond reach, even his own, as if he had cut anchor and set sail, the waters rough. He shucked off his shorts, which made his belly look bigger, and touched her for the first time, grazing the length of a leg. In no uncertain terms he wanted her open, nothing hidden from the eye, pink parts showing, and then, impulsively, he wanted her to flip over.

"I'm not an animal."

He examined her. "Pretend I'm a doctor."

"Mrs. Gately said you were a gentleman."

"Not with sluts. I don't care how gorgeous they are."

The words did not disturb her, merely made up her mind. "I think you'd better leave."

"Behave!" he told her in a parental tone, which triggered something within her. Her gaze unloaded too much upon him, all of it a surprise. "What the hell is it?" he asked in frustration. "My nose?" He touched it. "This?" He slapped his belly. It was a question of pride, conceit, dignity. "Maybe I remind you of somebody. Who?"

The answer was a foster father, which he had no way of knowing and never would.

"What don't you like about me?"

"Everything," she said with utter calm and abandon, almost with a smile of joy. Her breath blew sweet. "You're a pig."

His eyes tightened as if screws had been turned. Her eyes burned bright, too bright, and she shut them, squeezing the lids and breaking the rule. He made a fist without considering the strength in it.

Paige Gately took his call at her home and listened to him with anger and growing alarm, though she could not make total sense of him. "Not my fault," he kept interjecting. Then she got the gist of it and shivered. "You fool," she said, "you absolute fool. Will she be all right?"

"I don't think so."

"Can she talk?"

There was heavy pause. "Paige, I think she's dead."

The pause from her was heavier as she spread her fingers over her throat. Her legs went weak as if her own nerves and muscles were working against her. Then her mind, always her greatest edge, began to work.

"Paige, I'm shaking like a leaf."

She said, to herself, Now I know why I picked Biff. To him: "Has anybody seen you?"

"I don't know. I don't think so."

"Don't."

"Don't *what?*" His voice shook.

"Don't let anybody see you," she said. "Get a towel and start wiping. Everything you might've touched."

"I don't know if I can. Christ, if you could *see me!*"

"Ed, you don't have a choice."

She made herself a small drink, nothing strong. It was to calm her thoughts, not to dull them. Ed Fellows's voice replayed in her mind, and, though nothing in her face changed, she almost wept. She returned to the telephone and rang up the Silver Bell, surprised when the desk clerk answered in a female voice. She had forgotten that Chick was not yet on duty. "Any problems?" she asked and was told there were not. "That's the way I like it," she said. "When Chick comes on, tell him he can reach me at home if anything comes up."

Almost an hour later the doorbell rang, and she let him in. She expected to see trembling hands, but he was a solemn presence in his pinstripes, though his face was ghastly. "I wiped everywhere," he said. "Twice, to be sure."

"You're mistaken," she said, and he looked at her queerly. "You were never there. You and I never had a conversation on the phone. You know nothing at all about it, so you have nothing ever to tell me. If you do otherwise, even if we're quite alone, I'll walk away from you."

"I understand," he said in the tone of somebody granted rebirth.

"What you do now is go home. Take a bath. I recommend a long soak."

He nodded emphatically. "Yes, I will!"

"Then what are you waiting for?"

Now there was a tremble to his hands. "There is one thing," he said quickly, for she seemed prepared not to listen. "When I was driving away I spotted a car pulling into my space."

"Who was it?"

"A big blond kid. I saw him, but he didn't see me. He got out of the car and went in."

She whistled softly. "I think you've lucked out."

The boy crept into the room, his athletic jacket buttoned up to his chin, his sneakers tied tight. His purpose was to surprise her. The roar inside his head began when he neared the bed, and the cry from his lips was less a sound than a taste that came up on him. The nakedness, not the damaged flesh, appalled him. She seemed one with the white of the sheet, the fluff of the pillow, the ghostliness of the room. "It's not fair," he sobbed.

Her eyes had a lame look, as if scratched by a thorn. Her mouth was a wound. She said, "Help me, Wally."

"You lied to me!" She was dying, he could see that through a flood of tears. "I was ready. I could have done it!" he proclaimed, and a sense of betrayal and injustice cut through him to the bone.

Her lips parted. When she tried to speak again, he hit her, a helpless blow, only half his strength, which was more than enough.

She looked at her watch and picked up the phone, knowing that Chick was bound to be on duty now. She considered his brain no brighter than a twenty-five-watt bulb, but sometimes she suspected she was wrong. He answered the ring at once, his voice crackling with irritation.

"This is Mrs. Gately," she said. "Everything OK there?"

"Everything's fine," he sputtered, "except that damn Bauer boy nearly ran me down."

"What was he doing there?"

"I don't know. He didn't give me time to ask."

She made one more call, her last of the day, which was to Harriet Bauer, who listened without comment and then said, "Boys will be boys."

"I wouldn't even bother you with it except he did almost run Chick down."

After a moment's pause, Harriet Bauer said, "Can you connect me with Melody?"

"I'm not at the motel. I tried to call her myself, room forty-six, but she didn't answer."

"No matter," Harriet Bauer said in a tone of unconcern. "I'm sure it's nothing."

Twenty minutes later Harriet Bauer stepped into room forty-six. The sight of the body shocked her but did not stop her. She felt for a pulse, a beat, a throb and then did not touch it again nor look at it. She plucked a towel out of the bathroom, not the same one Ed Fellows had used, but she followed the same route and gave hard wipes to the same things.

No one saw her enter the room, and no one saw her leave. There was a roundabout way out of the lot, and she used it. The only one who noticed her pulling onto the main road was Attorney William Rollins, who had just come off the Route 93 exit ramp and was heading home.

Sixteen

The Bauers were buried in Spring Grove Cemetery next to their son. There was no known relatives of Alfred Bauer to attend the graveside service. The only one from Harriet's side to make the trip from Kansas was one of her brothers, a dour-looking Baptist with close-cropped gray hair, who spoke of his dead sister as a creature who had alienated herself from God. With eyes tucked deep in his face, he looked around and said to Attorney Rollins, "Who are these people?"

Rollins nodded discreetly. "That man over there, by himself, is Sergeant Dawson, a member of our police department."

"He doesn't look like a man who's at peace with himself. Nor, for that matter, do you. You have spirits on your breath. Who's the fat woman?"

"That's Mrs. O'Dea. And the lady beside her is Mrs. Gately. Both were dear friends of your sister and brother-in-law."

"Who's the one crying?"

"Miss James. She worked for Mr. Bauer."

"And the man with the beard?"

"Dr. Stickney. Another close friend."

"I notice you drive a Mercedes. You must be rich."

"It's an old one."

267

ANDREW COBURN

"The family would like to know how much money will be coming."

"That's hard to say at this point," Rollins said, squinting through his glasses. "There are claims on the estate, which could tie it up for years."

"Our lawyer will be in touch with you."

"Of course."

"Do you think we're ready now?"

"Yes, certainly."

He stepped past Rollins and positioned himself between the two caskets with a prayer book he did not open. He gazed at the assembled faces and raised his voice. "I'm a man of few words, so this will be short." He cleared his throat. "You toss a pebble in a pond and make ripples. That's life. When the ripples are gone, that's death."

Late that evening Attorney Rollins left the lounge at Rembrandt's and walked precisely toward his Mercedes, swinging his arms just so. Sitting behind the wheel, the driver's door left open and the interior dome light casting a pale glow, he patted himself down for two minutes in search of his keys. Ten minutes later, on Central Street, he failed to negotiate a curve and ran the Mercedes over a curb, onto a lawn, and into a tree.

Officer Billy Lord took the call on his cruiser radio and responded. He recognized the car, so he knew who was in it before he managed to yank the door open. "You all right, Counselor?"

"Yes, I'm fine," Rollins said. "But it doesn't look good for my car, does it?"

Billy Lord stuck his head in and got a whiff of him. "Look," he said, "I want to give you a break. Anybody I can call to get you home?"

"Sergeant Dawson's the only one I can think of."

"Gosh, I don't know, Counselor. Do you think he'd do that for you?"

"It's a possibility."

Sergeant Dawson arrived shortly, just before the tow truck, and guided Rollins into his unmarked car, which had gone through the wash that day. Inside it smelled of window spray. Rollins sat perfectly upright as they turned off Central Street, the headlights cutting a large swath.

"I appreciate this."

"Don't make it a habit."

Rollins opened the top of his overcoat and pulled at the knot of his tie. "Could you turn the heat down a little? Thank you." He rested his hands on his knees. "You know, Sergeant, I had fantasies of marrying Melody, but she never asked me to."

"You should've asked her."

"I couldn't do that. You could have."

Dawson made another turn and presently pulled up in front of Rollins's house, a light left on for himself. Dawson said, "I had a problem with that, Counselor. She was like a prize racehorse. Everybody had a piece of her."

"But you had the biggest." Rollins pushed at his door and let himself out. Then he peered back in. "I made meals for her, but *she* made them for you. That was a major difference. Goodnight, Sergeant."

Paige Gately called Chick into her office, gestured for him to sit, and offered him coffee, which she expected him to decline. He surprised her by asking for two sugars and a lot of cream. She indulged him, and he showed his appreciation with a smile that rearranged every wrinkle in his face. The cup clattered in its saucer. His grasp was sure, but his crooked finger had a problem with the cup's delicate ear. She placed her fingers in the shallow pockets of her blazer and leaned against the side of the desk, her legs close together inside her straight skirt. "As you know, Chick, the Silver Bell won't be mine after Friday."

"The place won't be the same without you," he said with sadness.

"I'm sorry to tell you this," she went on firmly, "but they're bringing in their own staff. I did what I could for you, you have my word, but they have their own organization."

"I kind of thought that was why you wanted to talk to me. Not your fault, Mrs. Gately, I know that. Those big chains don't have much feeling for the little fellow."

It was going too smoothly. She knew that and eyed him carefully. He slurped his coffee.

"This the cup Sonny gave you?"

"Not much gets by you, Chick."

"I keep my eyes and ears open and mouth shut." He spoke proudly. "When you hired me you knew you were getting loyalty. I like Sonny Dawson and all, but you're my boss."

She moved slowly from the side of the desk to the rear and leaned a thigh against the edge. "I'm not sure I follow that last part."

"When the girl got killed. That terrible day I never did tell Sonny I came to work early. I was snoozing in my car. In the lot. You know how I am. Never can keep my eyes shut for long."

"Yes," she said tightly. "I thought you might have been doing that." She lifted her fingers from her pockets and sat at the desk, her elbows firmly anchored. "You're quite right, Chick. I did indeed hire you for loyalty. You weren't really the sort one readily gave employment to, and I knew you'd be grateful."

"I am. I always will be."

"You will of course be entitled to severance pay."

"Yes, I'm grateful for that too." He drank more coffee.

"But being without a job kind of takes the fun out of life. I thought Mr. Fellows might want to do something for me at the bank."

"What did you have in mind, Chick?"

"I thought maybe a teller, so I can talk to people, see everybody who comes in and out."

She sank back in her chair and calculated the threshold of one man against that of another while taking into account the power of her own voice. Her mouth, pursed, was a bright spot on her face. "I have a better idea," she said with finality. "Why don't we add a bonus to your severance pay and leave it at that."

On a Tuesday eight inches of snow fell. In the next day's shivering beginning, Ralph Roselli arranged for a man with a plow to clear the sloping driveway. The graded walk he began shoveling himself, his coattails flapping, his long drag of a face reddening in the sharp blue air, which chipped the knuckles of his ungloved hands.

Inside the house Rita O'Dea was munching cinnamon toast and watching Phil Donahue, whose head of hair she admired but whose guests, polygamists, she soon tired of. Peeling apart the Boston *Herald*, she checked her horoscope and read "The Eye," in which her brother's name had once appeared with frequency. While munching a dark-skinned apple, she completed nearly two-thirds of the crossword puzzle. Eventually she lumbered to the window to see how far Roselli had progressed in his shoveling. She did not immediately glimpse him because he was lying on the ground.

She tossed her mink on over her voluminous lounging pajamas and went out the door in her bunny slippers. Much of the walk was cleared, the snow hurled high on each side. Roselli lay on his back, his coat twisted to one side. She had to step over the shovel to reach him. His chin had

271

settled into its folds, and his purple hands lay on his chest like cuts of meat.

"Your ticker?" she asked from her height, and he nodded. "This is a bad one, Ralph?" He blinked. "Can you get up?" He shook his head. His baggy face looked as if it had been filleted of all its bones. He spoke without moving his lips. He wanted an ambulance.

She bent over him, her hands stuffed into the pockets of her mink, and gazed into his misted eyes. Her words were soft. "Remember when the big boys in Rhode Island decided my brother was to be hit. Nothing nobody could do, the decision was made. You had to sit there in your car and watch Tony get it in the back of the head. Remember, Ralph, I told you I never blamed you?" She smiled down upon him. "I lied."

"Can I join you, Sonny?—'less you're expecting somebody and want to save the seat."

Sergeant Dawson looked up from his late breakfast of bacon and eggs and replied, "Be my guest."

The waitress came, and Chick said to her, "I wish I could eat like him, but I ain't got the stomach. All I want is a little tomato juice."

Dawson pushed aside the newspaper he had been scanning, mostly the sports pages, basketball scores noted and forgotten. He said, "How are things at the Silver Bell?"

"Haven't you heard, Sonny? I got no more job. The new people didn't want me."

"Then what are you doing here? You should be in the ground."

"I know that, but everything's frozen. So I thought I'd wait till spring."

"You'd better tell Mr. Wholley at Spring Grove. He might have the hole already dug."

"Jesus, you're right, I don't want to get on the wrong side of him. He's the one will be looking after me."

Dawson ate the last of his bacon. "Do you know what I think, Chick? I think you'll outlive me and the waitress."

The waitress delivered the tomato juice, which was ice-cold. Chick tossed off most of it with a single swallow, and it seemed to go down him like lump. Then he wiped his mouth with the bony back of his hand. "I was wondering, Sonny, can we talk confidential?"

"Sure, go ahead, I'm listening."

"It's something I should've told you before. About the girl. Melody. Tina Turner."

Dawson's jaw shifted. "What about her?"

"There was somebody else went speeding off that day."

The side streets in Boston were not as cleanly plowed as in Andover. Back Bay was a mess, and traffic was a horror, headlights flaring up in the tainted air. He navigated down a narrow street where pedestrians could not keep on the sidewalks and floated up beside his car like random ghosts. The search for a parking space consumed a half hour. With chill, wet feet, he climbed the steps to the brownstone two hours after he had telephoned. "I thought you weren't coming," Sue Bradley said, letting him into the apartment. She felt his hands. "Cold," she said and took his coat. "Do sit. Don't stand on ceremony." He dropped into a chair. She smiled, almond-eyed and fresh-skinned, the sleeves of her shaggy sweater pushed up to the elbows. "Natalie's leaving, did you know that?"

"How would I know?"

"She's been offered a job in Chicago, much more money. She's really very smart, smarter than me, though she doesn't know it. Did you know she's fluent in five languages?"

"No, I didn't know that either, but I'm not surprised."

"Mel's gone, now Nat's leaving. That leaves me all alone. Scary. Do you want a drink?"

"No."

"Hot chocolate, coffee?"

"No thank you."

She drifted forward and sat on the arm of his chair. "That job of yours, Sonny, do you really like it?"

"It makes me feel useful," he said. "I help keep the town safe for realtors and developers."

"But do you *like* it?"

"It's not what it used to be."

"Quit it."

He half smiled. "And do what?"

"I'll make you rich. Marry me."

"It wouldn't work."

She pushed an idle hand through his hair. "For a few years it might. A lot of people would settle for that."

"It's something to think about," he said and looked around. "Where is Natalie?"

"In one of her moods. In her room."

"I'm surprised she's leaving you."

"It's not me she's leaving, Sonny. It's Melody. It really hasn't been easy for her."

"I'd like to talk to her."

"Anything I should know?"

"I'll tell you later."

The door to Natalie's room was partly open. Her briary globe of hair was all he saw at first. She was bent double, squeezing on her shoes. Raising her head, she looked at him with little interest. "May I come in?" he asked.

"You already are."

"May I shut the door?"

"No."

"OK, it's not necessary," he said as if talking to an injured child. She was not wearing her glasses, which made her face look different.

"Contacts," she immediately explained. She played with the bracelet on her wrist. "Melody's," she said.

"I have some news," he said.

"What kind of news?"

He moved to her bed and sat on it. "Good news, but I need your help."

When he came out of the room several minutes later, Sue was sipping a drink in the shadowed kitchen. He went to her with his hair still mussed where she had run her hand through it. Her drink looked and smelled like Dubonnet. "Maybe I'll try one of those," he said.

She tilted her head. "What else would you like?"

"To stay the night."

Claire Fellows said, "It's for you, dear."

"Who is it?"

"I don't know."

"Then ask."

"Who is this, please?" She listened hard and then pressed the receiver against her breast. "She says she's calling long distance. Spring Grove."

"Where the hell is Spring Grove?"

She smiled. "The only Spring Grove I know is a cemetery."

He shucked himself out of the club chair that had belonged to his father, tore himself away from the television drama he had been watching, and shuffled toward her in leather slippers she had given him three Christmases ago. He snatched the phone from her hand. "Yes, who is this?"

"It's me." The voice was Melody's.